A Bridge
To Cross

Edward R Hackemer

A Bridge

To Cross

Edward R Hackemer

A Bridge To Cross

(Book 3 –Throckmorton Family Novels)

~ a novel ~
Edward R Hackemer

Hardcover ISBN: 979-8791807946
ISBN-13: 978-1494972820
ISBN-10: 1494972824

III

TITLES BY THIS AUTHOR

THE SIX THROCKMORTON NOVELS:

Sangria Sunsets
(Book 6 in the series © 2017)
ISBN-13: 978-1542615945

THE FLYING PHAETON
(Book 5 in the series © 2015)
ISBN-13: 978-1518707858

Dollar To Doughnut
(Book 4 in the series © 2014)
ISBN-13: 978-1505245110

A BRIDGE TO CROSS
(Book 3 in the series © 2014)
ISBN-13: 978-1494972820

The Katydid Effect
(Book 2 in the series © 2013)
ISBN-13: 978-1482669831

In A Cream Packard
(Book 1 in the series © 2011-13)
ISBN-13: 978-1482662801

PLUS

THE TWO TRUFFAUT TALES:

Phryné Isn't French
(Book 1 in the series © 2018)
ISBN-13:978-1975926397

Phryné Crossing
(Book 2 in the series © 2020)
ISBN-13:979-8581963524

AND TWO CHUNKS OF RELATIVE ANCESTRY:

Fables Foibles & Follies
(A quirky anthology © 2019)
ISBN-13: 978-1790613717

COBBLE TALES
(Sussex Stories © 2022)
ISBN-13: 979-8364639899

Titles are available in Hardcover, Paperback or Kindle® format.
Visit the author's Facebook, Goodreads, or Amazon page.

The Fine Print & Other Stuff

Sincere effort has been taken to ensure that this novel contains the straight stuff for 1927. Please realize that most of this story is fictional except what is not. The needle was changed to protect the record and only the record. The innocents are not guilty. The author used narrative license to alter the true schedule of Nickel Plate No. 1 by six hours.

Most of the characters in this book are fictional. Other than blood relations, any resemblance in the description or name of any real person (living or dead) is purely coincidental and unintentional. Any name specific identification, dialogue, or comments by any other character are used only for descriptive purposes. There is no endorsement and/or criticism made or implied for any Federal, State, or Provincial law enforcement, judiciary, or local witness protection program (past or present).

Lingo, be it colloquial, slang, slurs, or cultural, is just that; lingo used during the Roaring Twenties.

Brand named products or services (whether actual or fictitious) mentioned in this book are the trademark of their respective owners (past, present, actual or fictitious) and are used solely for descriptive purposes. The reader should feel free to turn down the volume when the commercial is on, or the credits are rolling.

Retail, government, service, or religious institutions mentioned in this book (whether actual or fictitious) are not included as an endorsement or editorial criticism of their products or services. They are included solely for the fun of it, or mere descriptive purposes.

Any lyrics or music mentioned in this book are the intellectual property of individual copyright holders and are referenced only for either mood music or descriptive purposes. The reader is encouraged to purchase the music, listen and begin to tap his or her foot enthusiastically. More information can be found at the end of the book under the heading called *Music To Consider*.

Slang and assorted colloquialisms are noted by single asterisks (*) and are defined and found in *The Glossary* at the back of the book.

Curiosities and notables are designated by double asterisks (**) and can be perused in the *Odd Stuff* section at the back of the bus.

The Jazz

The Players

Leopold & Nicholas Throckmorton: brothers, 23 and 17
Dillon Cafferty: 24, cohort of Leopold, beau of:
Eloisa Ashworth: 20, friend of:
Phryné (*fry-née)* Truffaut: 22, Leopold's love interest

The Stage

Buffalo, Niagara Falls, Canada, Chicago, Detroit, Los Angeles, The Nickel Plate Road, and The Atchison, Topeka & Santa Fe

The Set & The Story

August & September 1927
~The Roaring Twenties~

The Quotes

"The execution of the deed can be more exhilarating than its resulting climax."
~ Phryné Truffaut, July 2, 1927

"You know how fickle and flighty women can be."
Dillon Cafferty, August 20, 1927

"This train is a hotel ... a place going somewhere. A place going somewhere ... a flying vestibule."
~ Leopold Throckmorton, August 30, 1927

Acknowledgements

My proofer: Edny
My editor & pen pal: Letitia
My pen & inker: Amy
My audience, eyes, and ears: You

And:
The song writers, musicians, singers, flappers & dappers.
The Pirkle Woods Packard Parkers.
Miss Penelope Porque & the Flying Porcine Defense League.

Cover photo & design: ©2014 Edward R Hackemer
Photo properties:
Latitude: 42.9079394
Longitude: -78.9014292
From sea level: 613 feet
Date: July 2, 1999
Location: Busti Ave, Buffalo, NY, USA

Table of Contents

IX

Chapter One

Saturday Night Out

August 20, 1927, Buffalo, New York

Dillon parked at the curb directly across from the bungalow style home on Olga Street. He opened the rear door, and watched with hand on hip as Phryné** and Eloisa came bouncing down the steps. The women walked quickly, excitedly, across the street. He gave Phryné a smile and a nod as she neared the two-tone Pierce Arrow** sedan. He stood holding the door and was not giving her much room. She tried to avoid him, but when she brushed past him, she was unable to escape the bold, tawdry touch of his hand as she maneuvered into the back seat. Although Phryné would playfully tempt Dillon, and put up with his crude behavior, she thought of him as an inconvenient but necessary part of a very complex relationship. Eloisa lingered, and watched as her friend slowly stepped into the car.

Dillon shut the door behind Phryné, gave her a wink and a nod, and then brought his attention back to Eloisa. "Hey! Eloisa! My Ellie!" He took a step toward her, gave her a smile and a quick hug. "You are looking like the bee's knees, this evening, you are. Ready for fun are we, my little cupcake?" His actions seemed smug, slick and rehearsed. He pasted an open mouth kiss on Eloisa's lips.

She moved her head sideways. "You know I'm ready for fun, Dillon. Our Saturday soirées are the highlight of my week. I love getting all dolled up, all spiffy* and acting like a big egg* for a few hours. It's just too bad we can't do it more often. Wouldn't that be great? We could cross the border every week."

She took a few flippant steps to the front of the car, pushing her hips more than necessary, and allowed Dillon to open the

1

door for her. He moved close, gave Eloisa's backside a lingering touch, a rub, and a little push as she stepped onto the running board and into the car. She waited for it, curious if his touch would be the same or better than the one that he gave her friend a moment ago. It was impossible to tell.

She teased him, complaining coyly, "Dillon! It's a good thing my father is working! What if somebody saw that?! What if my mother saw that?!" He didn't take Eloisa's protest seriously. He'd had his hand there before -- plenty of times.

He leaned inside, placed his hand on her thigh and spoke devilishly. "Let me worry about your father, Sweet Cheeks. And a couple party trips a month is enough, Baby Doll. We don't want to go overboard and torpedo the *Lusitania*. I mean, this jazz has been working out good for us; all of us, I mean. We are having the time of our lives, and we sure as hell don't want to rock the boat. We go out often enough; just enough to be exact."

Phryné lit a cigarette, and interrupted the conversation. "Come on, Dillon, give the girl a break. There is no need to be a killjoy. Ellie just meant to say we're having fun." A whisper of smoke escaped from her lips as she formed the words. "We know what you mean. We've been doing it long enough." She took a tiny puff on the cigarette, blew a little cloud of smoke sideways and directed her remarks to her friend Eloisa. "But Dillon is absolutely right about one thing, Ellie. We all know that we need to limit our exposure to the bridge bulls* and coppers. I sure do not want to be on a first-name basis with any of them; none of us do. No thank you. We just need to keep it under our hats. All we want to do is have a good time. And like my Papa always says: *keep your nose clean*."

Dillon let out a guffaw, laughed and wondered if Phryné actually knew what that phrase really meant. He knew she could be so naïve at times.

Thinking that Dillon's laughter was directed at her, Eloisa became defensive, and quickly qualified her remarks. "Take it

2

easy, Dillon. Quit acting so hard-boiled*. There's no need to get excited. I just meant that I think it's fun to get all dolled up and go on the town. Not everybody gets the chance to do what we do. I enjoy having a good time, that's all. You know me: happy-go-lucky Eloisa."

Dillon was satisfied that he got his point across. It was gratifying to hear people agree with him. "That's settled, then. Every two weeks or so is enough. I am glad we all understand and agree with what I said. Now let's pick up Leopold and go get ourselves all spifflicated*." With that, Dillon shut the car door, stepped around to the other side, and got into the driver's seat. After a push of the button, the clunk and whirr of the electric starter, and the chattering of the six-cylinder engine, they were off to pick up Leopold.

Hot, humid summer breezes forced their way into and around the interior of the big sedan. The air carried a full load of summertime. Phryné held a small beanbag ashtray on her lap, carefully covering it with her left hand, keeping the ash down. The sidewalks along Fillmore Avenue were full of Saturday shoppers with their bags of bread, cold cuts, produce, pork shoulders, sausage, and cheeses from the Broadway Market. Some of the shopping sacks were so full of bounty, the limp heads and necks of freshly butchered and plucked chickens hung over the sides.

Talking to a newsstand vendor, Leopold was ready and waiting for them at the corner of Sycamore Street. He stepped to the street as Dillon slowed the four-door sedan to a crawl. Leopold opened the door, hopped inside, slid across the seat next to Phryné, and greeted them all, "Hey, hey, hey! It's Saturday!" Using his thumb and middle finger, he snapped a cigarette butt to the curb.

Dillon looked serious. "Yeah. It's Saturday. It's time for us to chase the good times down the road again … so, let's go catch some fun." He turned his head, checked for traffic behind him and swung the car left onto Sycamore, to Huron, and finally north on Niagara Street. Leopold leaned forward,

3

reached over the front seat and handed a ten-dollar bill to Eloisa. She folded it in half and passed it over to Dillon.

An enthusiastic Dillon announced, "Hey, thanks for the sawbuck*, buddy. Good investment for the night, I'd say, wouldn't you?"

"Cheap at half the price, Dillon." Leopold, glad that was over, sat back and put his arm around Phryné. When it came to money, Dillon always talked it up.

The quartet had been meeting up regularly on nearly every other Saturday afternoon for about seven months, since the first of the year. What originally began as a novel weekend party frolic became a daring, recurring and rollicking adventure under Dillon's tutelage. It developed into the popular, habitually hedonistic fun that was a ritual of nearly all the culturally nouveau riche of 1927. Every night they spent on the town together was like New Year's Eve. Dillon suspected the women were merely acting out their fantasies much of the time, but he was confident that Eloisa totally immersed herself into the clamor, hustle and bustle of the nightclubs, theaters, and dancehalls. She loved it, and told him so. Dillon could encourage young and impressionable Eloisa to do just about anything. Phryné cautioned her on occasion to no avail. Dillon had Eloisa wrapped around his finger like a string.

The four of them had encountered a few hiccups, bumps, and even a bruise over the course of things, but things had smoothed out since the drunken scuffle on St. Patrick's Day. Leopold drove everyone home that night, and Dillon promised that never again would he tout his Irish heritage in Canada -- especially in front of those puritanical Anglicans. After he settled that inconvenient debt with Leopold and squared things away with the Torricelli brothers, times had been good. Dillon wanted it to stay that way and would do his best to keep it so. He had realized that it was in his best interest to keep his companions happy, and the Torricellis off his back.

Leopold Throckmorton**, 23 years old and the eldest of five children, became the man of the house when his father died of tuberculosis in April of 1925, a veritable casualty of World War I. At the June, 1918 Battle of Belleau Wood, Leopold's father was one of many US 6th Marines to fall as mustard gas victims. Hermann returned home with damaged lungs and never fully recovered. He struggled to support his family with irregular employment as a handyman, laborer, street sweeper and even a rag-and-bone** man. In 1918, at the age of 15, Leopold began steady employment at the Urban Flour Mill on Genesee Street and helped support the family. He was hired on as a dockhand and subsequently was trained as a truck driver and apprentice mechanic. A year later, his sister Johanna started work as a stock clerk at Barr and Lepper's Grocery at the Washington Street Market.

After their father's death, their combined income still wasn't enough to sustain the household, and the situation forced his mother to convert the family home into a boarding house. Her action infuriated and insulted Leopold beyond tolerance.

His pride damaged, he pushed his 15-year-old brother Nicholas to get hired on at Russell-Miller Milling in the dreadful 'dust bins': the separator rooms. Deviously successful, this enabled Leopold to take a bold course of action. The ties between mother and son were already strained beyond tolerable limits. With the income from the rented rooms, his sister and brother, Leopold told his mother: "Well, you don't need me around here anymore, Ma." With that, he moved out and into a small apartment on Howlett Street. He was happy there; close to work and close to his dear Phryné.

Leopold was 21 when he became the first and only of five children to leave the Throckmorton home on Adams Street. His mother, sisters Johanna, Ottilie, Hilde, and brother Nicholas squeezed into the three rooms, bath and kitchen on the first floor while the four upstairs bedrooms were rented out on a weekly or monthly basis. Tillie was hired as a salesclerk at Gibson's Pharmacy and Hilde continued on her self-determined course to be the first in the family to finish high school.

Leopold had been wearing stylish three-piece suits, crisp white shirts, and spit-shined, white cap-toed brown oxfords. He'd begun sporting a pencil moustache a few months earlier. He stood tall, trim and athletic. He flatly refused to wear a hat during the summer, allowing the curls of his loosely cropped, dark brown hair to fall where they may, and used his fingers as his favorite comb. During his teenage years, he had spent hours of his free time at the Blackrock Boxing Club sparring with the semi-pros and newcomers. His enthusiasm for the pugilistic sport waned as he realized there was no glory in coming home black and blue, cut, mat-burned, and with sore knuckles. His father Hermann, weakened by illness, attended many of his fights, often sat at ringside, and was his biggest fan. His mother, Wilhelmina however, gave herself most of the credit for her son's decision to forego the bruising lifestyle. She nagged him incessantly about the sport; "Do you want to walk around the rest of your life with the mashed potato brains and cauliflower ears of a punch-drunk Irishman? Well, do you?"

The bridge of Leopold's nose was slightly crooked and offset to the left, a permanent memento of his teenage boxing days. Phryné considered Leopold's nose to be his second-best physical feature.

Dillon Ian Cafferty, the other man in the foursome, worked at the Iroquois Brewery on Pratt Street. It was, indeed, a brewery until prohibition, when the law forced them to change production from beer to soft drinks and 'near beer': an ungodly and inhumane concoction of one-half of one percent alcohol or less. Dillon considered the work to be beneath his qualifications, and often told others that it was only a matter of time until he latched onto something else. He boasted that sooner or later, somebody would recognize his unclaimed potential and snatch him up.

He was a tall, muscular young man of 24 years, with a physique that enabled him to easily handle the 15½ gallon beverage barrels and warehouse wagons.

He presented an energetic, cocky and sometimes very overbearing personality. His Adonis-like figure, of which he was very proud, was topped off with curly, copper-colored hair, scattered freckles and ice-blue eyes.

While among his peers, he bragged that his ambition in life was to launch a brewery or distillery of his own after the country came to its senses and ended prohibition. He loftily explained that naturally, he would be the one in charge, and would tell everyone else what needed to be done. Dillon's acquaintances often reminded him that his dream was not likely to happen; Prohibition certainly seemed to be permanent. His temperament and tendency to make hasty decisions had rewarded him with the occasional black eye, bruised knuckles and empty pockets.

Dillon was preening like a peacock in the driver's seat, his arm stretched along the seat back around Eloisa, with a big right hand resting on her shoulder. He could, and often did, prance like a stallion in front of a mare in season. Emanating the Hollywood actor Douglas Fairbanks, he wore a white shirt, brown tie, tan leather vest, brown linen slacks rolled up at the cuffs and brown wing-tip oxfords. His hat was a thick-brimmed straw boater, and for decoration only, a corncob pipe protruded from his left vest pocket. His ancestry on both sides was Irish, and he often boasted to anyone who would listen how his grandfathers helped dig the Erie Canal. He grew up in a struggling, proud, working-class environment in a rough-and-tumble neighborhood. The childhood scars of beatings and bullying that he received as a kid had yet to heal. Life in a waterfront row house in the shadows of towering grain silos was indeed growing up against the grain. He attended Danigan Grammar School until the fifth grade before he quit and hired on as an icehouse laborer. He walks with a slight but obvious limp, leaning to the left, due to an ice harvesting accident on

Lake Erie. He was 14 when he slipped under a horse-drawn ice sled and broke numerous bones in his foot. He continued to work at Superior Ice until he was 15, when he landed his current job at Iroquois. He held no family bond at all, having moved among boarding houses as a youngster, raised by an aunt, his maternal grandfather and whatever relative could provide him temporary food and shelter. His mother was unknown to him, and his father was a drunken no-account schlep who wandered between barrooms and pool halls, sweeping floors, and spreading sawdust for drink. When given the chance, Dillon would complain that families were like chickens: they constantly pick on one another, eat their young and, when it's least expected, they will shit on your head. Only recently has he shed his childhood nickname of *Spudsy McCafferty*. Unknown to him, thanks to his job at Iroquois, it had been shortened to *Sudsy*.

Eloisa (Ellie) Ashworth, the youngest member of the quartet, was a perky, energetic, blue-eyed, blonde 20-year-old from a family of three children. Like Dillon, she also grew up in the ethnic neighborhoods of South Buffalo's First and Third Wards. Her father George was a foundry foreman at the Bethlehem Steel complex in nearby Lackawanna. Less than a year earlier, he reluctantly allowed his youngest daughter to date the rough-and-tumble, gruff-talking and roguish Dillon. It did not happen until he held a long session of cautionary warnings with both of them.

Eloisa worked about 25 hours a week at Mama Farrachi's, an Italian bakery on Hamburg Street. As always, she was anxious to enjoy all the fun she could experience. She was dressed sharp, with green lace-patterned stockings, a flowing dress of yellow lightweight chenille, and a forest green, brimless cloche hat adorned with pheasant feathers. She carried a beige, fringed, sequined handbag and wore matching pumps with rhinestones on the toe. Four long strands of white beads around her neck, deep red** lipstick and nail polish rounded out her look. Her hair was in a bob, just like Phryné's, curled outward and up at the ends. She was aware that she could be gullible around Dillon, and often accepted Phryné's guidance.

Phryné Truffaut had had her 22nd birthday the past Tuesday, so this night she and her friends would celebrate that milestone. Leopold's gift for the hazel-eyed beauty was a cameo breastpin of sculptured silver. He had it wrapped in golden metallic foil, tied with a ribbon, and had it hidden inside his chest pocket. The bluenose clerk at Simon Jewelry assured him the carving was genuine African ivory.

Phryné and Leopold had kept steady company for almost two and a half years and considered themselves a well-matched pair. The subject of marriage had casually come up on occasion, but there were never any definite plans made. In the past, both Leopold and Phryné seemed to shy away from any sense of permanence in their relationship. Secretly, they both feared that any exclusive commitment could end the fun. Neither of them desired their lifestyle to change; at least not yet. They simply had so much to do, so much to enjoy, and life itself was an endless party. They played to each other; their mannerisms complimented their presence. They enjoyed dressing sharp and playing a billboard* almost as much as they enjoyed going out. Wearing the costume could be more entertaining and enjoyable than the fancy dress ball itself. In private, Phryné would tell Leopold, "The execution of the deed can be more exhilarating than its resulting climax." She meant it, and her lover knew it.

Phryné relished her sexuality and would tease Leopold at every opportunity. A touch here, a whisper there, a hand softly, seductively placed in his lap, or a squeeze of his thigh was not only a temptation for him, but also a thrill for her. She delighted in his arousal. He knew it, and sometimes would pretend to ignore her with detached indifference. This only encouraged her to make the tantalizing behavior even more direct, and his playful rejections to become stronger. Their foreplay could last for hours, ending with the predictable, passionate, prolonged and quaking rapture. She and Leopold shared an avaricious perspective on life that the couple vigorously practiced as the accepted norm in 1927. Living and loving in the 'roaring twenties' was exactly that: experiencing life with a resounding roar. Her father's parents were both Reformed French Protestant immigrants, and that allowed Phryné to blame some of her ardent devotion to life and fashion on her ancestry. Phryné dressed with attitude, wore her clothes with passion, and carried herself with prideful sexuality.

Dillon envied Leopold's relationship with beautiful and exciting Phryné. Earlier, Phryné would catch one of Dillon's thinly disguised lecherous glances and reciprocate with a look of disgust. She teased him, tempted him, but dared to simply ignore him as she did lawn snails after a spring rain.

She sat as close to Leopold as possible on the back seat. Phryné wore a black cloche hat with an upswept brim, over her curled, dark brown hair. She had red hook and eye ankle boots with black tassels and black, diamond-patterned silk stockings. Her dress was white chiffon with a wide red ribbon belt. She had it tied with the fringed ends hanging to just above the knee. She wore highlighting rouge on her cheeks, carefully applied mascara, a pronounced touch of violet eye shadow, and shining, crimson lipstick. Her deep red lipstick was the only color available, and the mascara was a thick, wax-like paste that was mixed with water before being carefully applied with a brush. Phryné used it well.

Five strands of black and silver beads in varying lengths hung around her neck. She had a delicate voice and a precocious, lilting laugh. Phryné was a cheerful jewel, a joy to be with. When she wasn't spending time with Leopold, she worked with her mother Selene, and Rita Palladio at Ritzy Rita's Beauty Salon on the corner of Main and Genesee Streets. It was at the beauty parlor where she first met her friend, Eloisa. Phryné's job at the salon gave her every opportunity to paint, polish, and perfect her flapper* style. Her father,

Bertram, was the Deposits Manager at Buffalo Savings Bank downtown, near the foot of Main Street, not far from the beauty parlor.

As the evening progressed, cooler air began to rush into the car. Phryné closed the window on her side, as did Eloisa in the front. They were driving north on Niagara Street, along the Niagara River, Blackrock Marina, and the Erie Canal. There was activity everywhere: fishermen, longshoremen, and street vendors. Canal barges, horse-drawn wagons, delivery trucks, handcarts, and automobiles crowded the waterfront. Trucks and automobiles jammed the ferry slips.

They all took particular notice of the bevy of federal Prohibition Police at the Blackrock Harbor. Leopold mentioned it as they passed, "It looks like the coppers are busy tonight."

As they left the city, Dillon slowed the car. The road surface was no longer a treated bed of stone and asphalt, but macadam with graded earth, pea-gravel, limestone and slag cement.

Towering, white, summertime cumulonimbus clouds filled the skies like cotton bolls in a quart jar. Shades of gold and orange tinged the edges as evening neared. Gulls squawked along the riverbank and swallows swooped gracefully over the swiftly moving water. In the front seat, Eloisa shifted her hips, set her head to rest on Dillon's shoulder, and closed her eyes. Dillon turned his frame a bit and allowed her to push into him. He placed his right arm around her waist and his hand on her belly. He began moving his hand and fingers wherever she would permit.

Phryné gazed up at Leopold, allowed her thoughts to drift deep into his brown eyes, smiled and gave him a playful nudge. In a soft, subdued voice, she started to sing *Tea for Two*; bobbing her head, and tapping her foot on the driveshaft hump. "Picture me upon your knee … me for you, and you for me … A lover's oasis, for you and me … Far from the city; nobody near us, to see us, or hear us ... Tea for two and two for tea ... me for you and you for me."

He smiled down at her. "It will not be long now, Phryné. We will be two-ing and tea-ing as much as you can stand. You will be bouncing your nifty body and wobbling your fantastic gams* all around the dance floor. And them gams go all the way up to Heaven! And me, well ... I will give you all the help you could ask for. We can bounce and wobble all night long, my Sweetheart!"

She picked up the double entendre and added, "Just you remember, Leopold Throckmorton ... you be careful ... I got one of them classy chassis* you hear about, and I aim to keep it that way, too!" She gave him a teasing poke in the ribs with her lacquered nails.

From the front seat Eloisa announced, "Hey! We can hear you loud and clear up here! You don't need to tell us all those secret plans of yours. Please! Control it back there! It's not fair you know; Dillon's driving!" Eloisa's pleas were of frustration, not jealousy. Dillon was playing his fingers up, down and sideways on her lower abdomen.

Dillon turned and looked to the back seat, snickered, looked over to Eloisa, pulled her to him, and gave her a quick kiss on her red lips. Dillon secretly lusted after Phryné's attention, her form, confidence, and carefree, casual mannerism. She was unconventional and sometimes daring with her clothes. She dressed as whim directed her, and often took inspiration from the magazines and fashion catalogs at Ritzy Rita's. She walked rhythmically to-and-fro, with her shoulders squared, back straight, and did not keep her breasts under the constraints of side-lacers or flat-chest corselets. Under soft crêpe or chiffon, her pert breasts could betray her nipples. She would roll down her stockings, and wore her dresses at 'knee knocker' length, and often with scalloped, handkerchief hems.

The bawdy talk brought on an impromptu, unpredictable moment of physical desire. In the back seat, Phryné placed her

12

hand on Leopold's upper thigh and gave it a sensual, prolonged squeeze before moving it slowly to stop and linger on his lap. She felt his desire rise and smiled up at him. She sounded out a soft sensuous moan and pressed her weight into him. "Later, I will have you purring like a kitten, Phryné," Leopold exhaled. She released three buttons on the front of his slacks and slipped a silk hanky and her hand inside. The back seat of the Pierce Arrow had become a passion pit on some of their return trips, but this evening Phryné could not restrain herself.

The city streets, brownstones, row houses, factories and Victorian homes disappeared behind them. The countryside opened up to grasslands and farms, and almost as quickly as Buffalo vanished, they were motoring along Buffalo Avenue past the brick storefronts of downtown Niagara Falls, New York.

Four young adults: Phryné, Leopold, Eloisa and Dillon were on an excursion that had become nearly a bi-weekly pilgrimage for them. Their destination was the Hotel Lafayette, a grand five-story structure with all the newest amenities and a spectacular observation deck on the top floor. The Lafayette's deck was a worldwide tourist attraction in Niagara Falls, Canada with its panoramic view of the American and Horseshoe Falls, rapids and the river below. The ground floor of the hotel boasted a large ballroom, restaurant, bazaar, museum, and an opulent public bath. It was a hedonist's holiday, the golden ring of life's merry-go-round, the treasured big door prize. It provided an enthusiastic escape from prohibition -- a veritable romp in a fantastic adult playpen. It offered a cultural immersion into New Orleans and Chicago jazz, Negro blues, scat singing, and the evolving sound of Big Band swing. Bluntly speaking, it was a wonderland of adult abandonment. Guests broke free of the shackles of the Eighteenth Amendment to the Constitution.

The four were not alone. Traffic across the Canadian border was brisk and the underground nightlife of Niagara Falls, Ontario flourished. Crossing the border for the

Americans was easy, no paperwork was required, and generally, no harsh questions were asked. Tearooms, dance halls, hotels, and souvenir shops were scattered between the varied storefronts that lined Portage Avenue and Lundy's Lane. Tucked in between were the so-called speakeasies, blind pigs*, or blind tigers, and the secret underbelly of basement bars and restaurants.

The Canadians worked to keep the streets clean and free of the horse plops and smell still common in other cities. Since the 1901 Pan American Exposition in Buffalo, both Niagara Falls, New York and its sister city in Ontario worked fervently to match the electric splendor that Buffalo displayed to the world. The streets were ablaze with incandescent lighting after dark. An occasional gas light, flickering blue and yellow, still adorned a singular entrance or obscure alleyway. Bustling foot traffic, sightseeing buses, and trolleys mixed with the automobiles and horse drawn tourist buggies.

Canada did not have the national ban on beer or liquor that the United States did. It was still legal to produce alcoholic products for export, allowing Ontario breweries and distilleries like Hiram Walker** and Seagrams to flourish, mainly from the illegal export of their products to the States. While it was perfectly legal to consume liquor inside homes and in private clubs in Canada, it was illegal for private citizens to purchase it. In 1924, the Ontario government, under the leadership of Howard Ferguson, studied the effects of beer, and determined that brew with an alcohol content of 4.4% or less did not have adverse effects on health and was not overtly intoxicating. So *'Fergie's Foam**'*, became legal in hotels and beer halls, but not in sealed packages. That meant draft beer could be drawn, but not bottled. Each of the separate provincial governments of Canada controlled liquor sales: there was none. Along the US-Canada border, the riff-raff, and rumrunners generally kept their high-volume, illegal trafficking of liquor away from the ferry and bridge crossings, and confined their illegal commerce to boats and barges across the normally calm waters of Lake Erie. Concentrating their enforcement efforts on the Detroit River, US Customs agents and federal Prohibition Police were spread thin elsewhere on the private docks and lakeshores.

The driver and passengers inside the maroon and black, 1925 Pierce Arrow, Model 80 touring sedan were ready for a night out on the town. The experience was not new to them, but highly exhilarating, nonetheless. Their pulses quickened as they approached the border. They had great expectations for another night of first-rate fun and frolic.

From Side to Side

As they neared the Ontario Street approach of the Whirlpool Rapids Bridge, all bodies inside the four-door coupe straightened up and temporarily put their randy shenanigans aside.

Just last year, a 10¢ toll was levied on automobile traffic, collected only on the American side, with the idea being that what traffic goes across must return eventually. *'Making millions a dime at a time'* became a localized topic for newspaper cartoons, editorials, and political candidates alike.

The Pierce Arrow was fourth in line. Dillon neared the tiny wooden toll booth, inching the big car ahead slowly. Eloisa sat up straight, and looked directly into the eyes of the toll collector. She fluttered her eyelids, tilted her head and smiled coyly. Phryné edged her dress up over her knee to her stocking tops, and moved forward on the back seat. She moved her hand to reveal a bit of bare thigh above her red garter. A small man in a white shirt, sleeves rolled up, bow tie, baggy cotton twill pants, and a tweed, button-down, newsboy cap stood behind the half-door. He was holding a small woven reed basket for the toll. He noticed Eloisa's gestures and moved his gaze to the back of the car. When he spotted Phryné's exposed stocking top and leg, his eyes moved skyward, and he focused only on Dillon.

Dillon asked him, "I suppose you hear all sorts of smart aleck remarks all day long, don't you, Jack?" He tossed two nickels into the basket. Dillon often talked down to service workers or laborers and named them 'Jack'. For one reason or another, he seemed to get a thrill out of it.

The toll keeper had a high-pitched voice that crackled as he spoke. It was irritatingly squeaky. "As a matter-of-fact, I do. I get all kinds of rude remarks. Sometimes I actually get a compliment, but it's not too often."

"Well, here's one you probably never heard before: *Don't spend it all in one place, Jack*." Dillon erupted in laughter.

"Bye-bye! Toodleoos!" Eloisa smiled, winked and waved. Dillon laughed louder. The evening's ribald entertainment had begun.

When the car drove onto the bridge, Eloisa smoothed her dress, and sat up straight again. In the back seat, Leopold and Phryné temporarily extinguished their fervor.

The Whirlpool Bridge was designed and built as a double-deck structure. The upper deck was the railroad connection between New York and Ontario. The lower deck was for automobile and truck traffic. It was an ominous experience to travel across such a massive piece of human engineering with the powerful, rushing Niagara River 250 feet beneath them. The wooden planks protested, rattled, creaked and moaned, echoing both underneath and behind them. Nobody talked during the crossing. Once the car was back on solid pavement, Phryné breathed a sigh of relief. "I don't think I will ever get used to driving over that thing. The new Peace Bridge is so much nicer to drive over that I really prefer that way across." Although Leopold agreed with her, he didn't say anything. Nothing would change the route that Dillon chose, so there was no need to fuel that fire. Besides, they would take the Peace Bridge next time or maybe one of the ferries.

Dillon saw a chance to stick in his two cents with a smart remark, "This bridge is a lot easier to cross after a couple of drinks, Frenchie!" Eloisa gave Dillion a gentle, cautionary elbow to the ribs, knowing that Phryné could take exception to his personal insults.

Just ahead, suspended across the road by cables, hanging between tall wooden posts, was a large sign in red letters on a crisp white background that read: "Welcome to Canada". A half dozen flags, blazing red, with the Union Jack in the top left corner, and the Canadian Ensign to the right, hung limp on their poles. Four booths, quite a bit larger than the tollbooth on the American side, were directly underneath. Dillon motored slowly and cautiously to the Customs and Excise checkpoint. Each booth had a neatly painted notice to the side of the door: *Visitors to Canada will be treated with constant courtesy by Customs & Revenue officers.*

A sharply dressed, uniformed officer with a service cap leaned into the car. "Good evening, folks. Each of you, tell me your place of birth, please." All four, almost in unison, replied 'United States'. The officer carefully glanced around the automobile interior with attentive eyes, and directed his next question directly to Dillon. "How long are you going to be in Canada, sir?"

"Just for the evening. We are going to The Lafayette right on the Parkway."

The officer took another carefully inquisitive look around the inside of the Pierce Arrow and added, "Have a good time, and be careful. Drive safe. Be careful."

With a "Thank you, officer", Dillon drove off. Once safely out of earshot, he added, "Applesauce*, Jack!"

Pedestrians, automobiles and buses were everywhere. The streets were wall-to-wall with people. There was activity all around. Looking out at the excitement, the crowd of people, and the traffic, Phryné thought about the border crossing this evening and all the others she had experienced over the last months. She and her friends always had an effortless experience on the Canadian side, but it was definitely a relief when it was over.

The trip home had always been a bit unnerving, too. While obviously the criminal population had absolutely no regard for men in uniform, ordinary law-abiding citizens often became very intimidated just by being near an officer of the law. The Customs and Immigration men on the American side always asked more direct questions than did their Canadian counterparts. They looked closely into the cars and sometimes nosed around under the seats, but Phryné and her friends had never had any problems or delays. *That must be what it is. It's the uniforms that make me nervous,"* she thought.

The traffic restricted their progress, and it was a slow trip from the bridge to the hotel. When they finally did approach the Lafayette, Dillon parked the car at their usual spot along the curb at the corner of Parkway and Ferry Street. A hand-painted sign read 'Hosted Valet Hotel Parking Includes Car Wash 25¢'. It was, indeed, a hosted valet service that parked the cars directly behind the hotel after they had been washed inside and out. There at the curb, there was a small staging lot, with room for five, maybe six cars. An Essex sedan and a top-of-the-line Peerless roadster had already taken two of those spots. Three men were seated on a wooden bench beyond the sidewalk watching the Pierce Arrow and its occupants. One of the men on the bench, a large fellow, got up, stood and approached the driver-side door. He had a two-inch cigar stub jammed into the corner of his mouth. He beamed a wide smile that exposed a mouthful of brown teeth. Dillon got out of the car, pulled a quarter out of his pocket and handed it to him along with the key for the transmission lock.

The attendant was wearing a black woolen beret, white shirt, sharply pressed black slacks, and a red vest that strained at the buttons around his rotund belly. His voice was harsh, raspy, like gravel rattling in a wheelbarrow. "Have a good evening, Mister Dillon. I will see you and your company later, and your car will be ready as usual, sir." He then stepped to the rear of the car, and opened the door for Phryné and Leopold. Eloisa exited the front seat unassisted.

Dillon helped Eloisa set her lace shawl in place around her shoulders, as did Leopold with Phryné. They started down the sidewalk to the Lafayette. Leopold turned back and spoke in a tone of sarcasm, "Nice to see that you are now on an exclusive first-name basis with the car jockey, Dillon."

The ladies' heels click-clicked along the sidewalk. "That fellow gave me the heebie jeebies," added Phryné. "We have all seen him before, but he never mentioned your name before, has he?"

"I know. I wondered where he got my name from, too. Maybe from one of the other men there at the lot, or he just recognizes the car. And he must think *Dillon* is my last name. The guy's just a rube*. I am not going to dwell on it. He's nothing, a nobody, and he don't know nothing from nothing." Dillon's manner was nonchalant, as though he wanted to put the matter to bed and forget it. It seemed to work. The subject was dropped.

Leopold and Phryné continued along the sidewalk, hand-in-hand, ahead of Dillon and Eloisa. The roar of Niagara's Falls was an incessant clamor, a roaring din that Leopold's senses struggled to ignore. The rumble in his ears was still present, but it inexplicably quieted, graciously allowing his other senses to function. Leopold could only accept his feeling as an unconditional surrender to the power of nature. With a perception of oneness, he began to see his existence as a merger, a unique type of union with the world. He could not explain his total submission to the noise in any other way. A sense of wonder came over him, and a stark awareness of the power and impunity of the Earth and Nature overtook him.

Suddenly, he was overjoyed by and delighted with the company of the woman walking next to him. The thunder of Niagara released a lightning bolt that jolted and lit up his world with absolute clarity. Leopold realized that Phryné was an integral part of his personal universe.

He released Phryné's hand, and placed his arm around her waist, holding her close as they walked. "See that? Feel that Phryné? We fit perfectly together. We fit. We're made for each other. We're dealing with the laws of Nature here, Phryné, so it serves no purpose to fight it. We have to surrender to the power of Nature." He stopped, leaned into her and placed a kiss directly on her lips. She kissed him back, standing on tiptoe and turning to embrace him.

She pressed to him and looked up into his deep cocoa eyes. "Right here in front of God and everybody?! Really, Leopold?! What in Heaven's name brought this on? The car ride? My hand?" She let out a silky giggle and kissed him again, lifting and bending a leg at the knee.

"Marry me, Phryné."

Time came to a screeching halt for the couple, and it stopped for Dillon and Eloisa as well. They stood watching the display in surprise and silence. Dillon pulled a packet of Camels out of his vest pocket and lit one. He looked frustrated and shook his head side to side in disbelief. For Eloisa, this was something she often imagined hearing second-hand, and never dreamed that Leopold and Phryné would act it out in front of her. She grabbed Dillon's cigarette and took possession, forcing him to light another. Eloisa's thoughts raced. She gave her full attention to the drama unfolding before her eyes. She wanted to be Phryné's maid of honor. It made sense; it just had to come true. It just had to. Phryné was her best friend.

Eloisa took a long puff on the cigarette and commented to Dillon, "I can see where this evening is going, Dillon. And the night has just started! Do you think they will get a room here at the hotel for tonight? What would they expect us to do then? Twiddle our thumbs? Leave them behind? Come back for them tomorrow?"

Dillon did not acknowledge her comment. He felt awkward, out of place, incredulous, and uncomfortable. He put his arm around Eloisa, and that seemed to help ease his insecurity. His thoughts were racing, and he hoped Eloisa would not expect anything like that from him, at least not in the foreseeable future. He also hoped any upcoming marriage between Phryné and Leopold would not alter his life too much. He was driving toward a goal of his own, and he did not desire any detours.

Phryné gave Leopold another long kiss. It was a kiss of commitment. "Yes, I will marry you. Yes, I will." He put both arms around her waist, lifted her off the sidewalk, and twirled her around in a full circle. Her feet flew out to the side, bending at the knees. It wasn't until he set her back down that he and Phryné acknowledged the presence of Dillon and Eloisa.

The couples faced each other, about three yards separating them. Leopold exclaimed, "Well, what do you think about that news, mates? She said *yes*! Me and my Phryné are getting married!"

Eloisa flicked her cigarette to the ground and sprang to Phryné. The women hugged and Dillon found it necessary to shake his head in disbelief before he walked up and gave Leopold a congratulatory handshake. Nobody noticed that for the moment, the deafening roar of Niagara had become nothing more than insignificant background noise.

Handshakes and hugs between friends were shared with best wishes: Eloisa's were heartfelt, Dillon's sounded hollow and flippant, but that was not out of the ordinary. Neither a date nor a timeline was mentioned. For the time being, it was all good wishes and happiness. The night's carefree festivities had suddenly become an impromptu celebration. There would be plenty of time in the days to come to talk about when and where the wedding would take place. Right now, the only thing that mattered was that he asked, and she said 'yes'. All the rest would fall into place all by itself. In a perfect world, it would have.

It was a few minutes past eight o'clock, and dusk was settling over the Niagara Escarpment. The mist rising from the rushing rapids and falling waters of the Niagara River mixed with the heat of August, and created an inverted bowl of humidity that cloaked everything in a haze.

An environment that made it impossible to distinguish any sharp outlines or clear boundaries within their otherwise normal daily lives temporarily surrounded Leopold, Phryné, Dillon and Eloisa. For the time being, the rest of the world was just a blur on the horizon, and almost completely obscured. It was party time. The situation was satisfactory and like they say, *'out of sight, out of mind'*. Leopold often proclaimed: "The situation is completely copacetic*; everything is just grand."

To The Ballroom, Cloakroom And Back

In black stovepipe hats, slacks, shoes and red jackets, almost like the Queen's Guards at Buckingham Palace, a doorman and two concierge staff members stood under the canopy at the leaded glass and polished brass entry doors. As Leopold and the rest of the group approached, the doorman nodded, reached into his breast pocket and brought out what appeared to be a small invitation-sized envelope. He smiled cordially and asked, "The usual, sir?" Dillon stepped forward, placed two tightly folded bills in the doorman's hand and took the envelope.

"Thank you! And good evening, to you, sir. Happy to have you back at the Lafayette once again, and have an enjoyable evening, sir. Ladies ... sir." The other two fellows, wearing welcoming smiles, held open both doors.

Inside, people were everywhere. Slowly and with determined effort, they made their way through the opulent lobby, around the brocade upholstered Queen Anne armchairs and divans, directly toward the ballroom. With a bump here, a brush of an elbow and a nudge there, they made their way across the welcoming hall. Brass Tiffany floor lamps with flowered stained glass shades, polished cherry accent tables, and plush ottomans adorned the sitting area. Persian rugs in crimson, gold, and sand patterns covered the shellacked rock maple floors. Polished brass accents embellished the check-in counter, railings and elevator doors. Large, potted parlor palms were in every nook and corner. Mixing with the clamor, the din of multiple conversations, subdued laughter and bawdy talk was a simmering stew of smells. The atmosphere bubbled over with the odors of cigarettes, cigars, cheap cologne and expensive perfumes, clothing new and old, shoe leather, stale beer and the distinct smell of gin. All of it was wafted through the immense room, churned and blended by three very large wicker-blade ceiling fans, integrated with five brilliant chandeliers.

A large advertising easel at the ballroom entrance displayed an art deco poster announcing an eight-piece band fronted by a trumpet player. Bold black lettering, edged in orange, proclaimed that the live entertainment for the night was *Al Kaye Hall and His Bootleg Jazz Band*, direct from Saint Louis. Walking past, Leopold flipped his thumb toward the sign, laughed and asked, "I wonder how many people will catch that knuckleball, Dillon?"

Dillon added, "Ted Lyons himself could not have thrown a better one, Leopold. Think of it, Leopold: Ted Lyons. All that talent wasted on a team like the White Sox. What a waste. Too bad the Yankees don't have him. If it was up to me, the Yankees would get him and sign him to a thousand dollar contract."

Neither Phryné nor Eloisa had any idea what the men were going on about, nor did they show any interest. The women were eager to get inside the ballroom and be seated so they could discuss things other than baseball: more important things like proposals, weddings and married life.

The ballroom was full of fifty or more round tables. They measured about five feet in diameter with room enough to seat four very comfortably. It was an impressive presentation. The tables all had white linen covers, votive candles aglow and place settings with a cup, saucer and sandwich plate. Not as brightly illuminated as those in the lobby, the chandeliers were not as large, or elaborate. Covered wall lamps glowed up and along all sides except the stage wall. The dining area floor was dark, polished, red oak parquet. The dance floor, like the lobby, was rock maple.

The room was buzzing with conversation and foot traffic. A swarm of men was milling around the beer bar. The noise level was a clear indication of the excitement for the impending entertainment and frolic.

The band members were setting out their stools and music stands. There was a set of drums with the band's name emblazoned across the front, a huge bass fiddle on its pedestal, and a lonely microphone standing as a silent, solitary sentry awaiting the company of a human voice. A coronet and trumpet sat straight up, bell-down in front of a cane bottom chair and a banjo leaned against another. Two trombones and a clarinet sat on three more. Snuggled inside a wicker basket were a kazoo, bugle, ukulele, tambourine and a washboard. The room was filling up, and at that moment, it was about halfway there. Wait staff wearing crisp aprons and napkins resting on their outstretched forearms were flitting around the room like scores of little white cabbage moths.

The group walked toward the front of the room, and laid claim to a table four rows back from the stage. The dance floor was the width of the ballroom and extended about thirty feet from the footlights and the elevated stage. A twelve-inch mirrored ball hung over the center of the dance floor, and benches lined both of the side walls. Already there was a tobacco haze in the room.

Immediately after the four took their seats, a waiter stood at tableside beaming an ear to ear smile in his own sincere attempt to appear ready, willing, and able. Dillon did not waste any time, "We'll have a pot of tea, four ginger ales, a quart of beer, and a plate of them fancy little finger sandwiches, Jack."

The fellow nodded eagerly in full agreement. "That's great sir. I will bring it right out." He turned on his heels as an army recruit and was gone.

Dillon lit a Camel and looked casually around the room. The cigarette was hanging from the corner of his mouth. "Good looking crowd here tonight." Dillon reached inside his jacket and brought out the envelope the doorman gave him. He opened it, took out what appeared to be a business card and handed it to Eloisa. The card had "2-OK" scrawled across one side and was otherwise blank. He put the empty envelope back into his chest pocket and gave instructions, "Bring back the usual, Ellie. You know, the gin and rye. That's a good girl." His cigarette danced between his lips as he spoke.

That neat little piece of manila card stock was their ticket for the night's liquor ration. It was automatic, exactly as it had been done for the last seven months. Phryné and Eloisa stood, grabbed their pocketbooks and walked to the far side of the room. They ended up beyond the beer stand, near the cloakroom and lavatories where they mingled with a dozen or more other men and women. The card that Dillon gave to Eloisa was the liquor ticket needed for two pints of alcohol. Inside the coat check, behind a rack was a convenient little cubbyhole where patrons could pick up the evening's personal libations. Eloisa and Phryné each had two half-pint pocket flasks that they kept secured under garters on their thighs. Here at the Lafayette they would keep them in their pocketbooks, and put them back under their dresses when they crossed the border later. Phryné called them 'The Pussy Cat's Meow' when she had them hidden. Eloisa called them her 'Garter Girls'.

The men sat smoking their cigarettes and watching the action in the front of the room. The Lafayette never disappointed them, and considering the billing poster on the easel, Leopold and Dillon hoped for a good show. The band members were rattling around on stage, clunking their instruments on the floor, chairs and themselves. A tall, thin, rawboned fellow stood at the microphone tapping and pecking at it like a chicken in a barnyard. Annoying raspy sounds and his nondescript pitchy voice poked through the room. "Testing. 1-2-3 Testing." Two men behind the drums and cymbals were drinking from a shiny new, German Dewar vacuum flask. They all wore seersucker suits with vertical blue pin stripes, red ties, spats over their shoes and straw hats with red bands; almost like the one Dillon wore. The jazz ensemble consisted of a mixed group: five white and three colored.

The waiter came with a large tray balanced up and over his left shoulder with the soft drinks, tea, beer, and sandwiches. He maneuvered it down to the table in one smooth motion. Dillon seemed preoccupied and didn't utter a word or acknowledge the young man. Leopold just had time to thank him before the waiter turned and walked away as quickly as he arrived.

Dillon directed his attention to the activity on stage. "Looks like a decent eight-piece band here tonight, Leopold. I wonder which one is the band leader ... you know, the guy they call *Al*."

Leopold couldn't resist offering a quip, "Probably the palooka* in the back with the Dewar Thermos. He's the guy that's getting all juiced up. His band is so bad he probably needs to get juiced." He laughed and poured himself a half cup of tea. "Pass your cup, pal."

"Thanks." Dillon looked across the room to where Phryné and Eloisa were last. "Still no sign of Eloisa or Phryné. There must be a line. Always is."

"Yeah, there's probably a line.   They'll be back soon enough."

"Tell me, Leopold, before our muffins get back.   What in the hell were you thinking of? I mean, asking Phryné to marry you like that? What got into you? Your life is going to go through the ringer now, bud. It's going to get all twisted up, upside down, and sideways. And it's not just you, either. It's me, too ... all our lives are going to change."

"I've been thinking a lot, Dillon. I got a good paying job at Urban's, damn good. I am making sixty-five a week, and it's about time I get my life squared away. My place is plenty big enough for me and Phryné for the time being, and well ... well, I love the dame. It's about time we do the middle aisle stroll* anyway. We've talked about it a couple of times, and I thought it was about time we go ahead and do it. Something came over me back there on Ferry Street."

"I don't know what came over you.   It seems almost a pathetic waste of time to me. I know you must be squashing that juicy French tomato* already. I sure as hell would. Twice a day or more. And when is all this going to take place? Have you thought about that yet?"

"No date yet, Dillon. And I still have to talk to her father. Phryné is old fashioned about that. She's not fussy about anything else, but like that, she is. She told me that before ... that I need to ask her father's permission."   Leopold felt insulted explaining all this to the rake* Dillon Cafferty. There were times that Dillon's comments could make Leopold's skin crawl.

"I just don't want to see you mess things up, that's all. Things are going good for me right now, and for us, I mean. And anyway, Leopold, maybe her father will tell you *no*."

"Maybe so. We could elope too. But me and her father seem to get on together. And besides, Dillon, you and I both know this cannot go on forever. Like they say, 'all good things come to an end'. And who knows? Maybe the Canadians will pass a damn prohibition Volstead Act of their own and outlaw their beer and booze over here too." Leopold took a sip of tea and grimaced. "This stuff is just plain awful. No wonder the Canadians look so miserable all the time ... damn lousy tea and shitty cigarettes."

Dillon laughed at that. "You should have known better, Leopold. You should have waited for the booze or had a glass of beer. You won't catch me drinking that Canadian noodle juice* without something good in it."

Leopold knew he could depend on Dillon to make a derogatory comment. He always had to have the last word.

Dillon spotted Phryné and Eloisa. "The women are coming, see? But, no matter what, Leopold, I guess I wish you luck. I can tell Phryné must be a bearcat*, and good in the sack. I hope it will work out for you. You can give it your best try, anyhow. Just don't go take no wooden nickels or rub that monkey's fur the wrong way. You know how fickle and flighty women can be."

Leopold bit his tongue over that remark.

Eloisa and Phryné returned to the table just as Dillon finished speaking. Leopold finished what little tea was left in his cup and passed it to Phryné. "Gin me, Phryné, Sweetheart."

Leopold looked across the table to Dillon, who gave him a nod and meek smile in return. Dillon looked nervous and that made his dime store smile appear even more insincere. It did not particularly concern him, but for a fleeting moment, Leopold wondered what could be troubling Dillon. He was not his usual self. His personality was corrosive enough, but lacked the wanton arrogance that had been the norm. Leopold assumed it was his impromptu marriage proposal that had set Dillon off balance and onto his heels.

Fun, Frolic and Flappers

The activity on stage was increasing. The band members were seated and setting up their sheet music. The drummer sat

28

detached, evidently daydreaming, with a blank look on his face and staring into nowhere. The tall skinny fellow had finished toying with the microphone and stood as if at attention.

He began to speak, and his squeaky, annoying voice of earlier magically transformed into a pleasingly smooth tenor. Dillon and Leopold exchanged glances in disbelief. Phryné and Eloisa paid earnest attention to the stage.

"Good evening, Ladies and Gentlemen. My name is Al, and this gang of hoodlums behind me is The Bootleg Jug and Jazz Band, and we've been on the run since Kalamazoo. The good news is that we are now safe and sound here in Canada, because before we left Kalamazoo, we drank all the evidence."

There was laughter and applause. Suddenly, Dillon was back to his usual self; very animated and enthusiastic. He put his thumb and pinky finger on his tongue and created a long, shrill whistle.

The bandleader continued, "We are here to entertain you with the finest music you can find in this great province of Ontario. We hope you will have a grand time and enjoy yourselves. If there are any special tunes that you would like to hear, I apologize ... because we don't know anything by *The Special Tunes*."

The drummer smacked four quick sticks onto the snare drum before Al continued: "And now I would like to introduce a special member of our band. She's our singer ... our sinful songstress ... our delectable doll ... our vocal vixen. She's originally from New York City, where she performed on stage with a troupe of gals called *The New York Knickers*. Lucky for me and the boys, she left New York and her knickers behind. So, let's make some noise for our singing flapper and give her a warm welcome to Niagara Falls ... Here she is ... so, let's hear a rousing welcome for Miss Rosie Bottoms!"

Again, there was laughter and applause. Dillon did a repeat whistle performance.

And yet again, the drummer smacked four quick sticks on the snare. The trumpeter then blasted *The Gang's All Here*, and the crowd continued with laughter and muffled applause. Rosie made her grand entrance. She pushed through the royal blue stage drapes, carrying a half-full champagne glass. The applause became outrageously loud. A few other enthusiastic souls whistled along with Dillon. Rosie was a big-busted blonde wearing a sequined white evening gown flowing to the floor and tailored to accentuate her chest. Such a buxom appearance was uncommon most everywhere else, but on-stage performers often flaunted their breasts. Her short hair had rows of curls, like soft ripples of water coming to shore. She stood at the microphone, did an abbreviated curtsey and waved to the very enthusiastic crowd.

The band started with *Ain't She Sweet* with Al and Rosie performing an effervescent, animated duet. The night was off to a fantastic start: the band in tune and the crowd in the mood. The ballroom floor filled up immediately and the good times began rolling along.

It was an atmosphere overflowing with fun and frolic. The ladies had their fringe flying in all directions on the dance floor and sequins sparkled on hats, dresses and shoes. The glitter ball reflected the festive, glimmering radiance from the light bulbs, votive candles and chandeliers.

The band was brilliantly rowdy, loud and boldly bawdy. Rosie kept the mood flying high with songs like *Six or Seven Times*, *Pussy Cat Blues,* and *I Wonder Who's Boogie'n My Woogie Now*.

Eloisa and Dillon were out on the floor at the first opportunity, enthusiastically moving to the music. Eloisa bobbed, Dillon weaved and together they created a superlative display of adult high jinks. The rousing entertainment on the floor and elevated stage was a clamoring diversion for Phryné and Leopold. They had come to the Lafayette to have fun, and the mood was heightened with Leopold's spontaneous marriage proposal on the sidewalk of Ferry Street. It was much more than fun after that. Phryné was euphoric. Her thoughts, dreams, and plans were rushing around like the white water of Niagara's Whirlpool Rapids. She had dreamed of this, confident that someday Leopold would propose marriage. He had been her steady escort and confidant for more than two years, since his father passed. They had shared laughter, excitement and personal drama together. For more than a year, oftentimes they had taken the opportunity and occasion to experience and share sensuous intimacy. Either spontaneous or planned, it was savored and cherished. Phryné relished it. Leopold yearned for it.

They both knew this would happen. Last month, while seated around the table for dinner, her father surprised her with an off-the-cuff comment he made to her mother: "Maybe Phryné's Leopold could start joining us for Sunday suppers." Phryné immediately responded with, "That could very well happen. Would you like me to arrange it, Papa?" Her mother quickly put an end to the conversation by pushing such talk off as nonsense. Her father, however, looked over his glasses across the table at his daughter and gave her a little wink.

She told Leopold about the interaction, and it was clear that it was very unlikely for her father to deny any marriage request. Seeing an opportunity, Leopold had taken a bold leap, like a daredevil in a barrel over the Falls. He had Phryné's pulse racing with his proposal. Leopold decided that he would dress for church tomorrow, attend services at Westminster Presbyterian on Delaware Avenue, and ask her father for her hand. Phryné excitedly agreed to his plan of action.

The band played on, the patrons drank, and hundreds of feet bounced and shuffled across the dance floor. Phryné and Leopold discussed their plans in between dashes to and from the dance floor for much of the night: bobbing, bouncing, waltzing, and wooing across the Canadian maple. They were enjoying themselves immensely in a world all their own. Somehow, all the uncertainty settled like old dust on new

31

furniture, and all the arrangements fell into place. Privately, Leopold explained to Phryné that he did not want to commit to asking Dillon to be Best Man; it did not feel right. He suggested that he should ask his brother Nicholas first, and she agreed. Phryné and Eloisa managed to discuss some early planning of the ceremony and of course, that Eloisa would be the Maid of Honor. It went without saying that Westminster would be the church.

It was perhaps eleven o'clock when Phryné asked, "So when are you going to give me my thimble**, Leopold? After my father gives you permission?"

With all the excitement, he had totally forgotten her birthday gift: the cameo brooch in his pocket. In a flash, his hand went into and out of his jacket. He put the shiny packet in her hand.

"Here's something better than any silly engagement thimble. Happy birthday, Phryné. I love you."

She opened it, gave him a kiss and immediately pinned it to her dress. "I love it, thank you, Sweetie." Awkward sideways kisses and hugs were shared across the wooden chairs.

Dillon could not resist. *"Thank you, Sweetie."* Eloisa gave him another jab to the ribs.

Just as Phryné knew it would, it was all coming together. Tomorrow, Leopold would attend church service, ask her father for permission to marry her, and the wedding planning could begin in earnest. There was a lot to look forward to.

Throughout the evening, Eloisa did her very best to duplicate for Dillon the feelings of happiness, infatuation and excitement that Leopold and Phryné were experiencing. She was ardent in her efforts, and managed to come very close, or so she thought. Dillon would give her attention only when it was for his satisfaction; otherwise, the closest Eloisa could get to Dillon was arms-length. She was generally happy with her own situation, but she could not help but envy Phryné's elation.

Turn Out The Lights, The Party's Over

Ultimately, the music had to stop. The melodies disappeared and wafted away into countless memories. The unrelenting murmur of idle chatter and errant laughter settled somewhere between the illuminated ceiling and polished floor. The annoying scrape of empty chairs and the shuffle of footsteps heading for the exits overtook the ballroom.

Their flasks, glasses and teacups empty, the quartet looked around the room and at one another. Phryné looked at each of her friends, smiled and made the announcement: "That was fun. Probably the most fun I ever had up here. And that's saying something. It was a fantastic night. I will never forget it." She slurred some of her words, but still managed to make it sound sincere.

Leopold stood and offered his hand, "Neither will I, Phryné. Neither will I."

It was just past midnight; the bell tolled, the curtain fell, and the funhouse door slammed shut tighter than a prizefighter's fist. All the neat, clean, round tables covered in white linen six hours ago were laden with lipstick-kissed teacups, dirty plates, empty glasses, saucers with food scraps, and ashtrays overflowing with cigarette and cigar butts. The ballroom emptied much more quickly than it filled. Normality returned. The Hotel's flood of music dissipated into a soundless ripple and the crowd's noisy clamor poured into silent, empty cups.

Out of the ballroom, through the lobby and entrance doors, Leopold, Phryné, Dillon and Eloisa didn't talk. A subdued feeling of melancholy washed over them, the proverbial wet blanket, and the realization that things were returning to normal, and the party was over. They held hands and maneuvered through the pressing crowd. Outside the doors, the exodus of bodies subsided, the mob thinned, and they took the sidewalk alongside The Lafayette and down Ferry Street toward the car lot. The resounding boom of Niagara's endless torrent of water returned and reverberated through their souls.

Two men were sitting on the cast iron bench at the valet parking lot. The smaller fellow was smoking a cigarette and drinking from a canvas covered flask. The big man still had that cigar stub hanging from his lips and his vest was still speckled with ash and still straining at the buttons. He stood when he saw Dillon's party approaching, stumbled over his own feet, and nearly lost his balance. Leopold cautioned him, "Easy there, big fellow. We're in no hurry, Jack."

The large man ignored Leopold and took a step toward Dillon. "Here you are, Mister Dillon. Your key. Your car is filled up, washed up and ready to roll. And I will see you next trip, maybe."

Dillon took the key and stuck a dollar bill into the big man's vest pocket. "You get one big 'Atta boy' for that, Jack. Thanks, good job. And I imagine that I will see you next trip."

"Thank you sir. Thank you. My name is actually John." Dillon ignored him and started toward the automobile.

Leopold took Phryné's hand and guided her into the back seat. He covered her lap with a cotton blanket and tossed another one up front for Eloisa. She walked to the opposite side and entered the front seat unassisted. Dillon did a quick walk-around the Pierce Arrow, kicked the tires, opened the trunk a bit and took a quick look inside. He finished his cursory checkup, got in, put the key into the lock and pressed the starter button. The car passed his inspection, clean and ready for the road.

Dillon squared his straw hat, loosened his tie, and put the car in gear. He let the clutch out with a short, sharp jerk and hung his arm out the door. He gave a wave of his hand and announced, "See you later, Jack!" The automobile trip back across the bridge to Buffalo, New York and the United States was underway.

There was no moonlight. It was the second night of the New Moon, and the sky emitted pure, unspoiled starlight. The

Milky Way spanned the shimmering heavens like a swath of sparkling silver sequins across a sensuous, black cocktail dress. Brief flashes of the Northern Lights temporarily dulled the glitter of the Big Dipper.

In the backseat, Phryné snuggled to Leopold, covered his lap with the blanket and teased him with her hands and fingers. Up front, Eloisa covered herself from shoulder to toe. The drive to the Whirlpool Bridge lasted only minutes.

On the Canadian side, there was no toll, but the structure of the bridge still required a very slow approach. Once onto the wooden deck, the ride itself set the speed limit at 5 mph. There was a light but steady flow of traffic.

Phryné wriggled her shoulders and tried to get closer to her fiancé, "This chilly night air gives me the opportunity to fully appreciate a car with windows, Leopold. I mean, your Tin Lizzie** is a fine car when the sun shines, but it sure is nice to have windows and a roof like Dillon's Pierce Arrow."

He lowered his lips to her ears and whispered, "My car is paid for, Phryné. It only cost me a hundred, and it's all mine." He stopped whispering, and spoke quietly. "I've been thinking of getting a new roof frame and canvas top before the winter sets in. Would you like that?"

"It would be an improvement," she twittered.

Phryné kept her eyes locked shut during the bridge crossing, but it still was an unpleasant experience. The creaking, groaning, cracking and rumbling was unnerving. She did not believe she could ever become accustomed to it. Leopold kept his arm around her.

On the American side, Dillon tossed a dime to the toll keeper and crept forward to the Customs and Revenue Service booth. It was well illuminated, with a flood lamp aimed at each side of the vehicle. One Internal Revenue agent walked around the car with a round twelve-inch mirror mounted on a broomstick, looking under the car. The other stuck his head partially into the driver's window.

"How long have you been in Canada?"

Dillon answered, "A few hours, since about seven thirty. We were in Niagara Falls at the Lafayette."

The agent pushed up at the brim of his cap. "All U.S. citizens?"

"Yes, sir."

"Bringing anything back with you?"

Dillon was polite, and spoke clearly. "No sir. Just what we crossed with … just ourselves."

The Revenue agent finished his mirror inspection, and nodded to the man outside the booth. He made one more check around the inside of the car, using a new, long, chrome and brass Eveready flashlight, looking behind the seat and on the floors. He looked carefully at all the occupants one more time.

"Anything in the trunk?"

"No, sir."

There was a five-second pause as the agent's eyes passed over the occupants of the Pierce Arrow one last time.

"Goodnight, folks. Drive safely." He tapped the windowsill, holstered his flashlight, stepped back into the grey booth and waited for the next car. They all learned early on that it was best not to start a conversation with border or customs agents and just let them do their job.

They were on their way home.

Back In Buffalo

After they cleared the border, traffic was nearly non-existent, allowing Phryné and Eloisa to nod off. The women met the previous year, on the Tuesday after Christmas, at the beauty parlor where Phryné and her mother worked. The situation was frantic that day; a Friday wedding was in the works for Eloisa's older sister, Virginia. Scheduled for New Year's Eve, it was a last-minute affair, arranged in haste out of what was deemed an urgent necessity. Virginia, Eloisa and their mother Esther were in need of new hairdos. Eloisa and

Phryné started talking, Phryné became a confidant, and a friendship was born. Shortly afterwards, Eloisa introduced Phryné and Leopold to Dillon, and it was not very long before the four of them began their cross-border party nights. They would go out on the town in Buffalo on occasion, to Shea's, The Gayety Theatre or The Hippodrome for a picture show, vaudeville, burlesque or off-Broadway stage show. Canada, however, became their favorite party destination, and exclusively, it was The Lafayette.

Leopold didn't talk during the trip back to Buffalo. He sat staring out the window with his right arm around Phryné. His thoughts were ten hours into the future. He was creating a timetable. He would get out of bed, wash and shave, then drive to Westminster Presbyterian and wait for the Truffaut family. That would be the easy part. Phryné's father would know something was up. Of course, he would. Oh, he got along well enough with her father Bertram and mother Selene, but what troubled him the most was exactly how he should start the conversation. Well, perhaps not. Maybe, just maybe, the most difficult maneuver would be the change from small talk about the weather and politics to the topic of marriage. Leopold was cautiously nervous, but he expected, rather, hoped for, a positive reaction. Well, at the least, the chances were good, he thought. After all, Phryné's father was always outwardly friendly toward him. It appeared that way. Generally, he knew that all the worry usually ends up to be just that: pointless, fruitless worry. Worse come to worse, it is never as dire as all the premature worry warrants. He was trying to convince himself of that.

He looked down at Phryné. At that instant, her beauty struck him, penetrated, curled, and danced deep within his heart. She looked more angelic, prettier and purer than ever. He wanted to keep her to himself -- close to him, tight to his soul, for all eternity. Tenderly, he pressed her closer, and kissed her forehead. He vowed that he would protect her forever. In the front seat, Dillon shifted his weight and stretched behind the wheel. Leopold knew that soon there would be some changes coming to all their lives.

Truth be told, Dillon was not exactly within the category of people he would consider as a close friend. He was more of an acquaintance, a pool-hall buddy. When Phryné's friend Eloisa first introduced them, Leopold got the impression that Dillon was an opportunist and a bohemian adventurer out to make a quick buck. The week after they met, Dillon asked him for a short-term loan to help purchase the Pierce Arrow sedan. He paid it back in a matter of three weeks, but the transaction made Leopold uncomfortable. The loan request took a measure of arrogance that Leopold did not appreciate.

In the front seat, Dillon took a deep breath, exhaled and stretched his neck from side to side. His thoughts wandered also, but unlike anyone else in the car, he knew he was required to keep his attention on the road, and ignore minor distractions. A cat sprinted across the street at one point, but managed to retain all of its nine lives despite Dillon's disregard. Around the Blackrock Canal, a pair of eyes was reflected in his headlights. *'Probably a dog'*, he thought; *well, maybe a raccoon.* Whatever it was, it stayed out of his way.

Like Leopold, Dillon could not totally ignore the scores of errant thoughts spinning in his mind. Driving south along the banks of the Niagara River, he was trying to put his wandering ideas and reflections together like pieces of a jigsaw puzzle. If the pieces did not fit perfectly, he would allow himself to smash them into place regardless. After all, some things naturally need adjustment in order to properly fit into the big picture.

Leopold's marriage proposal was as much a surprise for Dillon as it was for Phryné. He was concerned it could become a distraction, and a huge inconvenient roadblock to his own lifestyle. Dillon believed he could get along just fine without any distractions in his life. He felt he knew best, and allowing others inside could only muck things up. He did not need any volunteers. He kept friends and associates by invitation only.

Dillon believed that his relationship with Leopold was more of a necessary association than a friendship. And as for Eloisa, well, it's only natural to have their type of intimate companionship between adults. Ever since they got the Constitutional right to vote back in 1920, this generation of women believe they have the world on a string. It was obvious that Eloisa got just as much out of their liaisons as he did, and maybe more. It sounded that way sometimes, when they were doing the bedsheet waltz, and she told him she loved him. He was confident and knew that sooner or later his ship would come in. It would arrive either at the river or lakeside dock completely unannounced, but he would recognize it when it did. He did not need anyone's help figuring that out.

On any early Sunday morning, once beyond the border and its busy bridge, traffic was, understandably, nearly non-existent. Back in the city of Buffalo, other than the occasional streetcar or street sweeper, it was very quiet. However, two very vital participants in commercial traffic were still making their rounds. The milkmen and icemen were out and about the city. The rhythmic clip-clop of horses' hooves echoed between the brick and wood buildings, creating a sweet melodic contrast with the mechanical chitter chatter of the automobile engine.

For a little more than an hour, Phryné and Eloisa had been able to catch some sleep during the trip from Niagara Falls. The impolite clanging of the Main Street trolley's crossing bell rudely awakened them.

The sharp tintinnabulation also put an end to Dillon's and Leopold's early morning daydreams.

Dillon's usual routine was to drop off Eloisa first on Olga Street, then to Lombard Street for Phryné, and finally take Leopold over to his place on Howlett. Even then, Dillon could not call it a night. He still needed to drive the Pierce Arrow over to the garage on Prospect Avenue, lock it up, and hope that he could catch a streetcar up Richmond Avenue to Bidwell Parkway. If that worked, he could easily walk the last ten minutes to his two-room flat on West Delevan. If things worked out as well, as they usually did, he could be in bed by 2:00.

That night, Dillon decided to drop off Phryné first, and then Leopold. He took an intentional detour down Lovejoy Street into Sperry Park and parked under a large chestnut tree. Dillon slid from behind the steering wheel to the center of the front seat. Eloisa knew what was expected, reached under her dress and pulled off her chemise bias panties. Not a single word came from her lips before his heated kisses began. Dillon unbuttoned his trousers and slid them down over his hips. Eloisa straddled him, lowered herself and exhaled an impassioned sigh. She moved with lustful abandon, and welcomed each of his erotic surges with a soft murmur.

Dillon felt that a good deal of the effort he put into these party nights went completely unnoticed and unappreciated by Phryné and Leopold. It was different with Eloisa. Twice that night, she rightfully gave him the attention he deserved.

Chapter Two

Prayers, Pie and Preparations

Sunday, August 21

Leopold drove his Ford to Westminster Presbyterian and waited in the parking lot on Summer Street for Bertram Truffaut's green Essex to appear. He was fortunate enough to find a shady parking spot beneath a spreading Elm. His brown, wool tweed pants and coat jacket were too warm for the August sun, but it was the only conventional 'Sunday suit' he owned. When Phryné's family arrived, he tightened his tie, smoothed his jacket and pants, and crossed the street to meet them.

Phryné had told her family that Leopold intended to attend church with her, so his appearance at the Sunday services was not a total surprise. He met them at the steps, and after cursory greetings, smiles, nods and handshakes, they went inside.

As fate would have it on this particular Sunday, Reverend Barnes' sermon wandered through the Book of Corinthians, Chapters 7 and 13. He expounded on every possible aspect of virginity, marriage and adultery before finally outlining his message that 'love is gentle, love is kind'. Leopold caught Phryné rolling her eyes at one point and it was all he could do to keep silent, while struggling not to laugh. Phryné had no way of knowing it, but silently and in jest, he vowed revenge.

He and Phryné had assumed that he would be invited for dinner after church, and, as predicted, it came to fruition. Dinner was a simple, direct from pot-to-bowl affair: chicken and dumplings. Selene had set the pot over two pilot lights before church, so it was ready for the table when they got back.

Phryné's 16-year-old brother Robert knew something was in the wind. During the meal, his eyes traveled back and forth from Phryné and Leopold like the little white ball in a ping-pong match. After apple pie and coffee, Phryné and her mother disappeared into the kitchen. Her brother took off down the block to a friend's house to work on the ongoing repair of a 1910 Flivver. That left her father Bertram free to strong arm Leopold into joining him for a glass of grape juice** on the front porch. It turned out to be homemade wine, something that many people experimented with during prohibition. A whitewashed wickerwork settee, side table and two chairs were neatly arranged on the grey enameled porch floor.

To avoid any prolonged anguish, Leopold did not wait long to ask Phryné's father the inevitable question both men knew was coming. It was over in a matter of moments. Bertram Truffaut's response was, "Of course. You have our blessing, Leopold. We expected as much. You are welcome to join our family." Her father then stood up, grasped Leopold's hand, pulled him close and gave him a one-arm hug over the shoulder. "Welcome, my boy. Welcome. I will be right back. I am going to lose this vest and tie, and you should take that wool jacket off, Leopold. You must be cooking in there."

He disappeared into the house, leaving Leopold standing there satisfied, but still wondering what could happen next. He looked around him, out to the front yard, beyond the privet hedge, and back to the screen door where Bertram disappeared. A few houses down the block, a group of boys played stickball with rocks, and a dog barked somewhere on the far side of the street.

Leopold took off his jacket, loosened his tie and hung them over the seat back. He sat back down on the wicker love seat and waited like a patient in a dentist office: not quite certain what was about to occur or if it would hurt. He appraised his situation and allowed his thoughts to trail away. He was happy with how her father had reacted to his appeal for permission for her hand, and overly satisfied with his personal composure during the ordeal. Last night he was genuinely worried he would lose his composure, stammer or even forget a word. Countless times, he had rehearsed his little speech before he actually was able to sleep.

42

In the beginning, his apartment would be big enough for them, but they would eventually need something more accommodating, perhaps even a small house. And without doubt, he would need to put that roof on his Model T Ford.

The screen door banged shut, ending his daydream. Phryné and both her parents joined him on the porch. Her mother had a full pitcher of the wine; Phryné carried two glasses and a small candy dish of white peppermints. Her father Bertram had a box of Dutch Master *Presidents* under his arm. Before long, the front porch at 54 Lombard Street looked like a family reunion clouded in cigar smoke. Leopold and Phryné were seated on the wicker divan, with her parents in the chairs on either side.

Bertram, fulfilling his duties as the pragmatic bank manager and father of the bride, started a down-to-earth chin wag*, asking the standard 'when', 'where' and 'what next' questions. It did not continue for very long, leading Leopold and Phryné to believe that their responses had left him satisfied. Just as they thought the question and answer session had ended, a little misstep occurred. Phryné mentioned that initially they would be happy with the accommodations at Leopold's flat. This surprised her mother and prompted a direct question. "Really? Exactly how big is Leopold's walk-up?"

"Well, Momma, it's two rooms: one bedroom and a parlor together, a small kitchen with a hot water heater and a bathroom with a nice porcelain tub." Without immediately realizing it, Phryné's direct, swift reply let the cat out of the bag.

Selene looked genuinely surprised and incredulous. She raised her eyebrows, wrinkling her forehead. "Oh really, daughter mine? You have spent some time there already?"

Phryné knew she had just tied her shoelaces together. She flushed, looked quickly to Leopold, then to her father and back to Leopold again. "Yes, Momma. A few times."

Selene was sitting with one hand on her knee, daintily holding her glass of homemade wine in the other; her head slightly tilted to one side. Her eyebrows, however, remained cocked and it took a minute or two before they returned to normal.

Her father hurriedly came to his daughter's rescue. "Do you have an icebox, Leopold?"

"No, sir."

"Perfect. Well, that will be our wedding gift to you. I will get you two an icebox. Maybe from Montgomery Ward. You will need an icebox."

Leopold nodded in approval. "Thank you, Bertram."

Phryné agreed. "Thank you, Papa. That will be nice. Thank you very much." She and Leopold were clearly aware of what her father had just done, but he hadn't quite finished.

"So, when is this wedding going to take place? Do we have any thoughts on that yet?"

This very important component was something that Leopold and Phryné had not yet discussed, but it now presented Leopold with the opportunity to change the direction of conversation. "Phryné and I were thinking before winter, for sure. Perhaps late September or early October. You know, before the winter weather sets in and the snow flies. That time frame would allow us to set up our household and get settled before Thanksgiving. What do you think, Bertram?"

Bertram looked across to his wife and smiled. "Selene and I think that's fine. You two have been together now for well over a year, almost two. It sounds fine to me, so I think we should go ahead with it just like you said." He stood and presented his glass for a toast. "Let's drink to that then: September or October."

The entire afternoon was spent on the porch. After some additional wedding talk, some discussion on the bravery of Lindbergh and the no-nonsense politics of President Coolidge, Bertram brought out the tabletop Victrola from the sitting room and set it on an apple crate. Three *Masters Voice* records by the Paul Whiteman Orchestra, Bessie Smith, and Cliff Richards were played whenever Bertram would stand and take the time to wind up the record player. Since it was Sunday, Selene made sure the volume was kept low. In total, four Dutch Masters and two pitchers of grape juice wine went by the wayside.

As five o'clock neared, Leopold asked Phryné if she could accompany him to his mother's house and relay their news to his family. Perhaps in an attempt to keep everyone on the porch and the discussion going, Phryné's mother suggested that she could bring out the Ouija board.

Graciously, Phryné opted for the short ride to Adams Street to give Leopold's family the news. The Ouija board required a certain amount of wonton bravery that Phryné did not have, at least not then.

Best Laid Plans

Time passes quickly when you have a lot to do, and you are indeed busy doing it. Without a doubt, the days leading up to the wedding would be hectic. Realistically, even the best-laid plans can have either successful or disastrous outcomes. Neither a Ouija board nor Leopold and Phryné could actually predict the future.

Leopold's job at Urban Flour kept him occupied for 54 hours a week. Normally, it was a 44-hour workweek, but he made the additional commitment of two additional hours daily for his mechanic's apprenticeship. The extra time allowed him to hasten his preparations for the journeyman exam and the potential for higher wages. He had managed to sock some money away, but suddenly the need became more pressing. Now, with the upcoming wedding, the chance for extra income was a definite plus.

Leopold began to second-guess his decision to ask his younger brother Nicholas to be his Best Man. Nick was 17 years old and since Leopold moved out of the family home, his family ties were strained to say the least. He had not been back since Easter, Christmas and Thanksgiving before that. Nobody could blame him if he chose to select Dillon Cafferty to fill the bill; after all, they had been cohorts for about seven months now. And Eloisa, well, she would be Phryné's Maid of Honor.

Leopold was struggling with a decision that brought his loyalties into question. So many things weighed on his conscience. This, that, or the other -- such decisions are nothing but a headache before, during and even after the selection process is over. He allowed his thoughts to torment him; the conflict would force a decision, and the cream would float to the top. If he thought about it too much, it meant his indecisiveness was some sort of weakness, and his lack of conviction could be construed as an inability to correctly identify the moral choice. On the other hand, a quick decision could be nothing more than the disclosure of his insecurity, impulsiveness, and a willingness to please other people.

In the end, his initial choice for Best Man won out. Last night, he told Phryné that he would ask Nicholas. And that is what he would do. If his brother should decline, then he could ask Dillon. That was the plan: out of the trench and over the top*. He hoped that his brother would oblige. There was something about Dillon and his brashness that rubbed Leopold the wrong way.

From Broadway, Leopold turned left on Adams and drove halfway down the block before parking the Ford in front of number 31. Every window was open, some with curtains gently wafting outside in the summer breeze. The yellow house was faded, weather worn, and in need of a coat of paint. Leopold thought he should do something about that. He knew his brother Nicholas would certainly pitch in and help.

An unknown fellow, gruff looking and in need of a shave, was sitting on the porch swing of the Victorian home. He was wearing very worn shoes without laces, and reading Sunday's

Buffalo Courier-Express. No doubt, he was one of the tenants from upstairs. He looked up from his paper, surveying them over the top of his wire-rim spectacles. He smiled and gave them a nod as they took the five steps from sidewalk to porch. His eyes followed Phryné up the steps and across the porch. The heavy door opened with a piercing squeak from the rusty hinges. It was thick, weathered oak with a heavy coat of cracking, flaking and faded green enamel. Leopold held it open for Phryné. The hallway was long and dark with limited daylight from only one window. Dark lacquered wainscot rose from the painted pine floorboards to meet faded, flower-patterned wallpaper. A narrow side table sat along the bottom landing of the long stairway that led upstairs. Beneath their feet, a hand-braided rag rug lay in front of the parlor door. He knocked on the door, and took a half step backward. His sister Ottilie came to the door.

"Leopold! Phryné! Come on in." She beamed a wide, elated smile, and invited them inside with a broad, welcoming motion of her hand. His mother and sisters Johanna and Hilde rose from their chairs. They appeared happy to see him. His mother met her son halfway across the room and they shared a brief embrace. "Come in, son. And of course, you too, Phryné. Come in and sit down."

Leopold spoke only three words. "Forgive me, Ma."

She turned away, ignoring his words. "Come in and sit down, you two. There must be some reason you stopped in."

In the middle of the large room was a dining table with a bench and three chairs snuggled under board. A long, worn burgundy and gold tatted sofa sat against the front exterior wall with tall double-hung windows on each side. A pair of end tables and three armchairs were placed along the other exterior wall. Incandescent lamps with stained glass shades sat atop the tables.

The entire home had elaborate brass gaslights, with tall glass globes and mirrored reflectors on every wall of every room. They were rarely used now, since the expansion of electric service decades ago, and only on occasion during the cold months. In the summer, they emitted too much heat to be practical.

Leopold and Phryné took seats on the sofa, and Ottilie sat next to her brother. Johanna sat in the chair closest to Phryné and Hilde pulled the bench from under the dinner table. Leopold's mother was still standing in the middle of the room.

"Root beer, cream soda, coffee or tea? What shall it be, you two? And what, pray tell, brings you back here before Thanksgiving, Leopold?"

His mother's tone was not angry, but there was an unmistakable hint of mild acrimony in her question. Leopold was gracious, polite and openly apologetic. "We have some news, Ma, and I need to ask a favor of Nicholas, also."

Phryné, still in her flowery cotton church dress, starched lace collar and half sleeves, sat with her hands folded on her lap, eagerly awaiting a bottle of soda, a glass, or cup … something to put her hands around. The undeclared truce was unnerving, and she decided it was time to do something, to say something. "I would love a root beer. How about you, Leopold?"

"Yes, I would enjoy a root beer, also."

Leopold's mother sat in the armchair closest to the sofa. Johanna stood. "I'll go put the tea kettle on, Ma, and bring out the root beer. But first, I'll go get Nick and tell him you're here, Leopold. He's in the back yard cutting up all the branches that came off the poplars and pear tree in last week's wicked thunderstorm."

Once Nicholas had come inside and cleaned himself up a bit, the entire family was together in the sitting room. It was somewhat cramped, but perhaps that helped rekindle the sense of family harmony and unity that was burnt away years earlier. Leopold carried some guilt with him after the heated disagreement with his mother back then. That argument and his selfish arrogance pushed him to walk out on her, his sisters

48

and brother. On more than one occasion, Phryné had tried to spoon-feed Leopold some sense of humility and suggested that he should try to patch things up with his mother, but his pride was stronger than Phryné's common sense. Finally, he felt remorse and remembered what Phryné had tried to instill in him. It came back to him in a flashing moment of recall -- the feeling that he regretted his actions, but did nothing to rectify the situation. It was a moment of self-embarrassment and shame that only lasted a split second, but would stay in his mind forever. At that point, Leopold had the chance to correct his course, and he took it.

Their wedding news was received with excitement, and his young brother eagerly accepted the responsibilities of Best Man. Leopold tried to play down Nicholas' role, telling his brother that there was no reason to be nervous, and assured him it was not going to be a large-scale wedding. But, truth be told, no plans could be finalized, and no reservations could be made until Leopold and Phryné contacted Reverend Barnes, so the three of them could select a date. All they had agreed upon is a small traditional ceremony at Westminster and, of course, the reception dinner at Phryné's parents' home.

Leopold looked around the front room and watched the interactions taking place. His sisters had met and spent time with Phryné on a few occasions over the last year and a half, but today's get-together was different. Fifteen year-old Hilde sat wide-eyed much of the time, absorbing all the emotion, details and nuances that come with two people in love. Leopold noticed that his mother had an air of contentment that he had not seen since his father's wounded lungs took him away. His sisters Jo and Tillie were anxiously looking forward to new hairdos at Ritzy Rita's.

When the housekeeping, food, dresses, and makeup talk started up, Nicholas coaxed Leopold onto the front porch to share a bottle of the next-door neighbor's homemade beer. There was a little more to the invitation than beer. Nicholas was determined to let his brother know exactly how he had affected the family by leaving the household as he did. Nicholas handed the warm bottle of beer to Leopold and without hesitation, started talking.

"I want to let you know, Leopold, that when you moved out, what you did back then really hurt Ma. I mean, she worships the ground you walk on, and after Pa died, she believed that you were the one she could rely on. Pa's death hurt us all, not just you, big brother. I think Ma rented those upstairs rooms just to keep life in the house, to hear noise ... to know that people were around. It wasn't just about the money. She wanted company. She wanted the noise of people, the busy, the hustle, and bustle, you know. People have different ways of coping with death, you know. And I really want to forgive you, Leopold. Now I think I can. Ma forgave you a long time ago. She doesn't hold any grudges at all. I think she understands that leaving was your way of coping with tragedy and pursuing your destiny ... and your dream. And maybe you did us all a favor without even knowing it. You got me my job at Russell-Miller and then sister Jo got a job, then Ottilie and now Hilde is getting her education. I got dreams, just like you do. I don't want to be stuck in some dusty grain mill in Buffalo. I want to be a flyboy just like Lindbergh, you know, 'Lucky Lindy'**. You know, all the way to Paris. And I will … I know I can. Someday I am going to travel the world. That's my dream. Someday I will fly airplanes, Leopold ... and even go all around the world …to Siam and maybe all the way to China. It's all about dreams, big brother. It's all about family. If you ain't got family you ... you ain't got nothing ... not even dreams. You need to remember that, brother. If your family is gone, your dreams are gone. And let me tell you … that hard-boiled harp* you hang around with … that Dillon, he's not family … far from it, Leopold. You can't count on him like family … but … but … "

Nicholas bit his cheek, calmed himself, took a breath, and went on, "Aw … Applesauce, Leopold! You got to get back into the fold! Quit playing the big shot so much and start

50

coming home more often! And I could use some help around here sometimes." Nicholas blinked hard, and held his eyes shut for a second.

Leopold set the bottle of home-brew down, grabbed Nick around the shoulders and gave him a hearty hug. He spoke over his brother's shoulder. His voice was raspy, guttural, "That's the absolute best damn 'Best Man' speech I could ever get, Nick. It proves you are not just my kid brother anymore. You are not just a 17-year-old kid anymore. You are my Best Man. Thanks, brother ... thanks, Nicholas."

Nick regained his composure and ran a sleeve across his eyes. "Cut it out! Give me one of them Chesterfields you got, Leopold."

Leopold lit one and passed it to Nick. They leaned against the porch railing, finished the bottle of beer and smoked their cigarettes. Two brothers: united with beer, tobacco, and a Best Man bond.

Dusk arrived silently. A damp evening chill was coming off Lake Erie. Down the street, lights were becoming visible in parlor windows. They heard the mantel clock strike eight.

Leopold flicked his cigarette onto the lawn and gave his brother one last handshake. "Thank you, Nicholas. I mean that. But I need to get Phryné home. And take my word for it; you will see us again ... soon."

Quiet As A Church Mouse

Leopold reached across the seat, put his wool suit coat over Phryné's shoulders and pressed the starter button on the Model T. His family was standing on the porch, waving goodbye.

"That was nice, Leopold. We had a good visit." She had pestered him for weeks about his family ties and she enjoyed a sense of achievement, not just for herself, but for Leopold, too. He put the car in gear, gave a wave over his shoulder and they were gone.

"You were right, Phryné. Surprisingly enough, it was a good visit. I expected a cold reception, and Lord knows, I deserved one, but what I got was nice. I admit that I was a dolt, Phryné. But now I got to stop acting like that. It has to stop. What's done is done, so now we start over. Best of all, Nick and I had a long talk, a good heart-to-heart, brother-to-brother talk. And it made sense. We understand each other perfectly now. We wiped off the old chalk and now we got a clean slate to work from. I got a good feeling now, Phryné. Things are looking good … real good."

"I'm happy about that, Leopold, I really am. I would not want to get married with all kinds of tension between family. It never works out good when people are fighting. Do you know what I mean?"

"Yes, I do, and I agree. Today was a good day."

She scooted across the seat, closer to him. "Can we stop at your walk-up before you take me home? We have a little time, and we could look around and maybe get some ideas for setting up the place after we are married. We will probably need to rearrange some things at the very least." She had a perky, wry smile.

"Sure thing, Phryné." He made an immediate U-turn on Fillmore, and changed course for Howlett Street. He knew what she had in mind. It wasn't furniture.

Leopold's apartment at 101 Howlett Street had been his home since May of 1925. The boarding house was titled to Mildred Flannery, a sister of his shift foreman at Urban Flour. The house was one of hundreds of Victorian styled homes in South Buffalo: a two-story wood frame structure with a massive staircase to the second floor, elaborate woodwork, wide double-hung windows, heavy wooden entrance doors, cedar wood shingles and a wrap-around front porch. A small, circular stained glass window ornately glistened in the foyer. The rooming house had a covered portal attached at the side entrance and a large granite stepping-stone sitting at curbside;

both were architectural remnants of the vanishing horse and buggy days.

Inside the hall, Phryné slipped off her laced pumps and quickly scampered up the stairs in stocking feet. She waited at the door for him, hand on hip. "How was that, Leopold? Just like a church mouse! Quiet enough?"

He met her at the door and placed his hand firmly on her behind. He whispered, and teased her, "Good job, Phryné! Once again, Mildred will never know you were here."

She closed the door behind them and held him around the waist. "Maybe not yet, but I cannot promise that I will stay quiet!" She kissed him and roughly pulled him to her. One by one, fumbling along, Leopold worked on the buttons down the back of her dress, savoring a minor victory and strategic success with each one. Moving lower, his hands reached her waist, and Phryné wriggled, letting her dress fall to the floor. She stepped out of it, and took her turn with his trousers. She grasped each of his trouser suspenders, one in each hand, twisted the large leather buttons sideways, backwards until they came undone. In passionate zeal, Phryné pushed his pants down and onto the floor. Deep, sexually charged kisses continued. He worked feverishly to remove his shirt, socks and undershorts.

Her soft white cotton camisole fell to the floor. After three ... four ... awkward, backward steps, she was on her back and spread across the bed. She twisted her body under him and managed to move her head onto the pillow. His kisses devoured her breasts, and his lips teased, and bit at her stout nipples. His passion moved him down her belly, and his teeth pulled on her lace-paneled underpants. She stretched, squirmed, twisted, writhed and kicked them off.

She held him above her, defiantly daring him with her open palms pushing upward on his chest. Leopold was ardently pressing his hips to hers. She wiggled to him, teased, and writhed away again. She surrendered to his weight, and allowed his chest to cover her breast. His hips rose; her hands went to his buttocks; she pulled him into her, and purred softly into his ear. She wrapped her bowed legs around his hips, vehemently twitching and pushing herself to him.

He moaned, "Phryné".

For the better part of an hour, their bodies were entangled in an impassioned sexual encounter. Leopold and Phryné had a visceral, carnal relationship that they consistently pushed toward its, so far, undefined limits.

At about quarter past nine, he whispered, "Soon I can keep you here all night, Phryné."

She teased, "Then you can start making my breakfasts. And desserts!"

He rolled out of bed, gathered her clothes from around the room, and put them on the bed for her.

"But for the time being, I need to drive you home."

On Monday, Phryné planned to take the streetcar up Delaware Avenue to Westminster Presbyterian and talk to Reverend Galway Barnes first thing in the morning. The couple wanted only to be married without a long delay. When they left Leopold's apartment, Phryné mentioned she might like to be married by the end of September. He joked that a September wedding would be very workable with his social calendar. They knew there was planning to be done, but Phryné seemed eagerly ready to get things started. Like horses at the gate, they were pulling at their reins.

The race to the finish was about to begin.

Chapter Three

The Toast Of The Town

Wednesday, August 24

On Monday as planned, Phryné took the William Street and Kenmore Avenue streetcars to Westminster Presbyterian and was able to speak only briefly with Reverend Barnes. He explained that he was deep into constructing next Sunday's sermon on Nehemiah's rebuilding of Jerusalem, but fortunately, he and Phryné were able to plan a meeting at home with her family on Wednesday evening after dinner. She would invite Leopold for supper just to be certain he could also be there when the minister visited.

The anticipation of the wedding itself, and its planning had Phryné swimming in an invigorating sea of excitement. She returned downtown after her meeting with the reverend, went to visit Eloisa, and ended up staying well past lunch. Eloisa was already caught up in all the thrilling excitement of planning a wedding. She and Phryné had become the very best of friends after Eloisa's sister Ginny's wedding and they soon shared everything from sweaters to secrets. Phryné wanted to hurry things along, and wanted to have the ceremony as soon as practically possible; even two or three weeks seemed to be an unnecessary delay. Eloisa understood her eagerness, knowing that Phryné and Leopold had talked about marriage more than once. They wanted a simple ceremony with only close family as guests. Eloisa and Dillon would be the only non-family members in attendance and Phryné's mother wanted the wedding dinner to be at the Truffaut family home on Lombard Street. Eloisa said she was sure she could arrange to have the wedding cake made at Farrachi's bakery, where she worked, making the cake itself a special gift. Eventually, Eloisa and Phryné joked about a honeymoon in Niagara Falls.

They giggled about that, and suggested that Leopold could rent the honeymoon suite at The Lafayette for an entire week.

The progress she made Monday with the wedding plans left Phryné very satisfied, albeit only a scheduled meeting with the minister on Wednesday. She immensely enjoyed the time she spent with her friend Eloisa. Tuesday, it was back to the ordinary ebb and flow of events at Ritzy Rita's Beauty Salon.

On Tuesday, Phryné selected the style for her wedding dress: beaded sleek ivory rayon, fringed along the hips and bodice, with a handkerchief hemline, staggered above the knee. Gert Rothman, a seamstress she and her mother knew as a customer at the beauty parlor, agreed to have it done by the end of the next week.

On Wednesday, Leopold finished work at quarter past four and rushed back to his place. Hurriedly, he washed, shaved and changed for dinner with Phryné and her family. Reverend Barnes was scheduled to stop by right after supper, about five-thirty, and if all went as desired, a tentative wedding date would be set. Leopold eagerly awaited the newest developments; things were quickly falling into place.

Reverend Barnes arrived Wednesday evening as planned, just as dinner was over. In short order, the wedding date was set and the chapel reserved for two and a half weeks later: Sunday, September 11th, at three o'clock. The Reverend Galway Barnes was pressed for time, and stayed just long enough for a cup of coffee and a piece of apple pie. He mentioned that he was off to visit the widow Abigail Wilmot, a bed-ridden parishioner in Black Rock. He hastily wiped the crumbs off his herringbone tweed and scurried off in his rickety 1917 Monroe coupe.

It was late evening, just about seven o'clock, and things had settled down. Everyone was sitting in the parlor listening to 'The Cheer Up Gang' on WGR radio. The Federal Telephone & Telegraph receiver snapped, hissed and popped. Despite the static and wavering reception, the pearly smooth voice of young Buffalo Bob Smith was wondrous entertainment. Phryné, along with Leopold, her parents, and younger brother Robert were sitting on the edge of their seats, ears straining to pick up every syllable, particle, and nuance of sound that the radio magically emitted into the room. Bob was singing *Yes Sir, That's My Baby*, performing with the WGR Orchestra. As fate would have it, Bob and his cohorts were rudely interrupted by a knock on the Truffauts' door. At this time of the evening, it was truly an unexpected guest.

Bertram Truffaut opened the entry door to find Dillon Cafferty, standing nearly at attention, smiling, clean shaven, well groomed, and dressed to the nines with a new three-piece suit and tie.

"Good evening, sir. I wonder if I may impose upon your hospitality and ask if I may speak with Leopold and your daughter Phryné, please, sir." He carried a parcel wrapped in brown paper and secured with hemp twine.

Bertram Truffaut knew Dillon casually, but he was slightly taken aback by the impertinent manner of Dillon's speech and the flashy mode of his dress. Bertram dismissed his initial impression as mere amusement, and rationalized that guests could show up at the door just about any time now. After all, his daughter was getting married, and the young man was only being polite.

Phryné's father invited him in and offered Dillon his seat on the king-size Queen Anne chair. All eyes watched intently as Dillon walked into the parlor and sat down. Bertram switched the radio off with a loud electronic click, and remained standing by the buffet table. Phryné and Leopold were, perhaps, the two most surprised people in the room. Dillon sat like a kid in the principal's office, with the package perched on his knees and his hands folded on top. For Leopold and Phryné, it was unbelievable, surreal, and like a strange dream. Dillon Cafferty's behavior was generally as predictable as a Babe Ruth home run: deep and far out of reach.

Leopold sat flabbergasted. "What are you doing here, Dillon? I mean, now? What on Earth brought you here? And tonight?"

"Well, first of all, I want to thank the Truffaut family for their hospitality. I do not want to impose on anyone, so I will make this quick. We all know that Phryné and Leopold are engaged to be married, and this marriage is going to happen very soon. So, I wanted to stop in and ask them if they would like to join myself and Eloisa Ashworth this Saturday for a celebration of their engagement. And it will be on me, one hundred percent … on me … a gift to them, from me, for their friendship. Ellie and I want to do this because Leopold and Phryné are our friends, and I know things will be very busy during the coming weeks. And because I know how things can get hectic, this may be our last chance to do this for quite some time. Another thing: next week is the Labor Day holiday, on both sides of the border. It should be riotously busy fun"

Phryné had a look of surprise, a look of embarrassing surprise. The other members of the Truffaut family, mother Selene and brother Robert, did not seem to be as shocked. They were looking at Dillon wide-eyed and excited; like someone in the room just shouted 'Bingo'. Bertram stood with his arms folded. He was watching Dillon, the smooth-talking, uninvited, surprise visitor, with an amicable, amused smile.

Leopold quickly looked around the room, checking the response of everyone else. He had no idea what to expect next from Dillon. He decided to speak first, and maybe throw some water around on Dillon's little campfire and prevent a flare-up. "Well, that sounds like the berries[*]. Great. Thank you, Dillon. If Phryné is able to come, and if we don't have any other plans, it sounds like it would be fun."

Phryné turned and looked at her father. For a split second, Leopold thought she could be looking for an excuse not to go. "Do you or Mother have any plans on Saturday, Papa?"

"No, no, we do not have plans. You are free to go if you like, Phryné. Go ahead, you two, and have fun. That's what you young folks do best. This week is no different from any other. Niagara Falls is your sandbox, so go and have fun and make all the castles you can."

Dillon jumped at the chance to interject, and started talking immediately. "Well, that is just dandy. Just what I hoped for. I am sorry for the interruption. And hey, well, I brought this other gift just in case." He got up from the chair, and handed the package to Phryné. "Ellie and I ... well, it was my idea ... I got this for you, just in case. So, I guess I will see you two on Saturday, then. The usual time and everything. And we will go across the Peace Bridge, Phryné, and take a nice slow ride up the Niagara Parkway."

"Should I open this now, Dillon?" Phryné asked.

"Sure. Go ahead. It's really a grand gift. Show it off to everybody." He was all smiles, standing with his arms folded across his chest, proud as a peacock.

Dillon could blow his own horn without reason or encouragement, and it drove Leopold crazy. Dillon did not need any help with pushing praise his own way and was double-jointed just enough to pat his own back. He always did a fine job of promoting himself.

Phryné slid the strings off and opened the parcel, carefully removing the paper wrapping and revealing a shiny chrome object with an electrical chord attached.

Dillon saw his chance to embellish the gift and make the chrome shine even more. "That is one of those new *Toastmaster* automatic bread toasting machines. You put in your slice of bread, and it pops up all by itself when it's done. It's very modern!"

"I have heard about those." Selene stood and walked over to get a better look at the innovation.

"This is very nice. Thank you, Dillon. And I will remember to thank Eloisa when I see her." Phryné handed the appliance to her mother. Robert and Bertram came over to take a closer look.

Phryné and Leopold shared a glance of exasperation and curiosity. Dillon had an ear-to-ear grin, obviously pleased with himself. "Well, it's settled. I'll come and pick you up on Saturday, Leopold. The usual time. And you will go over to Ellie's place, and I can pick you gals up there, right, Phryné?"

He was not waiting for any answers, assuming everything he just said was exactly the way he wants it to be. He stood, and was ready to leave. "So, I guess I will be on my merry way." He took two steps toward Bertram Truffaut. "And thank you, sir, for allowing me to interrupt this special evening with your family."

Bertram stuck out his hand to a waiting Dillon. "You are welcome, young man. It was not an imposition at all. And thank you for the very nice gift. My daughter will love it."

Dillon turned and nodded to Phryné's mother and brother. Leopold walked with him to the door, stopped with his hand on the knob and quietly said, "See you on Saturday, Dillon," and opened the door.

Standing in the doorway, Dillon lowered his voice and spoke privately to Leopold, "I'll go ahead and plan on Saturday then." He turned with a snap, and spoke again to Phryné's family. They were standing inside the front room, watching him exit. "Good night, everyone." Leopold was holding the door open. Dillon was not quite finished, "I'll be seeing you, Leopold," and he was out the door, scampering down the steps like a kid headed for the candy store. His brown and white wing tips flashed like lightning bugs with each step. Phryné came to the door, put a hand on Leopold's shoulder and together they watched Dillon drive off in the Pierce Arrow.

"That man is as unpredictable as he is bold," Phryné observed.

Leopold added, "Hauntingly unpredictable, Phryné. You never know what's coming next. One big windsucker*, that's what he is."

Back inside the parlor, the new Toastmaster was still the main attraction. In the next thirty minutes, about half a loaf of white bread was toasted and spread with salted butter and grape preserves.

After work on Friday, Leopold purchased a new suit at Fleischman's Clothing, and made an appointment for a proper fitting the following Friday. Phryné's gown would be ready that day also. The wedding plans were moving along, and emotions were high. Leopold and Phryné had their heads in the clouds and at that altitude, they were enjoying the most memorable and exhilarating time so far in their lives.

The Yanks Are Coming (Again)

Saturday, August 27, Niagara Falls, Ontario

The Peace Bridge connecting Buffalo, New York and Fort Erie, Ontario, Canada was brand new. It opened to the public on the first of June, but the official international grand opening ceremony did not take place until August 7. Dignitaries from England, The United States and Canada attended. The crossing of the mile-long bridge for the Pierce Arrow and its quartet of travelers was nowhere near as exciting as that grand affair.

Dillon, Leopold, Phryné and Eloisa crossed the border again with complete anonymity. When they started traveling to Canada for their party nights and dancing, Dillon suggested that they mix up their routes, so as not to draw attention to themselves. As Dillon explained it, the idea was to avoid any suspicion of cross-border smuggling, and to make it appear that they were only casual travelers heading for the jumping nightlife in Niagara Falls. It sounded logical, and it didn't impose any great inconvenience. Between the ferry services and the two bridges, their trips all went off without a hitch. After all, they were just out for a good time, a spirited and peppy party night on the town. The fact that they could consume alcohol in Canada was just icing on the cake.

Tonight's outing would perhaps be their last one for the foreseeable future. They all wanted it to be a memorable night; a romp to rival all previous nights at the Lafayette. Phryné and Leopold especially were looking forward to dancing as they never had before. A week earlier, the exhilaration of his marriage proposal foreshadowed the dancing, so they planned to dance the entire night away … as fast as their feet could carry them.

Crossing the Peace Bridge rather than the Lower Steel Deck bridge in Niagara was a much better experience and nowhere near as traumatic for Phryné. True, it was quite a bit longer, but the quiet ride over a paved bridge rather than wooden planks on a steel deck, made all the difference in the world. The River Parkway from Fort Erie to Niagara Falls was much smoother than the similar trip from Buffalo to Niagara Falls; it had new pavement without ruts or chuckholes.

When they arrived at The Lafayette, Dillon immediately noticed one small change. The attendants at the valet parking lot behind the hotel were all new personnel, and Dillon deemed it necessary to make a comment to one of them, "I guess they went and hired a whole new crew of car jockeys and dressed you up in glad rags* and everything, hey, Jack?"

This fellow took exception to Dillon's snide remark and the name he gave him. He made it known, speaking in a steely tone: "My name is not Jack. And you do not need to know my name, sir. You pay me two bits and me and my crew will take care of your car. The same complete service as before, only better, and much more personal. We are here to do our job as professionals. Just so you understand, sir, I repeat: my name is not Jack."

Dillon did not say a word. He reached into his pocket, gave him a quarter, the key for the lock, and got out of the car to join the other three already waiting for him a few yards away on the sidewalk. The men were markedly more professional looking than the previous bunch was. There were three of them, all with snappy uniforms: black slacks, calf-high riding boots, red jockey caps, white shirts and red vests. The bench was gone, and replaced by a newly constructed, freshly painted, white shed with a red Dutch door.

It was another unusually cool late August evening. The women needed their shawls to hold the wind at bay. They hurried toward the hotel's entryway; their heels clicking cheerfully along the sidewalk.

The uniformed doorman took Dillon's cash with a broad smile, and welcomed them back to The Lafayette just as two other men opened the doors wide for the foursome. Inside, the sandwich board outside the ballroom proudly displayed the night's entertainment. A colorful poster pronounced *Fred Nichols and His Five Pennies* to be the best dance band west of New York City. That was exactly what Eloisa, Phryné, Leopold and Dillon went there to do: dance, drink, and party.

It promised to be an excellent evening. Their trips to Canada had become such a habit that much of it seemed to be mundane: their experiences at the border, interactions with the hotel staff, and even the trip itself. One thing that did vary, and thankfully so, was the entertainment. Never once did they encounter the same band over again. The Lafayette seemed to have an unlimited number of troupes to draw from. Several of the acts came to Niagara Falls either directly from New York or Toronto, or even through the vaudeville houses in Chicago, Detroit, or Buffalo. Leopold could not be sure, but he suspected that tonight's band was Canadian, judging strictly by their name. His guess was proven correct when the introductions were made. Fred Nichols had a female vocalist; a young lady hailing from New Brunswick with the very English name *Anne Howe*. By eight o'clock, the ballroom was alive with raucous conversation, dancing, and drinking. For Phryné and Leopold, it was more than just another evening of good times and dancing. They were truly enjoying themselves, living it up in the present and dreaming about the future. Tonight, for some unpredictable reason, the entire crowd seemed to know only one dance: the Charleston. Nichols, his Five Pennies and Anne Howe had a style of music that leaned more toward the popular dance tunes rather than the New Orleans Blues or Jazz numbers that opened up greater variety on the dance floor. Leopold and Phryné tried several times to break away and do the Black Bottom or Flea Hop only to be swallowed up by the crowd.

"Is that all this band can do? Nothing else? I can think of a lot of ways to have fun knocking knees together other than just doing the Charleston." Leopold's saucy argument got a salacious giggle from Phryné.

Regardless, it was another lively evening that had to end at midnight.

Bordering On Crazy

For the next nine months, the warm nights of summer would be a memory. The past week's cool, star-lit humidity was sharply different from the dark overcast and damp chill they felt that night. Despite her shawl, the walk along the sidewalk back to the parking lot sent a wave of goose bumps along Phryné's bare arms. Leopold felt the cool air, took off his jacket and covered her shoulders. The Pierce Arrow was parked down the street at the curb. Dillon was walking briskly ahead of them, with Eloisa close behind. She had her arms crossed, hugging herself and taking quick steps to keep up. As soon as she could, she opened the front door, slid inside and covered up with the blanket. Dillon approached the shed. Phryné and Leopold got into the back seat, sat close and covered their laps with the other blanket. They watched Dillon at the small valet stand and wished he could hurry it along.

From behind the Dutch door, the attendant announced, "You are ready to go, sir. All the usual; washed and cleaned up inside and out. Did you enjoy your evening, sir?" His tone was aloof, haughty and oddly puzzling.

As a matter of habit, Dillon passed him a dollar bill. "Yes, I did. I had a very good time as usual."

The attendant had an antiseptic, emotionless, smile and was holding the key to the Pierce Arrow against his chest. "That is good to hear, sir." He then gave Dillon a slight nod, handed him the key, and added, "The hotel management placed a very small token of appreciation in the trunk for you and your Buffalo friends. Don't worry; it's well wrapped so it won't present a problem at the crossing. Perhaps we will see you and your party again very soon, sir."

"You will. We are up here often. So, until next time ... toodles." He gave the parking attendant an acknowledging nod in return, studied him for a split second, and started toward the car. Dillon wondered what that fluffed-up conversation was all about and sloughed it off as some kind of promotional jazz for new and improved service. The valet's brash tone and overbearing manner were unsettling. Usually, Dillon was the one who could be disconcerting, but if anyone gave him a bad first impression, it stayed bad. He decided that he would complain to the hotel management about this fellow the next time they came up.

Dillon did his habitual, cursory walk-around the Pierce Arrow, kicked the tires and smacked the spare with his fist. As soon as he approached the driver's side, Eloisa had an urgent request, "Hurry up and start the car, Dillon. And shut the door! We're freezing in here!"

He got behind the wheel and talked down to Eloisa, "I really don't think it's all that bad, is it? We'll warm up quick ... before you know it." He unlocked the transmission, pushed the starter button, and with a click and a whirr, the car was headed south on the Niagara Parkway toward Buffalo.

"Hey, you two in the back seat ... you had a good time on my dime tonight, right?" Dillon lit a cigarette.

"Yes, we did. Thank you Dillon. That was nice of you to treat us." Phryné sounded tired.

Leopold echoed her thoughts, "Yeah. That was nice, Dillon. We had a good time, as usual." Then his curiosity took over. "The parking lot fellow, the new guy, he was talkative, wasn't he?" Leopold was probing for information. It was unusual for Dillon not to push his weight around with a service employee.

"Yeah. I think he had instructions to brag up the new so-called service. A pound of baloney is all it amounts to, if you ask me. He even said the hotel put a gift in the trunk, all wrapped up nice. Big deal … we'll see." He flicked ash from his cigarette onto the clean floor. "Anyway, I hope this trip will not be our last. Even after the wedding, you two are still going to come up here with me and Ellie for some good fun, right?"

Eloisa turned around, and Phryné quickly answered. "Of course. Sure … just because Leopold and I are getting married doesn't mean we won't be friends anymore. Certainly, we will still go out on the town with you. You cannot get rid of us that easily, Dillon!"

Eloisa smiled, and turned around. She cuddled under the blanket again, clearly pleased with Phryné's answer.

Streetlights were not as prevalent on the Canadian side of the river as on the American side. The midnight drive demanded that Dillon's attention be kept within the reach of the headlights. The dark skies, smooth pavement, the warm blanket and quiet, comforting ride of the Pierce Arrow, were enough to put Phryné and Eloisa to sleep. Eloisa was leaning against the door, using her shawl and pocketbook as a pillow. Phryné was balled up in the backseat, with her head on Leopold's lap. He awoke with his chin buried in his chest and his neck aching. They were in Fort Erie already, and Dillon was turning onto Queen Street, ready to cross back to the United States. The bright lights at the bridge approach flooded the interior of the automobile.

Leopold leaned forward. "Well, that was quick, Dillon."

"Yeah. Nice of you to join the party now, Leopold. You were snoring, you know. Wait until your baby vamp* Phryné finds out you snore. You might not be sharing a bed with that ripe tomato after all. Women can be funny like that. I don't snore … I got self-control."

Leopold was stiff, tired, half-awake and did not care to argue or hear any of Dillon's snide remarks. Phryné stirred and woke. She sat up, stretched, and arched her back. "Hey. We are almost home. Goody, goody gumdrops."

In the front seat, Eloisa was stirring. She straightened up, looked around and snuggled under the blanket again, hugging herself. Dillon made the turn from Queen Street and carefully approached the tollbooth. He reached into his vest pocket, grabbed a thin Canadian dime, dropped it into the toll keeper's little basket, and drove onto the bridge. Beneath them, the Niagara River seemed calm compared to the rushing water just thirty miles north under the Whirlpool Bridge. Light sparkled off the river's surface, creating countless twinkling, tiny flashes of light beneath the black, overcast sky.

Approaching the Immigration, Customs and Revenue Service Inspection Booths on the American side, Dillon slowed the car, and initially stood seventh in line. They casually watched as two agents performed the visual inspections, walking slowly around with their mirrors and peering into the automobile stopped at the booth. There were several floodlights mounted on wooden poles, lighting up the examination area like noon on a sunny day. One car at a time, they inched forward toward the booth. The inspectors were moving the line along. In mere moments, they were next in line.

Dillon crept forward, lowering his window. The inspector stuck his face into the car. "United States citizens?" Four voices responded: "yes". He stuck his head further into the car, forcing Dillon to lean back.

Another two officers walked around the Pierce Arrow, looking into the windows, and checking under the car with

67

their long-handled mirrors. They were finished quickly, and stood by the booth waiting for the next car.

"How long have you been in Canada?"

Dillon answered, "Just a few hours. We were dancing at the Lafayette in Niagara Falls."

"How about you, Miss? How long were you in Canada?"

It was Eloisa's turn. "Just like he said, only a few hours."

"Did you purchase or receive anything while you were in Canada?"

Dillon quickly answered, "No sir."

The agent persisted, "Nothing?"

Dillon again flashed a response, "No, nothing. And there's nothing in the trunk, either."

Dillon Cafferty immediately realized that he just made a mistake. He felt a tingle on his scalp. He wondered why he allowed those words to cross his lips. What did he just say, and why on Earth did he say that? He mumbled a profanity. The agent heard it.

Leopold was wide-awake by this time. His senses came alive.

The agent pulled his head out of the car, but kept his hands on the windowsill. He nodded to the right, and said, "Pull over there by the dock for a secondary inspection of the vehicle, please." He lifted his right hand off the car, and pointed. "Right over there, next to that parked Revenue Enforcement patrol car."

Dillon was unusually polite. "Yes, sir. Thank you." He rolled up the window, and cautiously crept away from the booth at a snail's pace.

Eloisa complained, "Of course this has to happen just when we want to go home and get to bed."

This was the first time they were singled out for an additional inspection. Dillon's senses sharpened. Electric charges were running up and down his skull. His skin prickled, his breath quickened, and his thoughts travelled at light speed.

Dillon always had a 'seed' package in the trunk: a paper sack with a quart bottle of Canadian Club rye whiskey tucked into the toolbox behind the tire jack, and covered with a rag. It had been there for months. Its sole purpose was to distract any snooping, blood-hound-sniffing federal officer off the scent of the real prize. The officer would confiscate the lone bottle, scold the driver, give him a stern warning and let him proceed. That was the intention.

Thunder clapped between Dillon's ears. He remembered something that bimbo* parking lot attendant back at the Lafayette said about a nicely wrapped package in the trunk for his 'Buffalo friends'. He thought, '*I should have checked the trunk*'.

In the flash of an instant, Dillon wondered what the valet attendant could have meant. His imagination flew out of control. There could be anything in the trunk: cases of whiskey, bottles of opium, bags of Indian hashish, jugs of beer, or even a drugged prostitute or two. He should have checked … and he didn't. Somebody could be setting him up. Maybe one of Lorenzo's greaseball* rivals from Tonawanda. There was only one thing left to do now, only one way out. The bulls forced his hand. Now was the time for action.

In the back seat, Leopold and Phryné were under the assumption that shortly they would be standing outside the Pierce Arrow in the night air while federal officers checked the car for contraband.

Dillon kept the car crawling toward the officer waiting for them at the dock. His eyes swept over the sprawling concrete lot, parked trucks, and warehouses to his right, back to the dock on his left, the wooden barricades and cement pylons a hundred yards ahead. He shouted out two words, "Hang on!" and pushed the accelerator pedal to the floor. The Pierce Arrow hesitated, the carburetor gasped, the distributor clicked, the engine sputtered and came alive, roaring with all six cylinders.

Eloisa's eyes opened as large as saucers. Phryné looked wildly around and held her breath. Leopold leaned forward, hanging onto the back of the front seat. "What's up?"

"We're running the border. Running it. Hang on, I said!" Halfway to the wood barricades, two uniformed officers stood with pistols drawn. The crack of a gunshot pierced the night. The officers at the barricades fired. They fired their pistols repeatedly. Dillon steered the car hard left, toward the docks. An officer jumped out of the patrol car with a drawn pistol, and he too, began firing. The unmistakable ding and ping of metal-on-metal echoed inside the car. Somewhere behind them, they heard the unmistakable pitchy sound of a siren growing, increasing its pitch, and reaching its crescendo. It was a hand-cranked siren, squealing from the inspections booth. Eloisa gasped, put her hand over her mouth and began to whimper. Phryné sank low in the seat, and held onto Leopold's thigh.

"What in the hell are you doing, Dillon?!"

He didn't answer, and swerved the car around, heading back toward the bridge. Officers appeared from nowhere, and came out of booths that looked empty, hands either on their holstered weapons, or drawn and aimed at the Pierce Arrow. A bullet hit the windshield and spider web cracks appeared in the corners, reflecting incandescent light in crazy, dancing patterns. Dillon swung the car around yet again, to see officers running toward him from the pylons and barricades.

"Get down. Way down! Hang on! I got them running! They're running!"

Eloisa bent at the waist, her head in her lap, and her hands over her head. She wasn't sobbing anymore. Phryné curled up on the seat, hanging onto Leopold's thigh with one hand and the other arm around his waist. Leopold raised his head just enough to allow him to peer over the seat.

"Son of a bitch! What the hell are you doing Dillon?" He didn't get an answer. There were more gunshots. Dillon held the steering wheel with both hands and kept his eyes aimed straight ahead. The Pierce Arrow was the only automobile moving.

More gunshots, metallic pings, loud growling from under the Piece Arrow's hood, men shouting commands, brass whistles and another siren were all mixed into an unintelligible soup of noise. Straight ahead, a Revenue officer stood, legs apart, pistol drawn and pointed directly at the car.

Dillon locked his jaw, stiffened his arms and held the wheel with white knuckles. He had his back pressed against the seat and foot frozen to the floor. His eyes locked on the officer and the barricades in his path. "I am going to drive this goddamn car straight through your guts and out your ass, copper!"

Together, in a boiling pot of noise, were repeated gunfire, a loud thud, a muffled scream, and crushing metal. The car rocked, bounced, and the Revenue officer was thrown under the car with a heavy thump. The car bounced again; more metal on metal pings, dings, and breaking glass. Dillon's straw boater blew off his head and out the window. Wooden barricades placed atop concrete pylons loomed just ahead. More noise was dumped into the boiling cauldron: crashing, cracking and breaking wood. He spun the wheel and drove into the makeshift wooden fence at an angle. A headlamp went out, lumber flew over the vehicle's roof, the car swung sideways, and the sound of sharp gunfire disappeared behind them like pops of July Fourth firecrackers.

The Pierce Arrow dropped from the curb of the Revenue impound lot and onto Front Avenue with a heavy clunk. Dillon turned and looked behind. Two pairs of headlights were bouncing up and down behind him. The hand-cranked sirens were still wailing.

Leopold turned to look, and determined that Dillon was pulling away from the Customs and Revenue patrol cars. The Pierce Arrow was gaining ground on the two cars behind them. Phryné was breathing heavily. Leopold carefully brushed glass fragments from her and onto the floor. The seat was wet. "Are you OK?"

Phryné took a breath, and talked loudly over the engine's horsepower, "I think so. Is it over, Leopold?"

Air from two shattered windows rushed inside the car. Dillon was driving the car as if possessed by the Devil, faster than any of them had ever experienced. It was an unexpected thrill ride through a shooting gallery.

"What the hell was that about, Dillon? For Christ's sake, what the hell was that about?" The wind whipped around; spinning, twisting like a Texas tornado inside the car.

"Wait until I shake these bulls off my ass. Then I'll tell you everything."

Phryné slowly sat up, and looked around. "Oh my God … oh my God … Eloisa … Eloisa! Are you all right? Eloisa!"

"I think I got shot … mmmm … in my arm." She slowly sat up, and held a bloody right shoulder. "Owww."

Phryné looked behind, and saw the pursuing Revenue cars in the distance, fading further and further back. Dillon had the Pierce Arrow flying down Front Avenue, and made a very sharp left onto Porter Avenue, almost flipping the car. The pursuing sirens were almost inaudible. The inside of the car stunk like a hospital surgery ward.

Phryné took her silk scarf and leaned forward to check Eloisa's shoulder. Eloisa shuddered and moaned. Phryné ripped the dress at the shoulder seam and held her scarf to Eloisa's wound.

"Dillon, you son of a bitch. Eloisa's shot. There better be a damn good reason for you acting like an idiot. A damn idiot. It stinks of whiskey in here!"

Dillon growled, "Shut up, Frenchie."

Leopold and Phryné sat close, clasping hands. They all tried to catch their breath, take stock of the situation and control their emotions. Eloisa winced in pain. Four hearts were pounding like never before.

"Take us home, you crazy Leprechaun. We've had enough. Take Ellie to the hospital and Phryné and me can go home. We don't have a dog in this fight of yours."

Dillon was in his own private reality, and did not hear what Leopold said. His eyes moved focus from the road to the mirror and back again.

The patrol cars could no longer be seen, and the siren was silent. Either Dillon lost the border bulls when he turned onto North Street or back somewhere on Porter. He dodged an oncoming car at the intersection of Main and Elmwood, and sped past another around Linwood. There was sparse traffic on the Sunday morning streets. Dillon slowed the car, continued down North Street to Masten Park, turned left into the park and stopped under a grove of Elms, right across the street from the city reservoir.

They sat without making a sound. The engine's roar settled to a purr. Each of them looked around the interior of the bullet-riddled car, sat quietly, thinking, wondering, and listening to his or her heartbeats and quickened breath. There was one dim streetlight down the block at the corner of Best and Jefferson. The Beltway trolley clicked past them.

"I lost them lousy Feds. They couldn't catch us with them cheap little four cylinder Chevrolets. Can't outrun a big six* straight Arrow with a lousy turd on wheels."

"You can find time to brag about a car now, Dillon? What the hell is going on? Eloisa's shot for Christ's sake." Leopold was incredulous, holding Phryné's hand.

Dillon opened the driver's door, and what was left of the window glass fell with a clatter and tinkle to the ground as he slammed it shut. He walked briskly around the vehicle and opened the other door to look at Eloisa's shoulder. He moved the scarf and her torn dress to reveal the gunshot wound. He put his face closer, covered the wound again and tried to encourage her. "You'll be fine, Ellie. Hold that scarf right there. I'll get you fixed up right away. Just around the block ... I'll get you to Doc Phillips over there on Locust ... and he'll patch you up. I can see the slug ... it's sitting right at the surface ... right below the skin. My car's steel slowed it down ... you'll be fine, sugar baby." Eloisa sat wide-eyed, staring across the street, and just barely shaking her head. Tears blackened her face with mascara. Dillon walked back around the car, got behind the steering wheel, and drove out of the park and south on Michigan Avenue.

Leopold was angry. "Well, Dillon? What was that all about back there? Ellie's shot, the car's a wreck, it stinks of alcohol, you drove over a copper back there, and I'm extremely pissed off. We got a trunk-load of bootleg* booze or what? What in the hell is going on, Dillon? And is all this shit worth it?"

"You shut up too, Leo. I'm taking Ellie to the Doc and get her patched up first. Then you and your flapper girlfriend back there can start asking questions. Until then, quit your bellyaching and complaining and shut the hell up, both of you!"

Leopold was quickly running out of self-control. "Are you mixed up in smuggling, Dillon? Are there jugs of whiskey in the trunk? Booze is leaking from somewhere ... booze! Are you mixed up with them Sicilians, the mob, the Black Hand?"

Dillon shouted. "I said, *shut the hell up!*"

Phryné pushed Leopold with her elbow.

Poor Bladder Control

Dillon drove the battle-scarred Pierce Arrow five blocks south to the Fruit Belt neighborhood of South Buffalo. He pulled into the narrow driveway at 56 Locust Street, turned the ignition off and immediately exited the car. He hurried around the car, "Come on, sugar baby. Let's get you fixed up." He helped Eloisa out of the car, and slammed the door behind him. Neighborhood dogs were barking.

He stuck his face halfway into the car and growled out the command: "I'll be out soon ... wait here ... this won't take long. You listen to me … listen up and don't either of you go nowhere."

Leopold protested, "Dillon, this is a veterinary office."

"You're a goddamned genius, Leo! And you think I don't know that? Just wait here with that Sheba* of yours, and I'll be back out as soon I got my Ellie patched up."

Side by side, with arms around one another, Dillon and Eloisa gingerly climbed the three wooden steps onto the porch. He banged loudly on the door with his fist, and pulled the bell chain as well..

Phryné huddled next to Leopold, and drew the wool blanket up under her chin. Both front side windows were shattered, the windshield had spider web cracks everywhere and a silver-dollar size hole in the upper right corner. The rear window was gone; shattered back at the border. The back seat and floor were wet with grain alcohol; its harsh, overwhelming, stench permeated everything inside the car. On the porch, the door opened. Dillon helped a wobbly Eloisa stumble inside. Before he slammed the door shut behind them, he looked back at the Pierce Arrow with a profound scowl. His harsh gaze brought an ominous chill to Leopold and Phryné.

Leopold felt threatened, angry and allowed his curiosity to take control. "I'll be right back. I need to take a look inside the trunk, Phryné. And whatever you do, don't go lighting any cigarettes. This whole car could ignite into a hell-fire storm."

Phryné turned and watched him open the trunk, lift and shuffle a blanket, tarpaulin or something. Leopold cursed, pushed the trunk shut, and got back into the car.

He looked at her in a vanishing moment and then fixed his gaze beyond the destroyed windshield to the veterinarian's porch and front door. He started to ramble, "There's a body back there, Phryné. A dead guy tied up with a hole in his head. Christ Almighty. And there are bullet holes everywhere. The trunk is riddled with them. Holes in the back of the seat, too. You could have been shot … we both could be dead. The trunk and the seat caught the gunfire. I'm done with this shit, Phryné.

We need to get as far away from Dillon as possible … we didn't expect this level of bullshit entertainment. Least of all, this particular goddamn horror show. This is trouble … it's big Torricelli brothers, Mafia trouble. This is the beginning of a mob war … that's what this is … the Sicilians are going to get their revenge for this. There's a body in the trunk. The shit is going to hit the fan."

Phryné hung on every word, blinking rapidly. "Leopold, we have to help Eloisa get home. We owe her that. She could not have known about all this either. I don't believe it."

He put his arm around her. They sat in silent anger, anxiety, worry, and wonder. Their thoughts were swirling, struggling to find reason in a chasm full of fear. They considered Dillon's dangerous, unpredictable, and violent response to everything that happened since they left the Lafayette, and could only guess what he would do next.

There was light filtering through two shaded windows of the veterinarian's one story bungalow.

Leopold looked at his watch and saw that it was 1:30. He was sorting through the broken fragments, bits and pieces of information, possibilities, shadowy probabilities, and fears hiding deep inside the dark, bottomless abyss of the unknown. He was trying to make sense of nonsense.

Sitting next to him, huddled under the blanket, Phryné was worrying on the same level. The ominous uncertainty of her immediate future pierced her dreams and chilled her soul. "Let's leave, Leopold. Let's think about this, and get out now. It's probably not safe here for us anymore. Not now. I'm afraid. Something happened tonight and it's not good."

He nodded, and did not say a word. Leopold reached under the blanket and held her hand. He sat thinking and staring out the windshield. Questions, situations, and histories were flooding his mind and pounding pieces of the puzzle into place. He shared his thoughts aloud with Phryné. His words flowed from his lips as soon as he retrieved them from memory.

He recalled the new parking lot attendants, and realized that should have been the first clue to the coming changes. He thought back to January, when Dillon boldly asked for, and demanded, a hundred dollar loan to purchase the Pierce Arrow. Dillon pressed him, and he literally would not take 'no' for an answer, assuring him that he would pay him back within a month. Leopold foolishly trusted him, gave in and loaned him the money.

A few weeks afterward, in February, Dillon appeared battered and beaten at Leopold's apartment on Howlett, desperately needing a ride back to his place on West Delevan. He said the Pierce Arrow was taken as collateral, a security deposit, for a gambling debt he owed to some low-life named Lorenzo Torricelli and his brother Vincente. Oddly, Leopold remembered that Dillon always parked the car off Prospect Avenue, three miles away from where he lived. That never made any sense to him, but he only gave it consideration just now. His mind was burning, churning with thoughts, uncovering one-by-one the lies Dillon created. Discovering one deception after another, the truth became clear and began to snowball down a slippery slope greased with Dillon's half-truths, fabrications and veiled falsehoods.

A Model 80 Pierce Arrow was not the type of automobile that an employee at a soft drink bottler would own. Now, even the reason and the mystery behind all their trips to Canada was clear. The car reeked of alcohol: crude, pure, straight grain alcohol. The gunfire must have punctured a reservoir of some kind somewhere inside the trunk or back seat. All the different routes they took across the border were likely taken to avoid detection. Leopold, Phryné and, without doubt, even Eloisa were a part of Dillon's fabricated identity and devious disguise. The snappy clothes, the movie star look that he emanated, the flashy talk, his aura of superiority, all of it was part of a clever deception. Dillon flushed his friends into a swirling sewer of lies; a demonic, devilish ruse. He took full advantage of their naïve outlook on life and pulled them into his world of duplicity and distortion.

"When we get out of this, do you still want to get married, Phryné?"

She did not expect that question, and was taken aback. "Of course. Yes. Yes, I do."

Together, in the passing moments, in silence, they pondered their future. They were in complete agreement without saying a word. Together, Leopold and Phryné woke up, and saw the truth.

The door opened on the veterinary's porch. Dillon came out ahead of Eloisa, holding her free hand; her right arm in a sling. He walked quickly, his arm around her waist, lifting and pushing her along toward the car. He hastily opened the passenger door. "There you go, sugar baby, get in. I'll drive you home now. Straight home." He slammed the door shut. Broken glass rattled and tinkled inside the door panels.

Phryné leaned forward, close to her friend. "Are you OK, Eloisa?"

Dillon was doing a walk-around the battle-worn Pierce Arrow, studying the bullet-ridden hood, and fenders, down along the driver's side, then to the back of the car, the trunk, and along the passenger side.

In a nervous, weakened voice, Eloisa answered. She spoke quickly as Dillon walked around the car. "Yes. I got my nerves shaken and my shoulder shot, but I'm OK now. Just like Dillon said, the bullet was just under the skin with no bad damage, just blood and bruising. I'll be OK. I just want to go home and get into bed. Tomorrow I need to tell my parents something. I don't know how I can explain this." She turned her head closer to Phryné and whispered, "I don't think I'll be going out with Dillon anymore. Maybe, but I doubt it. I really doubt it. I don't like this, and I know my father won't either."

Dillon got in, started the car, jammed the transmission in reverse and sped backwards out of the driveway. He started talking immediately. "Yeah, I was right. It was just a surface wound. Didn't even hit the bone. My sugar baby will be just fine."

Leopold had to ask, "A veterinarian, Dillon?"

Dillon rambled again, "Yeah. I found out about him a couple of months back after a dust-up at Flannigan's. Not too much work for those horse and donkey doctors now, what with all the cars and trolleys. Yeah, so Doc Phillips needs the work, you see." He had a sinister chuckle. "I told him to keep his mouth shut, if he wants to stay in the family, if you know what I mean. He knows who butters his bread."

Leopold was in the middle of a slow burn, and his patience was wearing thin. His insides were simmering and close to boiling over. "You just do not know when to quit do you, Dillon? You just keep the jazz coming and coming. You are nothing more than a bullshit artist. A low-life bullshit artist."

"Look, Leo, all I'm worried about right now is getting my Ellie home. Then I can deal with all your crap and two-bit, bullshit questions, Throckmorton. And your Frenchie Phryné's shit too. Whether you realize or not, I got us all out of a tough spot back there at the border. You can be thankful that you were in a fast car, and I can handle dangerous situations. I'm going to start carrying a gat from now on, a revolver. A 38 will be nice. I don't want no peashooter. A 38, that's what I need. I could have given them bulls a taste of lead for breakfast if I had me a realizer; a 38 realizer." He nodded as he talked, his words ran together, and he agreed with every word that came out of his own mouth.

Leopold and Phryné shared a quick glance, astonished at Dillon's arrogance. Everyone remained quiet the rest of the way to Eloisa's home. It was nearly 2:30, and the city of Buffalo was asleep except for streetcars and milk wagons. Leopold was constantly looking for a beat cop, and worried if anyone would spot the bullet-ridden car. Dillon turned into alleyways, along side streets, around vacant lots, and drove through city reservoir property. Eventually, his route led him to the curb at 17 Olga Place. He parked and barked an order:

79

"Go help your girlfriend out of the car, and up them steps, Phryné. Now, Frenchie!! Now!!"

Once Phryné and Eloisa were on the sidewalk, Leopold leaned forward and broke the news to Dillon about the contents of the trunk. "You got a body in the trunk, Dillon. It's wrapped and covered up nice, just like you said ... just like they told you back at the Lafayette. A surprise in the trunk. Nice and dead, with a hole in the center of his forehead."

Up on the porch, Phryné was giving Eloisa a hug and encouragement.

Dillon nervously jumped out of the car and opened the trunk. In mere moments, Dillon's situation dramatically changed; his life forever altered. He was jolted back from fantasy and into the real world. He stood motionless for five seconds, and returned to the driver's seat with a plop just as Phryné opened the back door, got in and slid over next to Leopold. She felt a piercing pain at her calf; a bullet-torn corner of the door had ripped through her stocking and cut her leg as she got in. Phryné reached down, and pressed her hand onto the wound, glanced to Leopold and quietly cursed in French, "Oh, merde!"

In a state of violent realization, Dillon turned around and looked at them. His cold blue eyes did not focus, and seemed to bulge from their sockets. He spit his angry words over the seat. "Son of a bitch! That's Vincente, Lorenzo's brother back there. Dead inside my trunk. Damn it! We're in the shit now. I sure as hell do not need this damn drama ... not now." He snapped his head back, and stared out the cracked and chinked windshield. His actions were mechanical, trance-like. He started the car, drove down the block and away from the streetlight, stopping in front of a vacant lot. He sat frozen, hands on the steering wheel with a blank stare. For a second or two, it was chillingly silent.

"Take me and Phryné to my place, Dillon, then I don't give a damn what you do. Just take us to my place."

Dillon once again jerked his head around and looked at them. "Well ain't that just the latest damn newsreel? You're going to jump ship like a diseased rat? It figures … it figures. The *ish kabibble** twins … Throckmorton and his Frenchie … the rats jump ship."

"Dillon, look … you need to think about this. You need to get this car off the street. Now. This car is a hot potato. Sooner or later a cop is going to spot this car, and I bet you a dollar to a doughnut that the Feds have already been on the telephone to the Buffalo cops and gave them a full description of your car. Think about yourself like you always do … think about yourself … you can take me and Phryné to my place, then get this car off the road, Dillon. You are a good driver. You know what to do. You keep calm in times like this. Park it in the garage where you do; anywhere, wherever, anyplace. Just get rid of it; just get this car out of sight and take care of things in the morning. Don't think about Eloisa or Phryné or me. Think about yourself and how you can get out of this mess. Do that for yourself."

Dillon turned his head again, appeared to focus on the dashboard and began to ramble. His words ran together, "In the morning Lorenzo is going to find out about his brother. We're in the shit. I need to get a wiggle on*. I need to think of something. I really need to think of something. We're really in the shit. It's up to me to fix this."

Dillon's blind arrogance sickened Phryné. She turned, looked down the street behind them and watched as a light came on inside Eloisa's home. The light was a flash, a signal, and she knew her friend would be safe now. She wiped away a tear and brought herself back to the drama inside the Pierce Arrow. She broke the brief silence, "You're in the shit, Dillon. Not us. Not me. Not Leopold. You're in the shit." She kept a hand pressed to the cut on her calf.

Dillon spun around yet again and hung his arm over the seat back. He spoke loudly, nervously with a cracking, wavering voice. "Oh yes, you are in the shit, sweet cheeks!

And your boyfriend back there, too! We all are! You don't know from nothing! I know better! And you can't bullshit a bullshitter! I've been running this flimflam* for six months now with the brothers. And now, Vinnie's dead. Don't you get it? Wake up!"

He lowered his voice and started to speak slower. His eyes moved from side to side and beads of sweat dripped from his forehead, onto his nose, and down onto his shirt. He started to lecture from the front seat. It sounded like a fire-and-brimstone doomsday sermon from the pulpit of a crazed preacher.

"You guys were my mask, my disguise. I've been using you as cover, you dopes. Live cover. The perfect disguise: a pair of Shebas and two Sheiks all dressed up and doing the town. It was all part of the perfect game, you know. You were my pawns, chumps*, snake charmers*, that's all. I cooked up the perfect scam. Dillon Cafferty had it all figured out and it worked good."

His waved his left hand and pointed a finger at them to prove his point, "And I got news for you two turtle-doves. That back seat you got your sweet asses parked on is full of damn near hundred proof grain alcohol inside bladders … bladders, you know, like hot water bottles, enema bags, only made out of canvas and rubber. I hand the Lafayette doorman a hundred and twenty clams* and them parking lot guys fill them bladders with hooch, then the next day, me and the brothers drain and refill them down here with plain water. Liquid seats, that's what they are; fifty-gallon liquid seats. What do you think of that? You got your sweet asses sitting on liquid gold! Me and the brothers water it down, dilute and color the stuff and flavor it; gin, scotch, rye, even vodka; any way we want. One of them Feds must have got lucky and shot a slug through the trunk and it hit one of them bladders in the back seat."

He paused and nodded in self-affirmation. "Damn … that's probably twenty gallons down the drain. And it was me, I myself beefed up the Arrow's suspension with a couple of leaf springs from that Stewart Motors truck plant on Delevan.

That was my idea, all mine. The brothers loved it. Shit! Now it's all shot to hell. Somebody else must want to take over the action at the Lafayette. Lorenzo ain't going to take this laying down. This ain't going to be good. The shit is going to hit the fan."

Leopold selfishly tried to throw some water on the fire burning inside Dillon's skull. "Let's worry about all that tomorrow, Dillon. Right now, think of your safety. Stay calm, and hide this car. You need to do that. Drop me and Phryné at my walk-up and hide this thing. We will work out all the rest in the morning, all right? We'll figure it out." He was trying to build on Dillon's ego and prevent any more disasters. Leopold wanted this nightmare to end. He knew it was necessary to take Phryné and get as far away from Dillon as possible. This situation was as dangerous as dynamite in a frying pan.

On the seat next to him, Phryné was confident that Leopold was only lying to Dillon about tomorrow, and all that talk about working things out was just talk; only talk. She trusted him, but this conversation was making her nervous.

Dillon sat motionless for a half minute, swore one more time and started the car. He stuffed the transmission in gear with a jolt, turned around in the narrow street and drove off, heading up Fillmore to Broadway and to Leopold's place. It was 3:00 when Dillon dropped them off at Leopold's second story walkup. He turned, looked around in every direction and spoke in a far-away, melancholy, and lonesome tone. "Goodnight … see you two tomorrow. I was right. I'll fix things. Things work themselves out. They always do, right?" His words were agonizing, terse, and sounded hollow. He nervously nodded in dubious agreement with himself.

Leopold shut the door, leaned onto the window frame and gave Dillon his veiled reassurance, "Yeah, they do. It always works out ... see you tomorrow, Dillon. Now go hide this car. You're smart … you know what to do." Leopold pushed away from the car and made a promise to himself: *I will not see that man again.*

Dillon mashed the transmission into gear. The Pierce Arrow lurched away from the curb, and disappeared down Sycamore Street.

Phryné waited on the sidewalk for Leopold. "You really are not going to see him tomorrow, are you?"

"Hell no, Phryné. Hell no. Neither are you. Ever again. From now on, Dillon Cafferty is nothing more than a bad memory."

Chapter Four

Twenty-Three Skidoo

Sunday, August 28

At the bottom of the stairs, Phryné and Leopold took off their shoes and walked up. Once inside the apartment, he shed his jacket and quietly set it on the floor with his wingtips. Phryné's shawl, pumps, and pocketbook followed. They stood motionless in the dark and held each other. Her chest was heaving against him. Through the alcohol, he could smell his sweat and her fear. Wet, cold and afraid, Phryné whimpered, and Leopold rubbed his hands up and down her back and shoulders. He was wet, cold, and fearful as well. He had never felt this way before. It was a horrific, torturous fear; the bogeyman lurked around every corner. He now feared for Phryné and loathed Dillon. whose existence and mere presence threatened them and their love.

Steadily, they regained their composure. Their heartbeats slowed and rational thought returned. He worked out a plan of action in absolute moments.

Leopold pulled the chain on the ceiling light, and lit the sidearm hot water heater. They knew their clothes had to go, even as they waited for the water to heat up. He urged her to sit at the table, and then asked to see her injured leg. She lifted her dress and gingerly slid her stocking down past her knee. He held her leg and examined the bloody but superficial wound, about a two-inch tear. "It's not bad, Phryné. Not bad. It hurts worse than it is, I'm sure. I'll put some Mercurochrome** on it." He stepped to the kitchen sink, dampened a towel and retrieved the little bottle of antiseptic. "This will sting a little."

She grimaced as he daubed her leg with the towel and applied the bright orange liquid to the injury. "You will live to brag about your war wound, Phryné. You are going to be just fine." She nodded and wiped away a tear, not from the antiseptic sting, but rather from the trauma of the entire evening.

The stench of raw alcohol in the apartment was everywhere, settling onto and into everything. Leopold was moving quickly, and brought a pair of his bib work overalls and a cotton shirt into the small bathroom for her. He poured some Fels Naptha out of a tin and filled the tub with two or three inches of cold water. Phryné got out of her wet, alcohol-soaked clothing and pulled on Leopold's work clothes. She removed the cameo brooch from her dress, slipped it into the pant pocket, then gathered everything else off the floor and tossed her clothes into the tub. Leopold brought his wet clothing from the bedroom and chucked it all into the tub along with Phryné's.

She lingered for a minute, looking at the bathtub of clothing. Her dress, torn stockings, underwear and camisole along with his coat, trousers, vest and shirt were in a porcelain tub, afloat and soaking in a couple inches of water and soap.

It was a dismal, despondent tragedy: the collected memories of a night out in Niagara Falls immersed in a bathtub of cold water on Buffalo's East Side. The entire night was a twisted disaster: saturating life with fun times and stretching it to the fullest only to watch it deflate and violently snap back mere moments later.

Phryné turned and noticed Leopold, seated at the kitchen table, watching her. He smiled and teased her, "Looks like you're dressed to the nines*, Phryné." She had the cuffs of his work pants rolled up halfway to her knees, his socks pulled up and over the pants, and his shirt over the coveralls, all bunched up and tied at her waist.

She playfully waltzed to him, hand-on-hip, and taking pronounced swaying steps. She mumbled, "Hubba, hubba, Big Boy," bent down and gave him a peck on the cheek. The flash of fun was short-lived.

They sat around the small table and took stock of the situation. Phryné recognized the opportunity to smoke her first cigarette since they left Canada, and pronounced, "Cig me*, Leopold." He dutifully lit a Lucky Strike for Phryné and another for himself. Sitting with an elbow on the table, she took a puff and exhaled. "I don't think I will ever drink again, Leopold. Right now, I could very easily become one of those tea-totaling, Bible-thumping, holy-roller prohibitionists. I've had enough booze tonight to last me a lifetime. Well … maybe not, but damn it, you have to admit, this has been a rough night."

They agreed on one thing: Dillon was poison, dangerous and unpredictable. It would be foolhardy to hobnob with him any longer. Their connection with him had to end. Phryné talked about the possible repercussions Leopold could face. Leopold knew it was time to explain his thoughts to Phryné and try to work out a plan of action.

"I don't think it will be safe for me here, Phryné. Dillon has had his share of run-ins with the Torricelli brothers in the past. Over the winter, right after we met, I remember he stopped by my place here all roughed-up and bloody, and needing a hundred dollar hand-out right away ... I should have realized back then that he was nothing but trouble ... shit.

"I need to skip town ... really. I really think so, Phryné. The coppers find bodies floating in Black Rock Canal almost every day now ... Torricelli will give Dillon his comeuppance over this … he won't be able to bullshit his way out of this mess. And I know damn well that Dillon will try and spread around the blame. Sure as hell, he is going to try. This mess is too big for me. We got Dillon to thank for that, but God knows it was partly my fault too. I got suckered in, for sure ... it was my fault for believing he was so damn innocent and harmless to begin with … and everything that we did together was on the up-and-up. We're behind the eight ball* now. I should have seen this coming and gave Dillon the bum's rush a long time ago."

Phryné piped up, "Dillon lied and tricked us all, not just you. I'm leaving with you, mister. I'm not staying here if you ain't." She crushed her Lucky Strike in the ashtray. "There's nothing here for me without you. So, it's simple. I'm going with you. Wherever you go, I go." Their eyes locked. At that moment, they understood they were inseparable.

They quickly developed and went over plans. Leopold began to ramble on to Phryné, putting his random thoughts into words as they crossed his mind. He would leave town, and so would she. He had a bit more than three hundred dollars squirreled away in an old oatmeal tin, and they could drive his Model T out of town and keep going, or even catch a train to anywhere. Whatever they did, they needed it done right away, before Dillon's acquaintances become aware of the night's mess, the night's disaster, and before the Revenue cops tracked him down. They realized that the outlook was ominous on all sides. It was a rancid stew of one catastrophic event after another. The problems would not end with Torricelli, either. The injury and possible death of the Revenue Officer who Dillon hit back at the bridge would bring severe Federal charges. Leopold and Phryné were in a threatening situation.

"Well, Phryné, one thing for sure … we need to get a move on. In a minute or so there should be enough hot water for you to wash. And while you clean that alcohol stink off, I'll go and pack some things … then we can go over to your place … and you can do the same. Do you think you can do that? Pack some stuff … I mean … tonight?"

"Of course. You are going to be my husband." She got up and kissed him, held him tight, and close. She pressed into him, holding on, capturing and saving a flash of time. "Go pack your bags, sailor."

He packed a denim clothes sack as full as he possibly could, taking only his better items, two suits, slacks, a jacket and leaving his worn and tattered work clothes behind. He finished by pushing socks, vests and under shorts inside, pulled the drawstrings on the sack, and paused in thought.

He realized that he had to leave a short note of some kind for his family. His brother would surely stop by the apartment. Sure, Nicholas would be angry, but perhaps if he wrote that he and Phryné were leaving town, eventually Nick would understand the circumstances. Leopold wanted to be careful, and could not go into detail about Dillon and everything else that night. That could create more questions than answers, and more trouble than solace. He would make the note short and to the point. His brother would figure it out. His younger brother never got on with Dillon, and would give him a big *'I told you so'* speech if given the chance. He decided to keep the note as simple as he could and would not mention the Torricelli brothers, Dillon or anything else. Should the worse come to worst, Nicholas would still be able to figure it all out.

Leopold turned and carried the duffle bag six steps into the kitchen and set it down with a thump. He sat at the table, flattened a paper lunch sack, and wrote in pencil:

Nick ~ Dillon stepped in shit. Phryné and me heading for Cleveland and getting married. In touch with you and family from there. Love to Ma. ~ Your brother

He wasn't sure of anything, but he knew Nicholas would not understand; at least at first. Cleveland was the only city that came to mind. It was like picking a name out of a hat or looking up a name in the city directory. He was thinking on his feet, planning his next move as he went along. Cleveland was as good a place as any, and it wasn't Buffalo. Leopold felt he was taking a gamble, a huge, but necessary gamble. His life, and perhaps Phryné's, depended on it. He had $338 from the oatmeal can, and $23 in his pockets. He was confident, and reminded himself that he could get a job anywhere with his truck driving, warehouse and mechanical experience. Things would work out just fine; of course they would. He looked around the room yet another time, and took the small framed photograph of his mother and father off the shelf and jammed it into the bag between his shirts.

In the bathroom, Phryné had finished her sink-bath, and put Leopold's coveralls, socks and shirt back on, and went into the kitchen. She stood primping her hair with his brush, and let him know that it was his turn to wash up.

There wasn't enough hot water for him, making an awkward sink bath almost unbearably cold. The alcohol odor was gone, and a bar of red Lifebuoy soap never smelled as good as it did that night. He quickly dressed in his best pants and shirt, grabbed his safety razor, brush, and soap off the shelf, and walked to the kitchen. He stuffed his shaving gear into the bag, and pulled the drawstrings again. He looked around the apartment one more time, and stood there, wondering if there was anything else he should stick into his bag. He realized then that it is not an easy task to pack your life into a sack, throw it over your shoulder, and hit the road running.

Standing beside his small kitchen table, he knew that he was not coming back. "Are you sure about this, Phryné?"

"Yes."

He glanced at the note he left for Nick on the kitchen table, and hoped his brother would understand. It would have to suffice. Just when he started to mend the family bond, he needed to pull away and break it again. He took a breath and let it escape as a sigh.

"This is it, Phryné, time to go. Old lady Flannery can have the rest. Let's grab a couple blankets, and take a ride to your house."

"I don't think your landlady will wear my dress, Leopold."

"She might. You never know." Phryné did not always understand his dry wit.

They went quietly down the stairs, out on the sidewalk and around the corner to an alleyway off Sycamore.

He gave Phryné his hand as she stepped onto the running board and into his Model T. His bag went into the back, along with all the bits and pieces of his life he could fit inside. Phryné immediately put both blankets around her. They were quiet during the short ride to her home at the corner of Peckham and Lombard Street. He parked at the curb and switched off the car. Phryné hopped out and onto the sidewalk as soon as he came to a stop.

She had a hand on the windshield. "Leopold, I'll be out in a flash. I'm going to bring only what I absolutely need, and I will do my best not to wake anybody. Either way, I'll be right back."

Leopold watched her walk toward the house, wearing his over-sized pants, holding them up on each side and wobbling just like Charlie Chaplin. She unlocked the door, went inside, and a minute later, a light come on inside her second floor bedroom. He checked his pocket watch, it was getting close to 4:30. He lit a cigarette and flicked the match to the street. Down the block, a milkman was making his deliveries, crisscrossing the street while the horse continued to slowly, deftly, pull the wagon unattended.

His thoughts drifted, darting to and from scores of unknown destinations. He had no idea where they would be tomorrow; other than it would certainly not be Buffalo. The suit he had ordered at Fleischman's, Phryné's custom-made dress, and all the promises that went with the wedding, would go unclaimed and unfulfilled.

What troubled him most was that the repaired relationship with his family would be once again shattered to pieces. He would write to them, or perhaps telephone as soon as he and Phryné were settled.

There was a hollowness, a fear within, and he hoped that Phryné's parents would understand their daughter's decision. He wondered when, if ever, Phryné's family, and Eloisa's as well, would discover the truth and learn the full story about what happened tonight. Every action has consequences, he thought, but we have so little control, if any, over the action of others.

His immediate concern about the fallout from tonight's events was stronger than his fear. Once he and Phryné were aboard a train, the rails would put Dillon and Lorenzo Torricelli behind them. Would Dillon and Torricelli follow them? The note he left behind could send them to Cleveland if they found it at his apartment. How deep could the fingers of the Black Hand mob search in Cleveland? He decided to use a phony name at the train station, and add another dead end for anybody who could be looking for them.

He wondered if Phryné would bring along his coveralls and shirt that she was wearing. She would not leave them behind, would she? He smiled at the thought of her parents finding them in her bedroom.

The moon was barely visible -- a narrow, curved sliver of luminance in a clear, starlit sky. He felt comfortable under the blanket, but a few minutes earlier, he realized that his breezer* Model T was not the best choice for long distance travel. He made his decision; they would drive to the Delaware, Lackawanna & Western Terminal and catch the first train leaving Buffalo. Their final destination would be determined with Phryné's help. He would leave his car in the parking lot, lock the transmission and put the key inside the right wheel well where Nicholas would find it; a hiding place their father showed them years ago.

The thought of a secret hiding place pushed his thoughts to Dillon. If the cops found him, how would he explain the tussle at the border and the body in the trunk? If Dillon got the chance, he would certainly implicate Leopold and perhaps even Eloisa and Phryné. The previous night proved one thing certain; Dillon consistently lied to them and could not be trusted. Leopold knew Lorenzo Torricelli would impose some revenge, some payback on Dillon. He wondered just how much revenge, and if Torricelli or the police would find Dillon first.

Leopold finished his cigarette, and saw the bedroom light go out. He closely watched the front door. It opened, and a suitcase was set on the porch floor. He got out of the car and went to help Phryné carry her things. She shut the door silently, carefully behind her. She was carrying a suitcase, a crescent-shaped, tan cloth tote over her shoulder, a folded quilt, and a good-sized handbag. Leopold grabbed the suitcase and took the quilt. They were off the steps and into the Ford in moments.

Phryné had changed into a knee-length knitted frock, white stockings, a vanilla bob hat with a loose, offset wide brim and hook-and-eye half-boots. She remembered to take her cameo from Leopold's pants and had pinned it to her dress.

Leopold passed the blanket over to her, and started the car. She wiped a tear with her white silk scarf. Her voice cracked. "I was quiet and didn't wake anybody up ... I brought what money I have, a hundred and forty ... and I left a note like you did, Leopold. But mine was a little longer. I told them we decided to elope, and I will write as soon as I can." She sniffled again. "Do you think that was enough?"

"Yes, I do."

"Have you figured out where we are going, Leopold?"

"The train station. We can decide when we get there."

Leopold was quieter than usual, and his mood was solemn. Phryné sensed his melancholy. She knew he was concerned about how she felt about leaving her family behind. She detected it in his manner and heard it in his voice. Phryné smiled at him. "I'm OK, Leopold... really ... I just know they will miss me, that's all. And I'll miss them too. But Mother and Papa know we love each other. We just made that clear, didn't we?" She knew he was struggling with leaving his family behind also. Their departure was more significant for him; he had just repaired his family ties.

Leopold drove the Ford right up to the train terminal entrance, and parked it near the long, wide portico. A very eager young negro, sharply dressed entirely in dark grey, with a bright red, pill-box hat, ran to their assistance, grabbing the quilt, suitcase, duffle sack, and shoulder tote. Within seconds, the porter had their belongings on a two-wheeled freight cart, and accompanied Phryné inside the hall to the ticket counter. Leopold parked the car deep in the adjacent lot, locked the gearbox, and stuck the key into the wheel well.

It was just after five o'clock in the morning when he walked into the main lobby of the Lackawanna Terminal, carrying the two wool blankets from the Ford. He had them under his arm and walked to join Phryné waiting for him at the ticket counter, second in line.

Behind the counter, a large chalkboard was mounted on the wall. It was simply separated into two columns, Eastbound and Westbound. It had a handwritten schedule, a timetable of sorts, smudged by countless erasures, cross-outs and was generally unreadable.

A portly fellow sporting an overgrown, wide mustache, wearing a wrinkled, worn, white shirt, bow tie and green visor, stood at the ticket counter window behind a little iron grate. He had a grand disposition, with a soft, soothing voice. When he spoke, his words had the sound of song: melodic and expressive, helping the travelers in line.

The terminal was a newer, three-story brownstone, sitting at the foot of Main Street and was fronted by the Buffalo River. There were waiting halls on the first and second floor and a ticket office on the first. A wide, double marble stairway curved up to the second floor.

They were next in line. "Good morning, where are we going?" The question was harmonic, like a nursery rhyme or limerick.

Leopold answered, "Cleveland, or anyplace down the line." He was standing alongside the woman he loved, at a gateway to the world with no particular place to go. In broad terms, he could have told the ticket agent "anywhere you want to send us."

Without hesitation, as if such indecision was the norm, the ticket agent went to work, and explained from memory that their earliest option was the westbound morning train to

Chicago. It was the Nickel Plate daily coach service from New York City to Chicago, and would depart the station in less than an hour, at 6:00, with an arrival time in Cleveland of 10:15.

On impulse, Leopold turned to Phryné and asked, "How about Chicago, Sweetheart? What do you think about Chicago?" He could not explain why Cleveland was his initial choice even to himself. He wrote that note to his brother in haste. That must be the explanation: a flawed first decision attributed to panicked thought.

"Sure ... why not? Chicago."

"Chicago it is. My wife and I would like tickets all the way to Chicago, please."

Phryné had a look of mild surprise, and instinctively knew what Leopold was doing. Like two children under the covers, they were hiding from the boogieman. This was a thrilling experience -- exciting, elusive, exotic, and just a little bit daunting at the same time.

The ticket agent gave them a quick single nod and continued, "Nickel Plate Number One does take on passengers in Buffalo but not beyond ... and I have the latest telegram here ... and yes, there are still four coach seats available to Chicago. This train offers Pullman** service from New York and Albany with limited coach availability to points west. You will arrive at Chicago's LaSalle Street Station tonight at 10:05 PM."

The cost for their coach tickets to Chicago was $23.75. Leopold fabricated their temporary name from his place of employment. Phryné had a beguiling smirk of amusement when she heard him say it. The agent listed them as Mister and Missus Stanley Urbanski in pencil. He methodically finished filling out the tickets, stamped and placed them in a ticket folder. He advised Leopold that he should take care and not lose them. Leopold and Phryné were excited, and anxious to begin their westward adventure.

"Your train will arrive at 5:55 and leaves at 6:00, so you will need to be ready to board. You will only have 5 minutes. The Red Cap has your bags, sir?"

"Yes."

"You can stow them on the luggage racks either above your seats or below, sir."

The young porter asked, "Would you like me to stow your bags or you do you wish to keep them with you, sir?"

Leopold looked to Phryné, did not see any objection, and answered, "I think we will keep them with us. We do not have long to wait at all."

The porter retrieved two tags from the ticket clerk and tied them to the suitcase and duffle bag. He quietly spoke to Leopold, "I believe you will be happy you have those blankets with you, sir. It can get uncomfortable and chilly in coach."

Leopold stuck a thumb and forefinger into his watch pocket, pulled out a quarter, and handed it to the young man. "Thank you. You have been very helpful, thank you." In a flash, the Red Cap grabbed their bags, put them onto the cart and wheeled them to an empty bench in the massive hall. Phryné and Leopold followed close behind. There were long rows of polished wood benches, back-to-back, with shaded lights mounted along the center. There were rugs on the terrazzo floors and smoking rooms with wicker furniture on both ends. The middle of the hall opened to the train platforms. A telegraph office, parcel room, newsstand, post office, and restaurant were at the far end. On the second floor were more traveler benches and an immigrant waiting room.

In less than an hour, they would be on their way, and then they could truly relax and begin to put the turmoil and violence behind them. They enjoyed a sense of relief and security, knowing that all they had to do now was wait. As they sat down, they each exhaled a sigh, glanced at one another and exchanged a look of comforting relief.

It was not long before Leopold and Phryné heard the unmistakable haunting whistle of a steam engine in the distance.   The noise rushed into the hall through the wide doorways leading to the platform and trackside. A long single blast echoed, then another.   A giant was approaching and getting closer.   Its breath huffed, puffed, spewed steam, and sent footprints of soot into the air above. Its bell rang and rang again, getting louder and crisper as it neared the platform. Louder, and stronger, nearer and nearer, it was advancing.   It was the sound of a dynamic, mechanical hulk, the sound of steam, the sound of rolling cast iron, the sound of unrestrained power, the sound of transportation, the sound of wheels on rails, the cold intimacy of steel on steel.

Inside the hall, Phryné and Leopold sat on a polished oak bench with goose bumps. It was a good feeling. He put his arm around her.   Three short, sharp blasts from the steam whistle echoed into the terminal … and were repeated once again.   The bell quieted, softened and transformed to a soft clang.

With a final hissing gasp, and the screech of air brakes, the machine came to rest, its breath constrained, its power controlled, resting on shiny ribbons of steel, and waiting for the opportunity to surge forward again. Just beyond the covered platform, four men worked fervently to quench the behemoth's thirst.   They frantically swung the spigot arm to the train's water tender and jerked the attached chain. Water flowed from the steel and wooden tower at trackside, and renewed the engine's lifeblood. Another team of men worked ardently to dump tons of clean burning West Virginia anthracite into the tender. In a mere five minutes, The Nickel Plate Road, No. 1 express service to Chicago would depart Buffalo.

Lackawanna Terminal was bustling with travelers from all points on Earth waiting to leave for their own personal destination, be it business, pleasure, or necessity.   An immigrant family from Italy was waiting with a letter of sponsorship from a cousin in Peoria, a leather satchel with a precious few belongings, and the clothes on their backs. A well-dressed   businessman   traveling   with   his   young stenographer was awaiting coach service to Binghamton, and scores of people on their way to places in and around Buffalo waited for the next streetcar around the Belt Line. Inside the terminal, countless stories were continuing, ending and beginning this August morning.

Leopold fingered the ticket packet inside his coat pocket. Phryné pushed closer to him and placed a hand on his thigh. In five minutes, they would begin their journey down a track that, until mere moments earlier, was completely unknown to them. Their destination lay somewhere beyond a horizon that was still out of sight and far out of focus.

A resonant voice boomed through the terminal echoing its message off the colorful mosaic floors, massive beams and plastered, vaulted ceiling:

"Now 'board! ... Nickel Plate service ... Erie ... Cleveland ... Toledo ... express service to Chi-ca-go ... now boarding at track two ... departure ... in five minutes! Come ... ABOARD!"

All Aboard

The 140-ton, iron behemoth stood at the ready, gasping breaths of steam, waiting to unleash its power once again, and continue its journey westward. A rush of activity surrounded the Pacific locomotive. The iron machine, with a coal fire burning in its belly, was prepared for a scheduled departure in mere minutes. Buffalo was the last passenger stop before Chicago. Red Caps scurried at trackside, loading baggage and freight, and Railroad Post Office clerks hurriedly handled sacks onto and off the baggage and mail car. The engineer was peering from inside the cab, elbow hanging out of the window, watching the swarm of activity. Steam whooshed from the underbelly of the black giant. Gold lettering adorned the side of the passenger car, simply but proudly displaying the gilded number; *25*. Also in gold were the words, *Nickel Plate Road*, stretched lengthwise along the roofline.

Leopold held Phryné's hand, and helped her onto the steel steps leading up inside the wood and steel, olive green, railcar. He followed directly behind her, and once inside, they walked down the aisle to an empty seat on the right side, near the far end of the car.

Number 25 was a 22 double-row, open seating coach car with a restroom at each end. Windows at the end of each seat row ran along the outside walls. The bench seats were steel framed, with fitted, bowed, rattan weaving on the back and seats.

Leopold stowed the duffle sack and suitcase on the overhead rack. Like the seats, the rack was also formed of steel pipe, curved up at the end, with woven one-inch canvas straps on the bottom.

Together, the couple quickly folded one of the blankets and the quilt as a makeshift cushion to fit across the bottom of the wicker reed seat. Phryné sat at the window, the other blanket on her lap, facing the platform side of the terminal. They were no sooner settled when the steam whistle sounded two long, steady blasts signaling their departure.

The steam engine came alive with thrusting motion and gushing sound. A tug … a clunk … a jolt … a bang … a surge … a groan of steel. The locomotive gulped a breath with a labored, mechanical draw, and exhaled in a loud, vulgar, guttural gust of escaping steam and a plume of grey smoke. The machine's passionate gasp echoed into the Lackawanna terminal. Two more, long whistle blasts signaled the train's unstoppable need to move forward, onward, to Chicago and back again to Boston.

The click-clack rhythm quickened. The rock smoothed to a sway. The powerhouse gained speed; the whistle sounded loudly. The locomotive powered the consist* past crossings, sidings, and switches. The throbbing of steam power overtook Leopold and Phryné's being, merging their bodies to the train itself. Every car was a cradle: rocking, rolling and carrying its passengers within a steel and wood cocoon fitted out with varying degrees of human comfort. Comfort was conditional to class; class to situation; situation to happenstance, and happenstance relative to determination.

Leopold and Phryné had ridden Buffalo's Belt Line innumerable times, but this trip was in a class by itself. It could be likened to a comparison of a horse-drawn buggy and an automobile: a world of difference.

The conductor passed quickly through the car, checking tickets, and closing the doors at each end of the car behind him with a thud. All along the length of the car, the curtains at the windows, like everything else, swayed with the train's rhythm. Steadily, the train left the miles behind.

They sat holding hands, knowing fully well that they were embarking on an adventure with a consequence so vast neither of them could imagine. The door to a new future was opening for them. Leopold and Phryné sat watching the countryside bullet by on their right. The farms, vineyards and small towns of western New York disappeared behind them. They leaned against one another, pressed their bodies close and nodded off, lulled into a numbing state of half-sleep by the train. They rested, content with their situation and the decisions that fate forced upon them.

Separately, their thoughts drifted from the previous night's trauma, their hasty departure from Buffalo, and their families, to an uncertain future in an unfamiliar destination.

Leopold again reflected on his relationship with the smooth, slick-talking Dillon and his ability to bamboozle the people around him. Leopold was embarrassed and angry, yet confident he could start afresh and begin a new life with Phryné.

Phryné was resting with her head on his shoulder, thinking about the ordeal her friend Ellie had experienced. She hoped Ellie could push Dillon completely out of her life. When Phryné left her wounded friend on the porch last night, Ellie promised she was 'finished with that bimbo, drugstore* cowboy Dillon forever'. Phryné would miss her family, too, but the bond she had with Eloisa was special, and dear to her.

They watched as the world flew by and did not talk much between Buffalo and Erie, Pennsylvania; the first water stop. They discovered that the train needed to make short, four or five minute stops to refill the water tender at least every eighty miles or so, and every three hundred or less to replenish the coal. The tender had a 6000-gallon capacity for water, and carried 7½ tons of coal.

As daylight broke, sunlight filtered through the closed curtains on the left side of the car. Some of the passengers who had been trying to sleep, either against each other, or leaning onto the windowed exterior walls, began to stir and awoke one seat at a time. A very few continued their awkward, uncomfortable attempt at slumber. Some arose from their seats, stretched and wandered to the toilet. Window curtains were pushed aside and morning cigarettes lit.

Everything was a new adventure, a fresh experience for Leopold and Phryné. Together, they decided to leave the only homes they had ever known and travel across the country at nearly sixty miles an hour. Their emotions were as varied as the myriad of fellow travelers on the train and the forever-changing view from the windows. Their ride on the Nickel Plate Road exposed them to a kaleidoscope of unique life experiences that ranged from attempting to get comfortable on a woven rattan seat to flushing the toilet onto the rails passing underneath.

Throughout the morning, they dozed on and off, leaning into one another and against the wall. It was Sunday, noon in Toledo, six hours after they departed Buffalo, that they decided to walk to the buffet car and get something to at least partially fill their bellies. Awake all night and most of the morning, they were exhausted physically and emotionally. They sat as long as they could in the buffet car, eating hard-boiled eggs, sliced ham, rye bread, and drinking black coffee.

While the train stopped for water in Wauseon, Ohio, they made their way forward to their seats in the coach car. Number 25 was third in the six car consist, behind the tender and mail and baggage car. The soot and smell of a coal-fired locomotive would find its way through any open window. The Pullman cars were further back, and further away from the by-products of combustion.

"Leopold, did you notice all those advertising posters in the station back in Buffalo? You know: all the different places the railroads go. The ones about California caught my eye. Did you see those?"

When those words crossed his ears, he knew immediately what was coming next, and with rekindled excitement, he welcomed it. It meant that Phryné wanted to go to California.

"California ... yes, I did. The California Limited** posters. They make California look good, don't they?"

"Well, California is supposed to look good. And I think Buffalo is a lot like Cleveland and Cleveland is probably a lot like Chicago. I was reading about California in a McCall's monthly at Rita's not that long ago. It's warm there, and it's a booming place. They say it's summer all the time in Los Angeles. And I was thinking that since we have our bags packed and already have our walking shoes on, we might as well just keep them on and go someplace that is worth going to ... instead of just going away from someplace. I do not think it is a good idea to leave someplace for another place that is just like the place you are leaving. Do you know what I mean? If you are crossing the street, you sure do not stop right in the middle, do you? It just does not make any sense to go only half way. I think Chicago is half way." Phryné was excited and her emotion was uplifting. "Let's go to California: Los Angeles, California, Leopold, love. It is supposed to be warm and nice. Exactly like that song, *California, Here I Come*. I think Al Jolson sings it. What do you think? How's that, Leopold? It's never winter in California."

She won her argument effortlessly and Leopold happily agreed, "California it is. I like Al Jolson … and hate winter, too." He did not need to be convinced.

"But we will need to get a Pullman, Phryné. No doubt about it … a berth or something. We cannot ride on wicker and reed seats all the way to California. I'm afraid that my backside could end up looking like one of those woven bread baskets at the Broadway or Washington Markets."

With that comment and the image it created, Phryné giggled.

There were still more than seven hours before they would arrive in Chicago, and the thought of a bed was more than tempting; it was irresistible. Their impending arrival in a new city and the anticipation of even more destinations to come mixed with the simple excitement of travel piqued their emotions.

Their arrival time at Chicago's LaSalle Station was about ten o'clock that night, and from conversation with the conductor, they discovered that *The California Limited* had a daily departure time of two hours earlier from Dearborn Station, which meant an overnight stay in Chicago. The conductor advised them to take either the short streetcar or a taxi ride to Dearborn Station after they arrive at LaSalle and purchase tickets for tomorrow's train before getting a hotel. After their ordeal in Buffalo, and the fifteen-hour train ride, they were looking forward to a good night's sleep.

Chapter Five

Justified

Sunday, August 28, Buffalo, New York

After he dropped off Leopold and Phryné on Howlett Street, Dillon cautiously drove the Pierce Arrow down the alleyways and neighborhood streets along Best and High, and kept off the mains. It was well into early morning, approaching 3:30 and that was yet another aggravation facing him. He carefully worked his way back to the garage on Prospect Avenue -- an old wheelwright, cabinet and ironworks that the Torricelli's used as a preparation, bottling and storage facility for illegal alcohol.

Dillon jumped out of the car as soon as he pulled it out of gear and brought it to a stop. He took six bounding steps, turned his key in the brass padlock, grasped the massive leather strap and slid the heavy wooden door open. He was back behind the wheel of the car in seconds, driving and parking it inside the dark garage. He could feel his heart steadily pounding within his chest. Dillon threw the key on the driver's seat, scampered out of the garage, slid the door closed, and clicked the padlock shut. His eyes moved quickly, from side to side, surveying his surroundings. He was experiencing a fear, a trepidation that was not new, but uncommon for him.

He continually looked in all directions and walked briskly down Prospect toward Porter. His distinctive limp bobbed his frame. Ironically, he was walking back toward the Peace Bridge, toward the Porter Avenue station for the Belt Line streetcars and train; back to the point of all the violence that had occurred about two hours earlier. He was pondering his situation as he walked, and constructing all sorts of scenarios that he could relate to Lorenzo. He was reliving the night's events, and shaping his descriptive interpretation of what happened. Since Lorenzo was not there, Dillon's inherent duty was to relay the events as they went down and explain in detail everything that occurred back at the Lafayette and the Peace Bridge.

This was his chance to plead his case for a pistol once again. If he only had one tonight, he could have had it hidden it under the front seat, within his reach. Then he could have beaten off any threat to either himself or the product back there in Canada and forcefully pushed back when the Revenue agents were in pursuit.

He planned to explain that if he'd only had some firepower, he could have corrected the ugly situation at the Lafayette. When he checked the Pierce Arrow and found Vinnie in the trunk, he could have knocked off those valet parking hoods with his realizer and avenged Vinnie's murder right then and there. As it was, he had been outnumbered, three to one, and without a weapon. He could not fight back. Instead, they forced him to skulk away in shame and bring Vincent's body back across the border to Buffalo. He'd clearly had no choice; he had to bring Vinnie back. It was the only sensible, responsible thing to do. He could not just leave Vinnie there; it would not be respectful to the Torricelli family at all.

There was another important point he wanted to clear up with Lorenzo: Leopold, Phryné and Eloisa were not the professionals he would have preferred to work with. The Torricellis should have listened to him when he suggested neighborhood talent: people closer to him, known to him, and people he could trust when the deal was going down.

Furthermore, Lorenzo surely could not fault his driving skills, not after tonight. He'd driven the Pierce Arrow straight through the Gates of Hell and back again. He had run the gauntlet, right down the middle and through a hailstorm of bullets. The Feds were aiming directly at him, with the sole intent of killing him. Scores of bullets missed their mark, one hit the windshield, but he managed to swerve around the worst of it. And he certainly did not panic in the face of adversity, despite the odds. When Eloisa screamed aloud, wailed and called out for help, he remained calm, quieted her hysterics and took her directly to Doc Phillips to get patched up. He had to control the frail and distraught Phryné as well, all curled up in the back and trembling on the seat. He would also need to mention how that cowering, whimpering coward Leopold Throckmorton kept his head low during the gunfight. Despite the danger and flying bullets, Dillon Cafferty had fought for their lives, performed well, and got all parties back safe and mostly sound.

The car sustained damage from the over zealous, trigger-happy Revenue cops, but it was repairable. Further, the trip itself was not a total loss. He was able to drive the car and its bootleg booze back to Buffalo -- battle-scarred, yes, but with more than half of the product intact. He drew on his instincts and experience to successfully dodge the coppers and completely avoid detection on the way back to the garage. He carefully negotiated through the city using side streets and alleyways, avoiding the beat cops while on the lam. Lorenzo would certainly appreciate his professionalism.

It was about 3:45 AM when he caught the West Side Belt Line to Elmwood. From there he could catch a streetcar to West Delevan, and still be able to get some sleep before morning. All things considered, he'd accomplished a hell of a lot in two hours. He could rest well until morning, and then he would go see Lorenzo, straighten all this out and let him know exactly what he'd had to go through. He was confident that once he gave him the goods about the night's events, Lorenzo would be pleased with his dedication and loyalty.

Rectified

Owen Healy opened the garage door right at 8:00 as he did regularly on Sundays. It was unusually cold for August, near freezing with a clear sky displaying a glorious autumn sunrise. Once inside, he spotted the Pierce Arrow through the shadowy darkness. It was leaning to the left, partially crippled with a flat tire on the rear. That was something he had not planned on. In disgust, he tossed his lunch pail on the bench and turned on the shop's four bare incandescent bulbs that hung from the rafters. The errant smell of alcohol was not unusual, but the bullet holes and shattered glass certainly were. Owen anticipated the inevitable. He walked around the car, visually assessing the damage. The dirt floor revealed the source of the alcohol smell: a three-foot diameter wet area in the dirt under the car. That meant that at least one of four canvas-reinforced rubber bladders leaked -- no doubt a direct result of the gunshots. He knew then that his day would be hellishly busy. When Owen opened the trunk, and realized whose body was inside, the morning went from bad to unimaginably worse. He was emotionally shaken, not because of his love for, or friendship with Vincente, but for the repercussions he knew would come: repercussions that would surely be felt by anybody who was deemed responsible, be it directly or indirectly. His pulse quickened, his stomach turned, and he broke into a sweat. He knew it was not going to be a normal Sunday. He was dreading it. His bowels twisted and he burped bile.

The big wooden door opened and was forced shut again by Michael Dunne, his co-worker. "Hey, Mike ... we got to make a telephone call to Lorenzo right away. There's a problem, a big problem; Vinnie is inside the Arrow's trunk, and he is dead as a doornail ... completely zotzed*. There's a hole clean through his forehead."

Mike did not show much emotion. "Damn ... no shit? Mary, Mother of Jesus, pardon my vulgarity on our Lord's day." His hands made the cross upon his chest.

"Do you want to get Lorenzo on the blower* or should I?" Owen's voice wavered. He could feel his brain churning like a pot of boiling potatoes. His eyeballs ached within their throbbing sockets.

"Not me. You are the one with all the pull and seniority with those guappo*, Sicilian wop* friends of yours."

107

Owen walked to the back wall, sat behind a dust-covered desk and stared at the heavy black pedestal telephone. He gathered his courage, picked up the earpiece and repeatedly clicked the receiver cradle. It was first necessary for him to chastise someone for tying up a party line, and when he was finally able to connect with Lorenzo, he was direct and on-point with the simple statement: "your brother is lying dead in the trunk and there is no sign of Cafferty or Throckmorton".

In fifteen minutes, Lorenzo Torricelli arrived at the garage with his cousin, Johnny Minello. They inspected the contents of the Pierce Arrow's trunk, counted over two dozen bullet holes in the car, and discovered blood on the front passenger seat, right front fender, and hood. There was extensive damage to the front of the car, windows shattered and just about a third of the cargo was lost. Lorenzo's fist came down on the roof of the car like a hammer, as the first attack on the problem at hand. In order to find out exactly what happened last night, he needed to check with someone who was actually there. He spit out commands, and ordered Owen, Michael and Johnny into his black, four-door touring sedan. His intent was to visit Dillon Cafferty, the occupant of an upstairs apartment at the corner of Elmwood and West Delevan. On Sundays, the pool, snooker and billiard hall on the first floor was closed.

On that particular morning, Dillon Ian Cafferty had a rude awakening. A handkerchief was jammed in his mouth, and then rousted out of bed, down a flight of stairs, tossed into the trunk of a 1925 Chrysler Six, and driven back to the garage on Prospect. At the onset, Dillon stood with hands tied behind his back and was interrogated at length. Lorenzo asked all the questions and allowed his cousin Johnny to physically encourage Dillon's responses. He was given the opportunity to clarify the events of Saturday night. Painfully gasping, Dillon collapsed into a writhing heap onto the fine dust of the garage's dirt floor. Lorenzo slammed his foot into Dillon's ribs with a cracking thud and roared one more question: "Where can we find this Throckmorton character and double-check

108

your damn story?" A final breath festered from his broken jaw, leaving his garbled words to suffocate in bubbling blood. Dillon was unable to answer.

In a frenzy, Lorenzo ordered Owen and Michael to drag Dillon's battered, broken, and lifeless body across the dirt floor and into the coal bin. Quickly, they all got back into the black Chrysler, and drove through the Fruit Belt and across to Virginia Street. Lorenzo was determined to find and talk to Dillon Cafferty's close friend Leopold. When they arrived at 31 Adams, there was a sharply dressed young man on the porch, seated on a steel clam-back chair and smoking a cigarette. Unsure who he was, they inquired about Throckmorton's whereabouts, and the young fellow introduced himself as Willy, an upstairs tenant. He continued to explain that the entire family was at church. His exact words were: "They're all at Sunday church. The whole bunch, and they're thick as thieves, they are." His response was helpfully enthusiastic and mildly apologetic.

Lorenzo lazily rolled a cigar stub from one corner of his mouth to the other and looked at his Waltham watch. The other men stood waiting for a command, a reaction, something. He pulled the wet cigar from his lips and crushed it into the porch floor with his polished oxford. It was Sunday, and almost noon. Lorenzo had relatives to notify, a funeral to arrange and product to prepare. Two bodies were back at the garage: his brother was still in the Pierce Arrow's trunk and Dillon's body was in the coal bin. He decided that he would deal with Throckmorton tonight, or tomorrow at the latest. "Let's go, boys." From the bottom of the steps, he turned to the young fellow on the porch and pointed a pudgy finger in his direction. "You can tell your landlord to keep the coffee pot on the stove, and that I'll stop back some other time."

Leopold and Phryné were about three hundred miles away on the outskirts of Toledo, Ohio. The train was stopped, and taking on water and more West Virginia coal to complete its run to Chicago.

It's All Routine

Sundays were special for Nicholas Throckmorton. It was the only day of the week he could enjoy the daylight hours, and attempt to live life on a normal schedule. Any young man of 17 years appreciates time off; genuine time off. *'Time off'* however, was a concept Nicholas never really understood or experienced. He had assumed the role of 'man of the house' nearly two years earlier when his older brother moved out. It was not something Nicholas wanted. It was not a position of familial standing, but rather one of imposed obligation and forced responsibility.

He worked nights at Russell-Miller, the graveyard shift 9:30 PM until 7 AM, Monday through Saturday. He was a foreman for the clean-up crew: the team that swept, removed and watered off the dust created by the production processes of the first shift. On the weekend, he was free from 7 AM Saturday until 9:30 Sunday night. As a rule, he was up with the birds on Sunday morning, and making breakfast for the family. His schedule was no different on the morning of August 28, 1927.

If anything works, and it works well, it can become routine. That was what Sunday mornings were for Nick: routine. Unlike many of the routines in his life, Sunday's routine was one that he enjoyed. He made breakfast for the family: corned beef hash, fried eggs, and bacon. On Saturdays he drew his pay, and on his way home from work, he would stop at Connery Meats at the Broadway Market to pick up a half-pound of corned beef, two pounds of potatoes, and a pound of fatback. After one final stop at Carlson's for eggs, milk and butter, he would bring home the family's Sunday breakfast and more. Generally, after the meal, the entire family would ride the Belt Line to Reformation Lutheran Church at eleven o'clock. Their full bellies lasted well into the afternoon without a midday meal. This Sunday there was no variation from the norm. It was breakfast, dishes, dress for church, ride the Belt Line, attend Sunday services and return home. Predictably, on a nice afternoon after church, it was lemonade or soft drinks on the porch.

Nicholas was sitting in a parlor chair, leaning back against the wall and nursing a bottle of Country Club cream soda. A Lucky Strike dangled between the fingers of his left hand. Willy McTell, one of the boarders, came bounding down the stairs, two at a time, and bounced onto the porch. His exuberance drew Nick's ire.

"Hey! This ain't no funhouse, Willy!"

The young fellow came to an abrupt halt, managed to regain his balance, and stand erect. "Sorry, Mister Throckmorton."

This interaction between the handsome, roguish Willy and their brother Nicholas was welcome and unexpected entertainment for his sisters. Their attention was piqued. Ottilie wore a smirk, and was watching Willy over the top of her wire-rimmed spectacles, dreaming of what it would be like to be held in his embrace and to be able to sense his muscular chest under his crisp, high-collar white shirt. Willy was a busy young man, holding down two jobs: as an usher and doorman at Shea's Theatre and as a pin sticker and ball runner at Broadway Bowling. He was easy on the women's eyes: curly black hair, with an athletic and daring demeanor. Johanna strived to appear disinterested, and she sat motionless in her cane bottom parlor chair. She discretely managed to admire the cut of Willy's pants, front and back. He was wearing a pair of oxford bags, wide-legged trousers with sharp pleats in front, and large cuffs. Hilde tried to ignore the scene and remain aloof by simply looking down the block. She could not understand why her sisters found Willy so attractive. She considered him an overbearing and pompous oaf, despite his dreamy blue eyes. Mother Millie maintained a steady pace in her rocker, while keeping a watchful eye on all three of her daughters and Willy as well.

111

Willy apologetically tipped his wool bowler to Nick's mother and sisters, flashed a smile and continued off the porch in slow, measured steps. He no sooner hit the grass of the front lawn than he stopped in his tracks, and mentioned, as a matter-of-fact: "A couple of mugs came by earlier, looking for you sir, and I told them you were at church."

Nicholas asked, "Mugs? Looking for me? What did they look like?"

"Two were dressed for the Ritz* and the other two were just dressed regular; like normal, like me, and like you, sir. That's it. They asked for Mister Throckmorton and didn't exactly say when they would be back, just 'some other time', they said. And then they left."

Nicholas was quick to fire off his next question, "What kind of car did they drive, Willy?"

"A black one, a big four-door sedan with a roof. One of them new Chrysler models I think."

"Thanks, Willy. Take it easy coming down them steps from now on, you hear me?"

Willy nodded, smiled and tipped his hat to the women one more time before he disappeared down the street. Nicholas did not want to trip any alarms. He worked to hold his composure, remain calm and quiet.

His mother was straightforward. "You don't think those men were looking for you, do you, Nicholas?"

"I don't think so, Ma. Must have been friends of Leopold and that Mick ... Dillon. Must have been."

Nick knew. Without a shred of doubt, there was some sort of trouble. He quickly thought of a lie to tell his mother. "I think I'll get over to Leopold's, Ma. Maybe it's important. It must be about the wedding ... something to do with the wedding, I bet."

His mother continued to gently push the rocker. "Don't be too long, Nick. You got work tonight."

"I'll be back by dinner, Ma. Quit worrying."

Nick checked his pockets for the nickels he needed for the streetcar fare. In an instant, he was off the porch and walking down the street to Sycamore. He was unsure of what he could find at Leopold's apartment, but his instincts told him that his brother would not be there. He smelled trouble. Willy's news triggered a sense of apprehension, an unfamiliar foreboding. He was fighting a sense of dire trepidation, and he always knew his brother's association with Dillon Cafferty was bad chemistry from the get-go. With every step he took down Adams Street, he sensed his heartbeat at his temples. After he came aboard the Sycamore streetcar and dropped his nickel into the fare box, his scalp tingled and the hair at the nape of his neck prickled. He was in an uneasy trance until he hopped off the streetcar, walked half a block down Howlett, and started to climb the steps, two at a time, to his brother's small apartment. He did not expect to find his brother, instead, he felt a sense of nervous urgency. There was a pounding deep inside his chest.

Nicholas did not knock, but roughly turned the white porcelain doorknob. The door swung open, and he entered the kitchen. He walked directly to the kitchen table, picked up the paper bag with Leopold's penciled note, read it, and read it again. His eyes went around the kitchen and into the bedroom where some of his brother's clothes were scattered on the bed and across the floor. Curiosity and the unmistakable smell of Fels Naptha laundry soap drew him to the bathroom. There he saw Phryné's things: dress, stockings, camisole, and dainties,. along with Leopold's entire three-piece suit and silk shirt. Every stitch of their clothing was soaking in the tub. Phryné's dainty pocket flasks, the ones she would strap under her garters, sat on the shelf above the sink. Back in the kitchen, he looked over the apartment one more time. It was clear that Leopold and his bride-to-be were gone. He did not understand the clothes in the tub or the little flasks that were left behind. The detergent had completely absolved the pungent odor of the grain alcohol, allowing yet another mystery to writhe its way into his brain.

He knew very well he would not get a response, but he asked aloud anyway, "Bathtub laundry on Saturday night? Really? And why did you go pick Cleveland, Leopold? What the hell is in Cleveland?" Bewildered, he shook his head and stuck the lunch bag in his pocket.

Back out on the street, Nick looked upstairs to the bedroom window. He did not expect his brother would ever be back there again. Somehow, he knew the note that his brother left behind said it all: "be in touch with you from there".

For the rest of the day, Nicholas' thoughts were about his brother. All the dusty memories, good and bad, melted together into a big ball of blended emotion. He showed his family the note, allowing them to speculate just as he did. His mother's only comment was "I expected as much", and she did not mention it again. His sisters considered the penciled note on the lunch bag to be exciting news, as some sort of adventurous postcard from a far corner of the Earth, and were awaiting the next installment with a kind of wondrous expectation.

After dinner, he went to bed to grab a few hours of sleep before he started another workweek in the grey dust of the grain mill. Before he slept, he wondered if there were flourmills in Cleveland and he realized that life goes on, whether it is routine or not. For Nicholas, the rest of this day, and the first part of the next, were quite routine: the repetitious, boring kind of routine he disliked.

The Last Shift

His job at Russell Miller made an imprint on Nick's personality. The dust settled into his clothing, hair and pores. More often than not, he thought the dust was even working into his brain, covering and dampening his spirit. As he explained to his brother just a few days ago, he longed to expand his

114

horizons, and even held the dream of piloting an airplane. When his shift ended that Monday morning, he walked through the gate and onto Ohio Street with scores of other men, shuffling their dusty shoes, clothes and souls toward homes scattered across the city.

It was no different from any other day; it was just routine. At the corner of Eagle and Pearl Streets, he stopped for his usual ten-cent breakfast at the Deco Restaurant: a hotdog and a cup of coffee. Every stool at the counter and along the walls was occupied, but it was only a minute before a spot at the counter opened up for him. Two City of Buffalo beat patrolmen were sitting to his left. One was evidently starting his shift and the other on his way home, just like Nick. His breakfast hot dog was served with catsup and mustard on a fresh bun, and his coffee arrived piping hot in a heavy white mug. It was indeed a normal day.

To Nicholas, what he was overhearing inside the little diner was a brutal testament of events past that proved to be a foreboding omen of things to come. But just then it was nothing more than idle chatter and back-and-forth shop talk for the beat cops, "Last night there was a gang fight in the Third Ward, with knives and clubs ... a ladle of molten iron spilled onto a rail car at Bethlehem Steel, killing a switchman ... a horrific fire burned a house to the ground, killing everyone inside as they slept ... a badly beaten body was found in the Buffalo Creek ship canal under the Michigan Street bridge."

Nick did not catch every word. He was too busy with his hotdog breakfast and Deco coffee. He was just not listening that closely to the policemen until he heard a name he recognized: *Dillon Cafferty.*

His senses sharpened. His muscles tightened. His sight was frozen on his cup of coffee, and his hearing latched onto every word coming from the policeman's lips, "After they pulled him out and dried him off, somebody from Precinct Two fingered him as Dillon Cafferty, one of them rag-a-muffin bog

115

Irish* from down here in the First Ward. He went by the name of Dillon Cafferty, yes, he did. It could be just coincidence, but there was a big dust-up at the new bridge on Saturday night too, you bet. And them Feds had a gun fight and lost the trail of a Cadillac that ran the border and drove over, and squashed dead one of them Feds, a Revenue agent, yes, they did."

Nick swallowed the last half of his hotdog in a large gulp. The bread and meat stretched his gullet so much it hurt, prompting a gulp of hot coffee that only accentuated his discomfort. The thin, narrow door of the diner slammed shut behind him.

Now he knew exactly what prompted his brother's hasty overnight departure and the visit to his home by those four men on Sunday morning: Dillon trouble. On the way home, he stood in the rear doorway of the Jefferson Avenue trolley, waiting for the exact moment he could jump off and get home. At Broadway, he did just that: he hopped out and hit the street mid-stride.

Three short blocks away he was walking north on Adams. That was when the smell of wet, burnt wood, smoldering embers, charred trees and scorched earth blanketed him. Three fire brigade trucks and a pumper were parked on the street. Farther down the street, he saw the smoke from dying flames and the water vapor from hot timber wafting up and hanging onto the cool, damp, morning air. Feeling his teeth tear into his flesh, he bit his lip until he tasted blood. His step was slow, steady and did not quicken. His eyes welled up with tears. His shoulders fell. His intestines twisted into a writhing mass. Like the hot black timbers on the ground, the words of two policemen back at the Deco restaurant continued to burn within his brain.

He stood on the sidewalk, directly in front of a smoldering pile of debris that had been his home for each of his seventeen years. The homes that stood on either side were reduced to broken, charred walls, collapsed roofs and scorched remnants of furniture. Towering shade trees were transformed into black

116

skeletons. He stood as close as the fire brigade allowed. Three firemen were walking atop the rubble of his former home and a few others were stowing equipment back onto the fire trucks. A handful of firefighters were still pulling along hoses, aiming streams of water at the pockets of smoke and the dying embers of three houses. Three men were making their way across the pile of debris, poking and prodding with metal poles. Two men in white coats were lifting gurneys, covered with blankets, onto a railed flat bed truck. Nicholas counted seven of them. His feet did not move for nearly half an hour, until he was coaxed by the Chief of Engine House No. 3 to either leave or state his business.

Nicholas was in a trance, a state of disbelief and grief. "This was my home." The fireman held him at the elbow, and led him down the sidewalk about fifty feet, beyond and away from the lingering firefighters and equipment. His eyes burned from not only tears and smoke, but also flaming emotional exhaustion.

"Nicholas. Nicholas?" The sound of his name jarred him from his catatonic stupor. He looked at the fireman and vaguely recognized the face, but could not instantly give it a name.

"It's your uncle. Me, Uncle Wilbur, your mother's brother, the fire-eater ... you know me. Are you all right?"

Nicholas looked at him with a blank, detached stare. It had been at least two years since he last saw this fellow.

"Your family, they died almost instantly, Nicholas. It started in your house ... the gas, the lines, the gaslights, all exploded, and the whole house went up in a fireball. They are still working on how it all got started ... the Battalion Chief is checking. Somehow, the explosion or fire bells or something, your neighbors, they woke up in time, and we think they were all able to get out alive, but we did not save their homes."

Nicholas looked back to the smoldering mass. He took a long, deep breath and gorged his lungs with the putrid air, held it in and exhaled, emptying them. He repeated this three, four times and started to walk away. Uncle Wilbur took him by the shoulder, but Nicholas twisted, turned away and gave him a defiant stare. He stood facing him, with his shoulders squared.

"Where are you going, Nicholas? Come on over to our house later, young man, and have something to eat or at least sit down with your aunt and me, and have a good rest, or talk, or something." Nick surveyed his rediscovered relative, checking his appearance and demeanor.

"Maybe. Maybe I will." Nick turned away again, and started back down the street toward Broadway. He had only a vague idea where Uncle Wilbur lived, in his grandfather's old house either on Kretner or Strauss Street. It did not matter.

He had no way of knowing that his brother Leopold and Phryné Truffaut were already well beyond Cleveland, and passing through Toledo, Ohio.

Chapter Six

A Thumb In The Breeze

Monday, August 29

Nicholas Throckmorton walked down the block, away from the smoldering ashes of the only home he ever knew. The hole in his stomach felt bottomless; the hollowness he felt within him was a chasm swallowing his soul. His head ached with unrelenting, piercing pain. His senses were numb, unfeeling, and left him aimlessly unaware of his surroundings. He was walking up Broadway toward his brother's apartment for reasons he could not understand. Perhaps Leopold did not leave for Cleveland after all, and he would find him there. But, if Leopold was still in Buffalo, wouldn't he be at his job, working at Urban's? He was so disoriented, so confused, he could not explain his actions. He could not make sense of anything. His heart pumped to the hoof beats of a thousand horses.

Ten blocks away from his destroyed home, his emotions overtook him. At the Fillmore Avenue streetcar stop, he collapsed onto a bench, buried his face into his hands and bawled like a three-year-old. Unseen by him, an unknown woman dressed in grey tweed and starched white cotton, approached and placed a comforting hand on his shoulder. He scowled, grunted and sullenly pushed himself down the bench and further away. He cried until he ran out of tears and his stomach ached with pitiful emptiness. When he collected himself and opened his eyes, he discovered that everyone else at the trolley station was at least six feet away from him. Nicholas lost all sense of time, and remained seated on the bench for most of the morning. Life went on around him unnoticed. He paid no attention to the weekday hubbub and the noise of Monday scurrying through the streets. It did not exist in his empty, heartless, frozen world.

119

Nicholas was now a young man without a home, without a family, stranded on a desert devoid of tears and deficient in emotion. Eerily, the melodious noontime Angelus sounding from the bell tower of Saint Stanislaus Church roused his consciousness. His tear-crusted eyes burned and stung with every blink. The front of his denim work shirt, covered in the grey dust of grains, appeared as a road map of falling tears and mental anguish. He stood, jammed his hands into his sailcloth work trousers, and continued on his journey to Leopold's walk-up.

From the sidewalk, he could see the curtains of a downstairs window part slightly and close again. He did not expect to find anything, and could only categorize his visit as pure grotesque curiosity. Inside, he closely studied the apartment again and discovered everything just as he left it on Sunday afternoon. Phryné's and his brother's clothes were still soaking inexplicably in the bathtub, and the single light bulb hanging from the kitchen ceiling was still lit. The apartment was silent; no sound, no life. It was vacant, empty and barren. There was one lonely, cracked coffee cup and an empty bowl in the sink. There was an ashtray on the small kitchen table with four cigarette butts; two with traces of lipstick. A lonely little bottle of antiseptic Mercurochrome sat isolated in the center of the table. The bed was messily made and some of Leopold's work clothes were strewn on top. The drawers of the ragged dresser were askew, and the window was left open about six inches. A yellowed muslin curtain wafted in the slight breeze.

He looked carefully around the place one last time, pulled the string and turned off the light. He did not look back again.

He went down the stairs and onto the street, following the exact path he made earlier. He walked to the alley off Sycamore to look for his brother's old Model T, only to discover that it was gone, just as Leopold and Phryné were. He imagined his brother driving away in the old Ford, turning around, and giving him and the rest of the family a wave and a big smile.

He could not fault his brother for leaving, but neither could he forgive him. In Nicholas' mind, his brother's association with Dillon Cafferty brought all this ruin and carnage. Dillon Cafferty blinded and poisoned his brother, and murdered his mother and sisters.

Nicholas was driven by fear, anger and loathing. He had made this visit by sheer mechanical impulse, to double-check his perception of isolation, to verify his loneliness, his devastation. He'd had no direction, no pre-determined destination. His older brother had abandoned him yet again, and this time it was thorough, complete and absolute. His entire family had been obliterated in a single day. Leopold had left while his mother and sisters burned to death. Nicholas' emotions were violently torn from his soul; vanquished by flame and a brief penciled note on a paper sack. His existence was blistered and branded forever by an early morning inferno wrought by the Devil's disciples. He did not believe the fire was accidental. He knew it was set by the mob, the Black Hand of Torricelli.

He blindly walked thirty blocks back downtown to the foot of Main Street. The morning had vanished, and it was nearing one o'clock when he walked into Yummy Lunch on the corner of Clinton Street. He carried with him a wretched mishmash of burnt wood, mill dust, sweat and tears. His bloodshot eyes were still ablaze.

He was sitting at the long counter on an undersized wooden stool, eating a hamburger sandwich with mashed potatoes and gravy. It could have been either the food warming him from within his belly, or the loud chatter and conversation around him, but he awoke from his stupor of self-pity and pathos. He looked around him, at the laborers, businessmen, shoppers and tradesmen. He quickly took stock of his situation, his predicament, his damnation, and his place in the world. A stark realization came to him: he had nowhere to go and nobody cared; he was a miserable, homeless soul. He looked around once again, and did a cursory study of the people inside the little diner. Nobody looked as pathetic as he felt, and nobody offered compassion. How could they, and why would they?

He jammed a hand inside his pant pocket, pulled out his folded wallet, shuffled the contents and discovered that he had one dollar and forty-seven cents. He glanced around the little restaurant in desperate anguish, in one final, futile attempt to discover humanity, and promised himself that he would leave Buffalo and not look back. He could stay at his brother's apartment, but he could not forget about the four men in the black Chrysler. Of course, Nicholas had no knowledge about the direct cause of the deadly fire, but there was a knotted, twisted feeling deep within his gut, and a foreboding in his mind.

Nicholas thought about finishing the week at Russell-Miller, but he didn't think about it long. Why would he spend another week, a day or even an hour by himself in an empty city? Only the week before, he'd told Leopold that he had dreams of travelling the world, seeing exotic places, and maybe even flying an airplane. It was about time that he began opening doors for himself, taking a giant step forward out of Buffalo and getting a fresh start. He muttered to himself: "I got to get out while I can." Years ago, he remembered how upset he was when his best friend's family moved away from the house next door. His tuberculosis-stricken father grabbed him by the arm and said, *"It's cheaper to move than pay rent."* Sometimes, without adding any further explanation, his father would say things like that. Occasionally, he could still hear his father's words.

He put two dimes on the counter for his lunch, and walked to the restroom at the back of the diner, where he washed his hands, splashed water on his face, and over the back of his neck. Seconds later, he was out the door, on foot again, wearing tear-stained, dusty flour mill work clothes, and walking toward the rest of his life. He was thinking as he walked, and he struggled to push away the shock, sorrow and self-pity. He had his head in the clouds and his nose to the wind, holding a carrot on a stick, tempting himself, prodding himself forward, placing one foot in front of the other. At the end of Court Street, the Erie Canal blocked his westward progress, so he turned right and walked north. Ten blocks away was the newly built and opened Peace Bridge, the gateway to Canada and Detroit. Canada was somewhere new and foreign. Detroit was a booming city full of automobile factories and without flourmills.

He was simply following his nose. Nicholas crossed the mile-long Peace Bridge on foot. Hundreds of pedestrians took to the bridge daily for cross-border business, shopping or employment. With just over a dollar in his pocket, his stroll across the bridge was the start of a journey without specific direction. Strangely, for the first time that day, he felt at ease. Perhaps it was the fresh air. The ache at the back of his skull was gone and he no longer felt the need to retch. As he started across the bridge, his attention was drawn to a set of buildings by a loading dock. A flurry of Revenue and Customs officers were milling about. To Nick, it looked like some kind of training exercise. He had no way of knowing: the agents were still investigating the ruckus and dust-up of the night before.

The Niagara River runs about a mile wide between Buffalo and Fort Erie, Ontario, and does not appear as ominous as its rapids are further north. The current pushes the water underneath the bridge with a steady, mesmerizing and almost hypnotic motion. The wind brushed past his face, refreshing his soul. Life returned to his limbs and he no longer was forcing his feet to move. He could actually hear the gulls squawking around him, and indifferently returned a greeting from a fellow traveler who was heading in the opposite direction.

His disposition was vastly different from what it was a few hours earlier. When he approached the Canada Immigration booth, he had a bland smile.

"Good afternoon, young man. Are you an American citizen?"

Never before had Nicholas been asked that question, and with surprise, he answered, "Why, yes. Yes, I am."

"And how long do you intend to stay in Canada?"

"I am just out walking across this new bridge, and I was thinking that I might go down to the riverbank and see what Buffalo looks like from this side." He did not know what prompted him to say that. He surprised himself with that answer.

The officer looked at Nicholas and smiled. "Have fun, young man, don't let the current hypnotize or fool you, and don't fall in."

Nick smiled back, "Thank you, sir."

He walked perhaps a half-mile away from the bridge, west on Garrison Road. He wondered if the officer at the border was watching, and if anyone would be following him to see if he actually did go and sit on the riverbank and look at Buffalo. After another half-mile or so, he convinced himself that the coast was clear, and nobody would be following him solely to check on his whereabouts. It was a strange feeling to be in a foreign land, on his own, and experiencing a sense of relief, a sense of freedom that came over him. He felt emancipated. He felt he was in total command of his fate for the first time in his life. With only the clothes on his back and the change in his pocket, he was indeed embarking on a life adventure.

He turned and began to walk backwards down the road, sticking his thumb high into the air at every passing buggy, automobile, truck or delivery wagon.

His first ride was an open-cab Fageol flatbed truck, with honeycombed, tubeless hard rubber tires, carrying black iron pipe and fittings. The driver was a crusty fellow, unshaven and wearing grease-soaked coveralls. He pulled the truck off the road and onto the dusty shoulder, mashing gears and kicking up gravel. After a brief introduction, and the exchange of destinations, Nicholas climbed aboard. He sat behind the driver's wooden high-back seat on a folded tarpaulin, his legs uncomfortably askew on the load of pipe. Ratchet chain binders and one-inch braided hemp secured the load to the truck bed. It was impossible to talk over the rattling load and rough ride, but the driver did manage to boast of his experience in the ways of the road and give Nicholas a warning. "If them pipe start shifting real bad, or you see me heading for the ditch, jump."

For the next four hours, Nicholas kept one hand firmly on the frame of the driver's seat. He rode atop the dancing pipes for 80 miles to Norfolk, Ontario.

That evening at about seven o'clock, he caught his next ride, and it was a marked improvement over the first. He was able to sit up front with the driver of a Ford panel truck loaded with freshly cured Burley tobacco. It was fresh off the farm in Haldimand, destined for a cigarette** processing plant in Saint Thomas, Ontario. After five hours traveling west on King's Highway 3, he spent the night sleeping on a pile of burlap sacks inside a storage shed at the plant. The next morning, Tuesday, he was awakened by a uniformed security guard brandishing a twelve-inch nightstick.

Chapter Seven

A Quickie

Sunday night, August 28, Chicago, Illinois

Nickel Plate No. 1 arrived on schedule at the busy LaSalle Street Station, the bellwether terminal of the Lake Shore & Michigan Railroad as well as the Rock Island Line. Leopold and Phryné were at the busy crossroads of America's rail traffic, situated almost exactly in the center of the nation. Chicago's LaSalle was markedly busier and noisier than Buffalo's Lackawanna. When they stepped off the train, the tired sting disappeared from their eyes, and their heartbeats quickened with excitement. They ignored the numbness in their backsides. Directly outside the train station, Leopold helped the taxi driver load their baggage into the trunk. It was a mere two blocks south and one block east to Dearborn Station, Chicago's terminal for the Atchison, Topeka and Santa Fe Railroad. Leopold handed the driver a quarter for the ten-cent dimbox* jaunt between the two gigantic railroad stations in the middle of a city, in the middle of America, separated only by two city blocks.

They stood in line for perhaps ten minutes waiting to purchase their tickets for *The California Limited*. The ticket agent was efficient and friendly, asking the questions he needed to assist them in their decision. He informed them that The Limited was the First Class rail service of the Santa Fe Railroad and offered a few options for their trip to Los Angeles. The flashy poster advertisements flaunted *Santa Fe All The Way*, with beautiful scenic views and comely female models. The agent first telegraphed for availability and confirmed that only two options remained open for purchase on the next day's train. Leopold knew the trip would be expensive, and the cold hard truth was confirmed when the agent clarified their choices and the costs. He picked up a massive volume, the railroad

'Official Guide' to tariffs and fares, and ruffled through the pages to the correct listing and mileage charts. Tickets for The Limited were $78.15 apiece for The Limited's first-class rail fare. Additionally, they had the option of a $17.25 Pullman charge for a lower berth and $13.50 for the upper berth in a curtained section or a private compartment for $44.00, with a three-foot wide lower bed and a fold-down upper berth. Leopold listened closely, nodded and told the agent that they were married yesterday in Buffalo and were travelling west on their honeymoon. He did not use the false name the way he did back in Buffalo, and with a sense of pride, informed the agent their names were Throckmorton: Leopold and Phryné. From the corner of his eye, he could see the quick glance Phryné sent his way. In an instant, she controlled her reaction, smiled and reached over to hold his hand. They quickly decided for the private compartment and were comfortable with their choice; the extra cost for the larger bed and total privacy seemed reasonable. Once their choice was made, the agent telegraphed the Santa Fe railroad to confirm availability and reserved the compartment. They were in the ticket office for fifteen minutes, exploring their options and determining their schedule. When it was all added up, the tickets written and their baggage tags filled out, the total was just over $200. Leopold quickly did the math in his head, and figured that they would have just about $250 between them when they arrived in Los Angeles. The agent confirmed their purchase with two more telegrams: one to the Santa Fe offices, and one more to the railroad, verifying that the private Pullman compartment was sold. Their train would leave Chicago Monday, at 8 PM and arrive in Los Angeles at La Grande Station on Thursday afternoon at 2:20 PM; covering about twenty-two hundred miles in three days.

Leopold asked about nearby accommodations and the agent recommended The Hotel DeSoto, a new tourist hotel just four blocks away on Jackson Street. He then assured Leopold that they would not need their blankets or quilt on the train, that their bedroom compartment would have everything they'd need. The agent called for a porter to wrap, tag and forward the blankets to baggage storage until their departure tomorrow. Leopold and Phryné watched as all this preparation was completed with military precision. Finally, the ticket agent stamped separate payment coupons for the Santa Fe railroad and Pullman Company. He placed their coupons and baggage tags in the ticket envelope, handed it to Leopold, thanked them for their patronage and purchase, and wished them a pleasant honeymoon journey to Los Angeles.

Leopold carefully placed the ticket packet in his billfold and buttoned his vest pocket closed. At the newsstand, Leopold bought a copy of The Saturday Evening Post and Phryné bought a 20¢ pack of Marlboro**, the new red-tipped filter cigarette for women, and a pack of Chesterfield for Leopold.

There were several taxis directly outside the terminal rotunda. They walked toward a sharply dressed driver standing alongside a polished, dark green, 1924 Auburn Brougham, waiting curbside with the rear door open. He tipped his hat to them, stowed their bags and drove them the four blocks to their hotel. Neither Phryné nor Leopold was accustomed to this level of personal service. Leopold determined that it would be necessary to have a pocket full of silver for the rest of the trip, and thought it was a curious but convenient coincidence that so many hacks* were waiting outside Dearborn Station.

The DeSoto hotel was an attractive ten-story steel and concrete building in the French Renaissance style, with a decorative façade of vitreous red brick and white terra cotta trim. Inside was a spacious, opulently decorated lobby of wood, marble, and plaster work, its pressed tin ceiling rising to the second floor. Leopold paid three dollars for a double-bed room and for the second time since their arrival, checked them in as husband and wife. Out of the corner of his eye, he caught Phryné nervously pretending to study the collection of postcards on the counter. Without question or comment, the desk clerk thanked them and handed a complimentary copy of Saturday's *Chicago Tribune* newspaper to Leopold. He summoned the bellboy by tapping on the round chrome bell, telegraphing its melodious ring; which went echoing throughout the large lobby.

The bellhop loaded the suitcase and duffle sack onto the baggage trolley and accompanied them to the elevator for the ride up to the fifth floor. The hallway had Persian-patterned burgundy and gold carpeting with lacquered cherry wainscoting and textured magnolia cream wallpaper. Wall lamps with upturned, maroon china shades cast a soft glow onto the walls and ceiling.

Once inside their room, the bellboy set their bags onto the floor, switched on a table lamp and exited the room. When the door clicked shut, Leopold and Phryné smiled at one another and embraced, allowing themselves to savor their newfound tranquility. The previous twenty-four hours constituted the most tumultuous, traumatic, dangerous, and disturbing day of their young lives. The quiet of the hotel room was a serene, welcome contrast to the rumbling, rolling motion of the train. They took seats on the small divan. Leopold opened a bottle of ginger beer from the side table, poured some into a glass and passed it to Phryné. They sat in silence, his arm around her, serenely, privately reflecting on their first full day of travel.

"What are we going to do tomorrow, Leopold? I mean, we have a whole day before the next train, don't we?"

"Just about. We can sleep in, that's for sure, but I have an idea."

"Really? An idea?"

"Think about what I'm suggesting, sweetheart mine. When we bought the railroad tickets, and when we signed in downstairs, registered at the desk, I got to thinking that we might as well go ahead and tie the knot, you know, get married." He gave her a squeeze across her shoulders. "That way, we will not need to pretend that we are married when we check in anytime, anywhere, anymore. No matter what, we are not going to have the wedding that we were planning, that's a fact. That sure got all ballocked up. So, what do you think about getting married tomorrow?"

She looked into his eyes, smiled and nodded. "Chicago is as good a place as any to get married, I suppose.

"So, let's do it ... go ahead and do it. We will get one of them quickies they talk about. We will have a Monday wedding." With that, they were in complete agreement. It was decided that tomorrow they would seek out a Justice of the Peace, a judge, anybody, who could legally unite them as husband and wife.

Like a mild headache, outright exhaustion dampened their excitement about tomorrow's impromptu wedding and the upcoming trip to California. They sat and sipped the soft drink, glanced through the paper, and ended up sorting through their clothes, spreading them all out on the bed. Leopold discovered that Phryné had packed up the overalls and shirt that he gave her on Saturday night and did not leave them behind after all. On that hectic night back in Buffalo, they each packed things on impulse, and stuffed things away without much thought or regard. The next day's planned wedding was a welcome distraction that required them to put a little effort into looking their best. Phryné laid her beaded white chiffon party dress on the bed and pressed the wrinkles out with a damp washcloth. She carefully placed the dress on a heavy wooden hanger, hooked it over one of the armoire doors, and went to work on Leopold's dress shirt. He carefully brushed out his vested Sacque suit and hung it over the other door of the mahogany cabinet. They sorted the remainder of their clothing into two groups. The things that should be folded: shirts, blouses, dresses, trousers were arranged, tucked and re-packed into Phryné's suitcase. All the rest was co-mingled and placed in the duffle sack.

Leopold expressed confidence that he would be able to quickly find work in California and they could find a suitable

130

apartment by simply checking the newspapers upon their arrival in Los Angeles. The classified advertising pages of the Chicago Tribune contained scores of both job and apartment listings, so it was only reasonable to expect the same in Los Angeles or any large city in California. They recognized that their situation was uncertain at best, and notwithstanding their confidence, they still needed to be very careful with their spending. He promised her that he would buy a wedding ring made from California gold as soon as he landed a job.

By midnight, they had showered and gone to bed. They teased one another for about fifteen minutes, but Leopold ultimately surrendered and allowed Phryné to taunt him further. She told him that she was saving herself for the wedding night. He accepted the challenge, and as a condition of the cease-fire, he vowed that revenge would be his.

That night in Chicago they had time to reflect on their lives, their decisions they had made, and their future together. They were still agitated and angry over the deception that Dillon wielded on them and realized that it would be quite some time, if ever, before their hostile attitude toward him would subside. His ability to use their association and friendship with total disregard for their well-being or integrity was only part of what was bothering them. The genuinely disturbing truth about what happened Saturday night was the fact that neither of them had even the slightest hint that something suspicious was going on. Dillon displayed his roguish, gruff and 'let the devil take the hindmost' attitude so well, that when taken in context, it was such an obvious overstatement of his personality that he was consistently able to deceive everyone. Leopold and Phryné selfishly put up with his officious bravado for the sake of the good times, the dancing and partying they all enjoyed both in Buffalo, and mostly, across the border in Canada. They were still very anxious over Eloisa, but Phryné reassured Leopold and herself that knowing her as a close friend and her family as well as she does, Eloisa's situation would work itself out.

Everything else that had happened back in Buffalo since they got aboard the train (Dillon's demise and the deadly fire) was completely unknown to them and would remain that way for some time to come.

Going All The Way

Monday morning, August 29, Chicago, Illinois

They slept soundly that night, barely moving a muscle. Leopold woke first, and lay there watching Phryné in her deep sleep. Sunlight was pushing through the drapery, and his curiosity got the best of him. He turned and grabbed his pocket watch off the night table and quickly set it back down. The hands were stretched straight across the dial; quarter past nine. He swung his legs around and sat at the edge of the bed pulling on his socks. Phryné stirred, "Leopold?"

"Good morning, Phryné. I looked at my watch and got nervous for some stupid reason … it read nine-fifteen. But that's wrong. We're on Central Time here, so it's quarter past eight, that's all. I forgot about the time zone change. You slept well?"

"As a pure matter of fact, I did. I sure did. And it felt good."

It was the first time they awoke in the same bed. Never before had they had the opportunity to sleep through the night together. She slid across the bed, tossed back the blanket, sprang to her feet and stood in front of him, hands-on-hip. The soft subdued light of morning put a warming glow across her form. He stood, they embraced and shared a kiss. "We better get our wiggle on, Mister. We have a wedding to attend. And I don't know about you, but I am definitely getting into that shower in there. You can help me figure out how to work it, won't you?"

It took patience and a few minutes to get the water temperature adjusted, but it was a delight for her. The oilcloth shower curtain hung over the tub on a circular rod. Never before had Phryné experienced a shower. As a young girl, she remembered a large galvanized washtub that her mother would fill with hot water from the stove. Years later, after her father was promoted at the bank, they moved to their home on Lombard Street with its large, boat-shaped, claw-foot, porcelain-on-cast iron tub. Leopold often showered off the Urban Flour dust and grease in the locker room, but the water pressure and temperature were highly unpredictable, if not completely unreliable.

Leopold's shaving brush clunked inside the mug as he worked up the lather and slathered it onto his face. He studied the chrome safety razor he was holding, turned it slowly between his fingers, and thought of his father. The water coming out of the faucet was piping hot, and heated the razor and its blade with every rinse. His father purchased that chrome razor while he was in the Marine Corps, before he left for France, and used it for the last five years of his life. Leopold had used it every day since his father died, and this day, for some reason, it brought on a melancholy daydream, and allowed his thoughts to wander.

Phryné shared the bathroom mirror with him, putting on her lipstick and working patiently to artfully form Cupid's bow*. She smiled at her reflection: perfection once again! She used Max Factor mascara, the only brand that furnished a little brush with the paste product. As she powdered on her rouge and finished her 'face mask', she thought about her parents. She wondered about their reaction to her note and absence. She knew her father would comfort her mother, have his coffee, and take the streetcar to the bank as usual. Her brother Robert would eat his oatmeal and walk to Grover Cleveland High, impatiently awaiting the end of the year when he planned to quit school, hire on as crewman, and sail the Great Lakes for American Steamship Shipping. She was not sure about her mother; she may or may not open the shop in time for the usual Monday nine o'clock appointments. Unlike Leopold, she clearly knew why her thoughts wandered this morning: her life had drastically changed.

Leopold and Phryné dressed in the clothes they'd laid out the night before and wore them well. It was 1927 Chicago, and they fit right in. Together, no one could doubt that they enjoyed flaunting fashion. Anyone who saw them would find it difficult to imagine that he drove a truck, and she cut hair and applied makeup at a beauty shop. Phryné looked ready for a party in her white chiffon with the tiered hem and lace trimmed collar and waist. She wore her red ankle boots, black patterned stockings and a red, offset brim cloche hat, with a long pheasant plume. Inside her pocketbook, she had a pair of red half-length opera gloves for later in the day. Leopold's midnight blue three-piece pinstripe fit him perfectly. His trim jacket was nipped at the waist, his vest held his trunk like a chamois glove, and his slacks were form-tailored from the waist to the hip, full to the calf, and narrowing at the cuff.

After a small breakfast of eggs and toast in the dining room, Leopold and Phryné stopped at the reception desk for assistance.

The hotel clerk was a tall and lanky fellow, his black hair and eyebrows slicked with hair crème. He had round, wire-rimmed eyeglasses, impeccably manicured nails, and wore the slightest touch of lip wax. He took his job seriously, and eagerly presented an elegant, professional appearance for the hotel. His starched cotton shirt was as white and stiff as a frozen rope. "How may I help you this morning?"

They stood in front of him, waffling their fingers together and holding hands. Leopold asked, "Where can we get married?"

"You would be surprised how often I am asked that question by honeymoon couples." He smiled nobly, nodded once, carefully pointed his index finger to the left and continued, "Six blocks up on Washington Street, you will find the Cook County Offices building, Courthouse, Register, and Permits Office. Right inside, you can get everything you need.

They will be happy to help." Leopold thanked him and paid fifteen cents for three two-cent postage stamps and Phryné's colored picture postcards of downtown Chicago, the Mercantile and LaSalle Street's business district.

Their morning was planned. Upstairs in room 517, they sorted and packed up their belongings and prepared to leave. They were killing time, fidgeting like youngsters in the front pew at church. Neither of them mentioned it, but, without doubt, there was nervousness, the typical wedding-day jitters.

Phryné sat at the desk and brought out the bottle of Parker ink and fountain pen from the side table to write brief notes to Eloisa and her parents on the postcards. She found it difficult to dance around the truth for each tidbit of correspondence, and she had to choose her words carefully. Short and to the point, her cards contained only brief platitudes, a little white lie and words of well-being with absolutely no mention of Saturday night's debacle. She told them that she and Leopold were married that morning in Chicago, and were on their way to establish their future and find fortune in sunny southern California. She explained that she would write a lengthy letter as soon as opportunity permitted. It was not easy to hide the truth from her best friend and family. She felt genuine relief as she finished the last address.

Leopold's postcard to Buffalo was very simple, and he had no reservations about his message. The only problem was an unfamiliar Parker Duofold pen that leaked. The fountain pen left an ink spot as big as a quarter above his short message:

On our way to California now, love to everyone. More when we arrive. The Ford is at Lackawanna Terminal. ~ *Leopold.*

He had no way of knowing, but his picture postcard of LaSalle Street would never get delivered in Buffalo. It would end up in a Post Office Department 'dead letter' office somewhere in New York City.

Phryné was sitting on the edge of the bed, legs crossed and watching him as he finished his postcard. She teased him, "There is no hurry, but as soon as you finish there, Leopold, we can get married. But you go right ahead, and take all the time you want. Our train does not leave until eight o'clock tonight."

He smiled at her, nodded, got up from the little desk and slipped on his jacket. "All right then. Let's go and get married, Miss Phryné Truffaut." He snugged and straightened his tie.

Once outside their room, they playfully scurried to the elevator; his right hand resting on her backside. Inside the elevator, behind the brass accordion doors, they shared a passionate kiss; their hands pulling, pushing their bodies together for a few fleeting seconds.

They crossed the street at Adams and mailed their postcards inside the busy post office. It was nearing eleven thirty, the sun had already passed its zenith, and was waning in the August sky. The street noise was markedly louder than what they were accustomed to in Buffalo. The click-clack of the rails and the ringing bells of trolleys and streetcars echoed between the tall buildings. People crisscrossed the street everywhere, dodging heavy truck and automobile traffic, and even an occasional horse-drawn wagon or cart as they rattled across the pavement. Walking down Clark Street, toward the Cook County offices on Washington, they held hands and talked about the day ahead of them.

Leopold once again justified the purchase of the Pullman extras. The cheapest coach tickets to Los Angeles would have totaled nearly eighty dollars apiece, and considering the distance and three full days of travel, it would be an unbearable trip without sleeping accommodations. Briefly, he second-guessed his decision to leave his Model T Ford back in Buffalo, with or without a roof. Perhaps he was even trying to convince himself that the cost was reasonable and not over the top. There simply were not that many options when it came to transcontinental travel. It was either hopping aboard a freight train and riding the rails as a hobo, buying a coach-class ticket for an uncomfortable seat on a hard wicker bench, or a luxury train like The California Limited. They both heard stories about automobiles running out of gas on the prairie or breaking down in the Rocky Mountains. He and Phryné convinced themselves that since they already knew what Niagara Falls looked like, they should consider this as their honeymoon trip. Together, they agreed once again that they could find jobs and a suitable place to live in Los Angeles soon after arrival. When they were nearing the courthouse steps, Phryné expressed her confidence once again with the light-hearted comment: "It's warm out there in California, Leopold. We can even sleep right outside, under a blanket of stars, if worse should come to worse." Of course, their mood was buoyant and cheerful; it was their wedding day.

They took the marble steps of the Cook County Offices with cautious determination. Leopold held the heavy oak and glass door open for Phryné. Once inside, they stopped, and together, they studied their surroundings. Subconsciously, they were giving one another the chance to escape, to think about this just one more time. They were silent, and not as much as a whisper crossed their lips.

It was a large, imposing gallery, with polished pink and grey granite floors, brass railings along massive stairways, large chandeliers hanging from a domed, plastered ceiling, and grand, polished wood wainscot and trim. He held her around the waist. "Are you sure about this, Sweetheart?"

Phryné did not hesitate, and answered with confidence, "Yes, I am."

Chapter Eight

Rock And Rye

Tuesday, August 30, St. Thomas, Ontario, Canada

The security guard who woke Nicholas waited patiently for him to gather himself and rise from the pile of burlap sacks. "Where are you heading, young man, eh?"

Nick stood, arched his back, ricked his neck and stuck both hands inside his pockets. "Detroit. Port Huron. Wherever my thumb can carry me."

"You're a Yank, eh?"

"Yessir. From Buffalo."

The guard studied him carefully, running his nightstick along Nick's form, and looking into his eyes. He paused, holstered his blackjack, and breathed his words into Nick's face. "Tell you what, Yank. Here's two bits."

He took a half step back, flipped a quarter to Nicholas and stood with his arms crossed. "It was a Yank that saved my soft pink arse in October of '18 in some hell-hole of a farm field. It was right at the end of the war; over there someplace in France called Arras." His voice trailed off briefly. "*Hundred Days Offensive* they called it afterwards, when it was over and all the bodies were buried. *The war to end all war*, that's what they called it. I don't think so. It was Hell on Earth, that's what it was." He nodded at Nicholas, grabbed him by the shoulder and pushed him out the shed door. "Now, get out. There's a food wagon just outside the gate; get yourself something to eat on me, Yank. Then keep walking. I don't want to see you back here again, you hear me, eh?"

Nicholas turned, gave him a gestured salute and walked off the property of St. Thomas Processing Limited. Directly outside the gate, sat a food wagon, decorated and trimmed in bright green and blue. The line was ten or twelve deep, and for just a moment, he toyed with the thought of skipping a morning meal, but quickly thought better of it. The meal wagon had one young fellow working over an exterior charcoal griddle and another older chap pouring the drinks, slinging sandwiches and shouting out hot plate orders. Nicholas wolfed down a fifteen-cent, paper-plate breakfast of hash and a cup of broth before he stole away behind a growth of maples for his morning constitutional. His ten cents in change meant he could eat again tomorrow.

So far, good fortune was his travelling companion. The weather had been fair, and his thumb had served him well. He was on the road again, walking along the shoulder of King's Highway 3 for no more than five minutes before a Buick Standard touring sedan braked and pulled off the road, and onto the berm.

The Buick's driver reached across the seat, and opened the door. "Get in, kid. You'll get rocks in your shoes walking along this cow path."

Adding irony to fate, the driver was a fellow American, another traveler, driving to Walkerville, Ontario, just east of Windsor. He introduced himself as Lester Mayfield, sales manager for the Pillsbury Company, the second largest grain mill in Buffalo. Nicholas let him ramble on, listened like he was interested, nodded in agreement, remained quiet and did not add anything to the conversation. He was in good spirits and so far, things were going his way -- a free breakfast and a ride that should take him the rest of the way across Ontario, Canada. He did not want to do or say anything to put that in jeopardy. More of his father's words wafted through his memory: *"Don't speak until you are spoken to."* He ran his tongue across the self-inflicted gash he'd left in his lip the day before.

Lester Mayfield continued with his narration, "I am tasked to convince Hiram Walker that they would be better served to purchase Pillsbury rye from Buffalo, rather than transporting an inferior product from Watherby Mills in Minneapolis. Ours is cheaper, cleaner and we can get it there faster -- right across the International Rail Bridge right there at the Black Rock Canal and deliver it straight to their railroad siding in Windsor." Lester talked as if he had been deprived of human contact for six months. His words were coming without pause, one after the other, continually, for what seemed like an hour. When he did eventually stop for a breather, he turned to Nicholas and asked, "So, where are you from and where are you going, young man?"

Nicholas knew that eventually that question would be coming, but cringed anyway. He had time to think about it, but he did not need or want anyone else involved in his life now, and he certainly did not want to volunteer any information unless absolutely necessary. "I'm from Buffalo, too, and I'm headed for Detroit. I got a job lined up."

Lester nodded, and looked at him across the front seat. "There's plenty of work in Detroit, that's for sure. Anything in particular? What kind of work did you do in Buffalo?"

Nicholas' thoughts raced, looking for the answers he hoped would satisfy this fellow and stop his questions. Nicholas wanted to avoid questions about himself, his family, everything. He wanted to be left alone in his misery, and to work things out for himself. There was nothing anyone could do for him. He remembered another of his father's quips: *"Nobody is better at self-pity than yourself."* Considering everything that was taken from him, no one on Earth was able to give it back, but he rationalized that this fellow was good enough to stop and offer him a ride, so some kind of response was required of him. He hoped that a short answer with minimal information would suffice. Reluctantly, he started, "I lost my mother suddenly and there is nothing to keep me in Buffalo any longer. I worked at Russell-Miller for the last two years, but I'm done. I quit on Saturday. I have a cousin in Detroit that works at General Motors and I'm on my way to his place. That's the story of my life. Now you know." Nick was comfortable with the lie.

Lester was quiet, thinking. "Well, you must know a little about the grain business, working at Russell-Miller. What's your name?"

"Nicholas. You can call me Nick."

"Well, Nick. Like I was saying, I am on my way to Hiram Walker, they make Canadian Club whiskey, and they have their own flour mill, but they need more rye than they produce, so that's what I am trying to sell them. They have been buying their rye from Watherby's in Minneapolis. We have the best rye in the entire Northeast United States at Pillsbury."

For a while, it had developed into a very good day for Nicholas. Lester kept talking as Nicholas listened with one ear and watched the flat, fertile farmlands of southwest Ontario pass by. The monotonous drone of Lester's voice put him into a timeless trance, and his thoughts wandered back through childhood memories of his brother, sisters and parents. Growing up on the East Side was worry and trouble free until his father's health began to steadily worsen. His brother Leopold quit school at the age of thirteen and did whatever jobs came his way. His father struggled with menial, insecure jobs that lasted only until his next regression. His older sister Johanna started work after their father passed away, and his brother pushed and helped him get a job. Somehow, the family hung together and struggled through. Food was on the table, and they could afford nice clothes for church on Sunday. All in all, squabbles and hurt feelings aside, things could have been worse. He caught himself in time; he was beginning to tear up. Quickly, he lit one of his six remaining Camels and drew the smoke deep inside his lungs, coughed, and wiped his eyes on his sleeve.

"Take it easy there, Nick. Don't inhale so deep. How about we stop for a sandwich or something? It's about one o'clock, I think." Lester looked across the front seat and knew something was troubling the young man. Try as he might, Nicholas couldn't hide it.

"I'm not hungry. But, yeah, I could shake some water off the lily and straighten my shoelaces, I guess. It will be good to get out of the automobile for a while and stretch … I suppose." Running away just for the sake of running, he worried he could trip on those shoelaces of his. He regained control of his emotions.

"That's the ticket, Nick. We'll stop and wash the road dust off our hands and face with some soap and water and then rinse our gullets with some coffee. How's that?"

"Sure."

They had been driving a little over four hours when they stopped at a small roadside hash-house in the little hamlet of Essex; a converted home no more than twenty feet off the road. Weatherworn wood steps led up and onto the porch of 'Mom's Meals'. Lester would not accept Nick's refusal to eat lunch or have coffee, and insisted he pay for his plate of fried eggs and potatoes. Nick's thumb-power tour of Canada was graced by good will. He realized it, and there was a hint of hope for his future. He knew that eventually, the smell of burnt timber would drift away from his mind.

Lester's sales appointment was scheduled for the next morning, which was another touch of fortuitous fate for Nicholas. Lester drove him directly to the Sandwich Street ferry slip at the Windsor docks situated right on the Detroit River. When they parted, he told Nicholas that if things did not work out for him in Detroit, he could return to Buffalo and get a job at Pillsbury just by mentioning his name. Nicholas thanked him, but did not mention that there was nothing back in Buffalo to return to.

Ferriage across the river to Detroit cost Nicholas ten cents. His trip across Canada was free. It would be nearly thirty years before he would appreciate how free it was.

A Grand Canyon

Leopold and Phryné walked hand-in-hand down the steps of the Cook County Offices as husband and wife. Included with their marriage certificate was an exuberant sense of permanence and commitment that was new to them. They felt security also, a feeling that together they could conquer the world and withstand any misfortune that could come their way. The world belonged to them now, and the only things that mattered were themselves, their love and devotion to one another. Only seven hours and seven blocks away, they would begin a cross-country journey to their new life together. Their circumstances had drastically changed since Leopold proposed marriage on the sidewalk outside the Lafayette Hotel in Niagara Falls.

When they arrived back at the DeSoto, Phryné was in a world of her own. Oblivious to everyone else in the bustling lobby, she nearly danced across the foyer and playfully showed their marriage certificate to the desk clerk. She placed the document on the counter, pointed to it and tapped her finger. Proud and elated, she said, "Look at this! We are one hundred percent legal now!" The fellow was not the blue nose* as his waxed hair and impeccable clothes presented him; nonetheless, he was prudent and restrained his reaction to her exuberance.

He smiled, cautiously looked around the hotel foyer and spoke softly, "Come back and visit us the next time you two get that honeymoon feeling." Together, they shared a quiet laugh, as if it were a normal occurrence on a normal day. Leopold and Phryné's mood celebrated life as joyous, natural fun. It felt good to behave wildly, and enjoy life with a champagne glass full of humor, regardless of Prohibition.

Between constrained giggles, small talk and joviality, the clerk recommended the smorgasbord buffet in the dining room before they check out. It was an experience beyond comparison for Leopold and Phryné. The dining room was full of businessmen, bankers and travelers. Many of the diners came from the Chicago Board of Trade, Butter and Egg Board, and some of the nation's largest banks which lined both sides of LaSalle Avenue, creating a cosmopolitan wall of brownstones, concrete and wooden buildings that gave the street its nickname, 'The Canyon'.

The dining room was directly off the lobby, opulently lit with ornate chandeliers, decorated with paneled walls, a white tin ceiling, long, narrow windows on the street side, and oil paintings of agrarian and continental landscapes on the other. Long, linen-covered tables were along one wall, with a wide variety of English style fruit and curry chutneys, smoked salmon, kippered herring, jams, jellies, deviled eggs, and unlimited types of breads, bagels and biscuits. One table had pots of coffee, carafes of hot cocoa, steaming tea, pitchers of juices, bottled sodas, milk and a vulgar, spiced punch. An army of a half dozen waiters in black slacks, white shirts, bow ties and royal blue jackets stood against the wall at military attention, at the ready, for any request, and for any reason. Leopold and Phryné knew they were definitely not at the familiar Broadway or Washington Street Markets. The selection could be the same, but the presentation was certainly not from the East Side of Buffalo. The stylish Hotel Lafayette in Niagara Falls couldn't come close, or compare with this display. The meal, the experience and the memory cost two dollars.

Upstairs in room 517, they checked one more time for anything they might have overlooked, and closed their bags.

The lobby was a bevy of activity. They waited patiently at the desk to check out, and once again, the desk clerk proved to be a friendly, helpful fellow. "When are you leaving Chicago?"

Leopold was ready to walk out the door, baggage in hand. "Eight o'clock. We're leaving for Los Angeles, California, from Dearborn Station."

"You have six hours, then. This is what I suggest: take a taxi or walk to the station, store your suitcase and bag with the railroad, and take the Adams Street trolley six blocks back in this direction to the Art Institute of Chicago. It is a top-notch gallery with art galore from all over the world. There are oils, watercolors, sculpture and all that French nouveau jazz, and it is really worth your time. That is, if you do not want to sit around a train station for six hours. That is my suggestion, anyway."

Phryné and Leopold shared a glance, nodded in confirmation, and thanked the young fellow with the waxed eyebrows and hair. Leopold set the bags down, and shook the clerk's hand. It was small, narrow, cool and pasty. Leopold then thanked him, "That was kind of you to think of us. It sounds like you know your onions*. We appreciate it."

"Oh, you are welcome, sir. Enjoy your honeymoon, delight in your romance, and tell your friends that Chicago is a great city to get married in."

The California Connection

The newlyweds wandered the long hallways, open foyers, secluded chambers and concealed nooks of the art gallery. It was indeed an impressive exhibit, but three hours of culture was about all that Leopold could tolerate. He would remember the beautiful oils, watercolors, portraits and landscapes, but not the names of Degas, Monet, Cézanne, Renoir, or some American named Winslow Homer.

They decided to forego the trolley and took a leisurely walk back to Dearborn station. They stopped at Colosimo's Italian restaurant for a light afternoon meal of veal scaloppini and new asparagus, followed by coffee, biscotti and a dish of fragola gelato. They had dressed to the nines that morning, and with the addition of her red half-length, fingerless opera gloves to her white lace and chiffon frock, red boots, black stockings, and red hat, Phryné turned more than one head that afternoon. She walked with flair, flashing red and black like a matador. Hand-in-hand, they walked in step and kept their bodies drawn together. People watched them. They knew it, and savored the gaiety, the razzmatazz, and the attention their spontaneous celebration was getting.

Dearborn station was an imposing three-story structure standing strong with pink granite and red pressed brick exterior walls, and a twelve-story clock tower crowned with a steeply pitched roof. Visible for blocks, the station stood as a symbol of the powerful, prosperous railroads. For Chicago, it stood as an exhibition of civic pride. The first floor waiting hall bustled with foot traffic. Ladies' heels and men's leather soles echoed within the expansive, multi-colored marble hall, blending with the subdued tonal buzz of hundreds of human voices. The ceiling was two and a half stories high, vaulted in the center with massive skylights running along the length of the passenger atrium. Black cast iron railings brought the symbolic power of steam locomotives along the mezzanine of the second floor.

They spent the early evening hours inside the terminal. There was a Harvey House restaurant with a delectable menu featuring varied choices available at reasonable prices. The wait staff consisted exclusively of comely young women, known as Harvey Girls**, specially recruited and trained by the company. The wait staff dressed in black and white uniforms tailored to accentuate the female figure. With their hemlines not more than eight inches from the floor, they wore black stockings, and black shoes. Each had a white apron that triangled upwards from the waist to the shoulders, and their hair was tied back with a white ribbon. A piece of pie and a cup of coffee cost 25¢: a piece of pie that was fully one-fourth of the pie. The restaurant carried such a reputation that the Santa Fe railroad had exclusive contracts with the firm for Dining Car meals on their Pullman service and trackside restaurants at equipment switch-out locations. The railroad proudly advertised 'world famous Fred Harvey' food and

146

service on their trains; *The California Limited* being the first of Santa Fe's named trains to offer the Harvey service.

There were two sections of The Limited leaving Dearborn station that evening. A 'section' was a separate train, commissioned as needed, that ran on the same schedule, each independent of the other and running a few minutes apart. The California Limited was the flagship, the showpiece service of the Atchison, Topeka and Santa Fe. Leaving from Chicago every day, it was the fastest and most direct route to California, and traversed 2,231 miles in 66 hours. Scores of passengers, a uniquely special clientele, awaited The Limited's departure that day. The express to Los Angeles was affordable first class travel that catered to the businessman, socialite, mogul or worldly traveler. Leopold and Phryné were dressed the part, but they did not have the social standing that normally filled the seats of The Limited. They had not known that the day before, but became aware of it while waiting there in the terminal.

Inside the waiting room, there was a large, colorful, Santa Fe Railroad poster on the wall that was illuminated by three small, shaded lamps along the top edge. Pictured were two fashionably dressed, smiling young women. It proclaimed: *The California Limited is for first-class travel only. This train of luxury and speed will take you away from the cold weather to sunny California. All other trains to Southern California via any line carry tourist sleepers and second-class passengers. Travel first class Santa Fe all the way.*

Privately, in their back and forth conversation, Phryné expressed her concern that they would either need to fit in as honeymoon newlyweds on a quest for their future, or simply be taken as a misdirected truck driver and his beautician wife from Buffalo, traveling willy-nilly on a wild westward jaunt, blindly hobnobbing with the upper crust. Phryné told him that nobody should settle for or accept the monikers of *'tourist class sleeper'* or *'second class passenger'*. "I think my money is just as good as anyone else's. My Papa told me they do not separate the money inside the vaults of Buffalo Savings Bank; no matter who makes the deposit."

"You fit in just fine, Phryné. I love you. You are beautiful, and someday I will buy you all the nice things you desire. These hoity-toity people cannot hold a candle to you. You light my way, Sweetheart. You are the ticket to our new life."

She leaned over and kissed him. He had her heart.

The public address system crackled to life at 8:00 PM. It was a resonating, but smooth, silvery voice resounding through the waiting room, terminal, and platforms that announced: *Atchison, Topeka and Santa Fe ... Train Number Three, The California Limited ... First Class Pullman service to Kansas City ... Albuquerque ... Grand Canyon ... San Bernardino ... Los Angeles ... and San ... Fran..cis..co ... now boarding ... Track ... Seven ... Board! ... Track ... Six ...Board!*

Honeymoon On Lake Union

Monday night, August 29.

Dozens of large white reflecting shades hung from the lofty steel awning above. Incandescent light flooded the concrete platform between tracks No. 6 and No. 7. A black giant stood at each track, ready to power the Pullman coaches, baggage, Parlor, US Mail, and Dining Cars on their way westward. Steam hissed from pressure ports under the locomotives, small puffs of smoke and tiny bits of soot escaped and wafted skyward from the stacks. Waiting, ready and eager, the rhythm of the machines merged with human emotion inside the cavernous train shed.

Leopold and Phryné mingled with scores of other passengers on the platform. Their tickets were for *Compartment C* on *Lake Union,* a sleek seventy-foot long heavyweight sleeper, the fourth car behind the locomotive and

148

tender. It was dark olive green with *Pullman* in gold lettering stretched along the roofline, and the car's name, *Lake Union*, in gold, below the windows and centered on the car. The Lake Union rolled the rails upon three-axle trucks, or wheel sets, on each end. The Santa Fe conductor took a quick check of their tickets, smiled, nodded and welcomed them aboard. An impeccably dressed colored man, a Pullman** porter, an employee of the Pullman Company, greeted them at the car steps. He wore a dark blue uniform and service cap with a brass *Pullman Porter* nameplate sparkling over the brim. Gleaming brass buttons adorned his jacket, and a gold braided band ran around the cap.

There was no way to gracefully or gallantly carry hand baggage down the narrow hallway of a Pullman compartment car while walking sideways, but the porter managed it magnificently, and was able to effortlessly open the door for them. He palmed the silver dollar Leopold gave him, smiled ear to ear, and said he would be back soon, thanking them for choosing Pullman and riding Santa Fe.

Once inside, the anticipation of travel and the excitement of new frontiers sent tingles through the couple's bodies. They were starting their future together within the confines of a forty-two square foot rolling bedroom pulled by a coal powered, piston-driven steam engine. 'Compartment C' was the first room past the ladies' salon at the rear of the car. The door was hinged on the right, and opened to the inside. Straight ahead, against the outside wall, two upholstered bench seats sat facing one another, a curtained window at each. A wardrobe closet, mirror, and sink were on the right-hand wall. The compartment had baseboard heat, electric lighting, fans, hot and cold water, and an electric bell to summon the porter.

They sat looking out at the hectic activity on the platform between their train and the second nine-car consist of The California Limited. It appeared as a twin, configured like theirs: Ninety feet of Baldwin locomotive power and tender pulling a baggage, Buffet and Club Car, two Pullmans, a Dining Car, Lounge Car, and three more Pullmans. Coupled together, the consist was over seven hundred feet of iron and steel. Conductors, Pullman porters and Red Caps directed and assisted the cross section of America that was travelling that night. The vast majority of the travelers was businessmen or professionals; some accompanied by either a wife, secretary or some uncategorized acquaintance. A select few looked as though they would not fit into any mold at all, and appeared aloof and mysterious, either attempting to hide their identities, or ignoring everyone else around them. Notwithstanding, they were all dressed well; a select few were decked-out flamboyantly well.

At exactly a quarter past eight, two long blasts from the four-chime Baldwin steam whistle let it be known that the first consist of The California Limited was ready to depart from Dearborn station on its way West. Leopold and Phryné were certainly not the only ones, but they felt their pulses quicken and the hair at their temples prickle. He took her hand. The engineer pulled the cord again, and released two more long bursts of steam-driven sound. With a smooth, gentle tug, their journey began just as the porter knocked, asked if he could make up their bed and if they would like him to make up the upper berth also. Leopold asked if the lower berth would accommodate newlyweds. The porter smiled from ear to ear and politely told him that it would open to three feet wide; they could try it and if they needed the top berth, he could come back and make it up. Another long whistle blast was followed by two short ones as Santa Fe No. 3 cleared the station, and rolled through the maze of track outside the shed. The porter introduced himself as 'William' and said that he would be with the Lake Union for the duration of the trip. Leopold and Phryné stepped outside the compartment, walked toward the front of the car, down the short, narrow hall past the next compartment, and the larger drawing room on their right. The short hall ended, and the car opened up to ten sections of double seats on each side. Each section broke down to an upper and lower berth with privacy curtains; a few already closed up for the night. They walked about halfway through the sections before turning around and returning to their room. The porter was just leaving.

The bed was impeccably made, and turned down. A brick red, woven wool blanket with 'Pullman' embroidered in white script, and perfectly centered covered the crisp sheets. Two small lamps were lit on each side of the windows, two next to the closet, and two more by the sink. Leopold took off his jacket and hung it in the small closet. Together, they emptied the small suitcase and hung shirts, dresses and slacks on hangers along with his other suit out of the duffle bag.

They settled in for the night. Phryné sat on the edge of the bed and began to undress, and Leopold was at the sink. He turned on the spring-loaded hot water tap to a burp and sputter, and allowed the cold tap to offer an encore performance. A small, cast brass sign was on the wall: 'This water not for drinking.' Small bars of Palmolive soap sat neatly on the top ledge of the compact sink. Washing off the dirt of a Chicago day was as refreshing as a spring rain on his face, neck, arms and hands. The hand towels, neatly folded into triangles, sat on the sideboard.

Phryné was down to her lace trimmed, combed cotton and silk crêpe camiknickers*. She took her turn at the sink while her new husband disrobed to his underwear and hung his slacks and shirt on the cupboard door. The click, click, click of the rails underneath telegraphed their speed. She locked the compartment door and switched off the lights by the cupboard and sink.

They sat together on the bed, watching the city lights of Chicago disappear behind them. She was leaning on him, and he against the wall. Leopold closed the curtains, turned off the last two wall lamps and allowed their passion to take control. Her lacy top went down off her shoulders as his mouth and hands moved over her breasts and belly. She quivered from

151

the tickle of his tongue and the poke of his fingers on her nipples; aroused, sensitive and as big around as nickels. He slid her undergarment past her hips, down her thighs, calves and onto the floor. He teased and tempted, slowly moving his fingers back up her leg and stopping between her thighs. He gently explored her warmth, and they shared a soul deep kiss. He made a discovery and whispered, "Something new there, Phryné?"

She continued twirling her fingers in his thick hair, and whispered in his ear, sending goose bumps across the back of his neck. "I did that on Friday, before that disaster trip to Canada, and was hoping to show you on Saturday. I read about it at Rita's in that *Gazette du Bon Ton* fashion magazine, and it said that most of the fashionable ladies and cuddlers* in Europe are doing it, and it is getting more popular every day. It's for cleanliness and freshness and it even feels better. So, I went ahead, and I did it with some scissors and a little *Milady* razor. It really sounded exciting, and I was thinking that I like kissing you with that John Gilbert mustache of yours trimmed so nice that maybe you would like my mustache shaven and trimmed too."

There was not much more conversation.

Some Place, Somewhere

On a plush new innerspring mattress, between fresh linen, under a woven wool blanket and upon goose feather pillows, they slept soundly throughout the night, spooned together, front to back. After last night's heated intimacy, it was not long before the train lulled them into a refreshing, restful sleep. Leopold slept against the wall with Phryné resting on his arm. Entwined on the secluded bed, secure within the sleeping nook of a Pullman compartment, they slept deeply for nearly eight hours.

Phryné woke first, and watched her husband push back the darkness of sleep, opening his eyes to her smile. After a soft morning kiss, a cuddle and soft intimate touches, they pushed back sleep's comforter and allowed the day to begin. Phryné stepped into her dress, and took four steps down the narrow hall to the ladies' salon. Leopold pulled the curtains open and witnessed bright morning sun flooding over brown, rolling fields of corn ready for harvest. In the distance, an oasis of green shade trees, a barn and weathered farmhouse disappeared from view. The train was rushing past the trackside telegraph poles, cloaking them in a blur of motion. The telegraph lines that stretched between them appeared as a wavering thread in a tornado. Flying past a water tank and a loading platform, a single, long muted blast lamented from the steam whistle. Leopold was barely able to read some letters of the sign on the green clapboard rail station; guessing that it could have been Carrolton. In the flash of a half second, the little building disappeared and reclaimed its place in obscurity, inanimately unaware that its name does not matter. Leopold estimated that the train was traveling at least fifty miles an hour.

Leopold met the porter, William, as he was leaving the men's salon at the far end of the railcar. After the exchange of pleasantries, William said they were an hour and a half outside of Kansas City, and the train would be in the station for forty-five minutes. He suggested they forego the Dining Car and instead have breakfast at the Harvey restaurant inside Union Station.

"Not to disparage the fine food and service of the Harvey folks in the Dining Car sir, but breakfast in Union Station would be a pleasant break from the train, sir. Your next opportunity will be in Albuquerque, at noon tomorrow."

Leopold agreed, thanked him and accepted his suggestion to have coffee and perhaps a breakfast pastry in the buffet car while he made up their bed. Mornings were the busiest time of day for Pullman porters. Curiosity pushed Leopold to ask how fast the train was going.

"Maybe sixty, but at least fifty through here. Gustav, the Swede, is the engineer; you can tell by his whistle. Each driver gots his own technique, you see. He has the Kansas City leg, makes this rattler* roll, and he's always on time. And his fireman, Fitz, he knows how to stoke the fire box and keep it hot. We got a good crew; always got a good crew." William spoke with pride. "Have a pleasant day, sir."

They took the porter's advice, and opted for something light before lunch. Walking through their car and the next, Leopold and Phryné noticed that quite a few sections still had curtains tightly closed and secured. It was as if some passengers were hiding, ignoring the bright sun of morning and desired to be transported directly through time and distance to their destination, be it St. Louis, Los Angeles, or San Francisco. As with even the smallest trip, some wanted the travel to end as soon as it began.

In the Buffet and Club Car, they sat at a small window table for two, enjoyed coffee and shared a buttered biscuit. The restaurant china and silver plate sparkled equally brilliantly in the morning sun, adding flashes of light to their tinkle and chime. Closer to Kansas City, small stations appeared much more often, evidenced by the numerous times the engine whistle sounded a single burst as they flashed by. It seemed the rails clicked more loudly, and the rocking rhythm increased in anticipation of the upcoming stop. Viewed from the window, the rows of corn were a golden brown blur under a soft cerulean sky.

Their room was restored to its pristine condition while they were in the buffet car, with new linens, pillowcases and towels. The valet took charge of their soiled laundry, Leopold's suit and Phryné's dress. It was apparent that The California Limited was, in fact, a hotel on rails that offered unequaled service and anything imaginable from soup to nuts. The world flew by their window as they sat close and snuggled on the seat. Every blade of grass, each telegraph pole, and each trackside signal was new to them. Every click of a rail set rhythm to their journey. Everything had the shine of new, the sparkle of wonder and whispered a hint of destiny.

154

Two nights and a thousand miles ago, in Buffalo, New York, the cold darkness of night fell hard and crashed down around them; changing their lives forever. They were still unaware of just how dark that night had been.

A day earlier, in Chicago, Illinois, they joined their souls in marriage. This morning, aboard a train travelling past Independence, Missouri, the warming glow of daylight lifted their spirits.

"This train is a place, Phryné. This is a place … we are not on a train, this is a hotel … a place; we are here … in this place, with all this glass and steel and people and steam; together with the noise and motion ... time and life joined together as one. And we are a part of this place … a piece of this time. This train is a hotel … a place going somewhere … that is what we are: *A place going somewhere … a flying vestibule.*"

Phryné was quiet, and tried to understand what he just said. It was easy to agree, and not necessary to know why. She said, "As long as we are together, Leopold. That is all that matters now."

Leopold could not argue with that. He did not fully understand what he said either, nor why he said it. He thought he could be drunk with travel, euphoric with love, confused by motion, or simply exhausted. Perhaps it was a wild combination of all four crazy ingredients. Whatever the explanation, his flash-in-the-pan moment of philosophical reflection disappeared back to from where it came; lost in time, movement, and perception. Perhaps it was stored in a cabinet, somewhere inside that flying vestibule he talked about.

A burst of the steam whistle was followed by several shorter ones as the train slowed. Rapidly, one by one, steel girders flashed past the windows with a dynamic whoosh. They crossed the Missouri River at Sibley, over a long three-span steel railroad bridge, painted a dull, grey tint of celery green. Looking out of the windows, they witnessed the gradual appearance of Kansas City, Missouri, with its stockyards, corn silos and lumberyards.

Union Station was the second largest train station in the United States, behind New York City's Grand Central. More than a dozen rail tracks meandered toward and into the station. A massive passenger waiting hall ran perpendicular to the main building. Inside, a ninety-five foot, art deco ceiling vaulted over the square-patterned marble floor and supported three gigantic, two-ton chandeliers. In the center of the hall, a huge seven-foot diameter clock hung from the ceiling, styled like a pocket watch, with bold, black Roman numerals. Arched gateways were tucked into the walls and fitted with rounded windows stretching to the ceiling. The noise of a thousand travelers created a constant, unintelligible din.

They spent fifty minutes in Kansas City, enjoyed a hearty breakfast at the Fred Harvey Restaurant and walked through the terminal checking the wares of countless souvenir shops and newspaper stands. The Santa Fe Newsstand had newspapers from every major city on display, some were days old, but there was a paper from just about anywhere the railroad reached. Phryné spent five cents and made time to write another picture postcard to her family in Buffalo, mailing it from the post office inside the station.

In Kansas City, The Limited got new power along with a fresh engineer, fireman, conductor, brakemen and flagman. Newer Baldwin, Berkshire type, eight drive-wheel locomotives were hooked to both consists to speed the express trains across the prairies to the southern Rocky Mountains. One Pullman sleeper with Chicago passengers for St. Louis was switched out with another Pullman assigned from St. Louis to Los Angeles. The changes in manpower, rolling stock and passengers went smoothly, as intended, like a well-greased machine and on-time, exactly as scheduled. It went largely unnoticed, just as the dancers in a Swan Lake ballet performance can flutter on and off stage in complete anonymity. A seventy foot, seventy-five ton, olive green piece of equipment changed out with another with the identical flow and grace of a five-foot, ninety pound ballerina in white tights and a pink tutu.

Once The California Limited left Kansas City, the conductor walked through the car, no doubt double-checking for unpaid or misplaced passengers. The stop broke up the day, allowing the afternoon to pass quickly. Their bellies, full with their breakfast at the Harvey Restaurant, they made one short trip to the buffet car for a sandwich and bottled soft drinks. Leopold and Phryné gave some hours to sleep; at first leaning against the windows and walls with a scrunched-up pillow, then sprawled across the seats in an uncomfortable fetal position; knees at awkward angles. Leopold called for the porter about two o'clock, outside of Emporia, Kansas, and William cheerfully made up the bed for the night. Leopold was second-guessing and questioning his obligations, and was unsure if he should tip the porter at all, and if he should, how much. The day before, he passed William a silver dollar and the porter seemed to be appreciative.

Underneath the porter's dark blue, woven wool jacket and pants, it was apparent that he was a formidable man, perhaps thirty years old. His demeanor was affable, his tone sincere, and his words were on point.

"William, to be perfectly honest, this is a new experience for my wife and me … as I am sure you have noticed … and you seem to be a man who knows his onions, and shoots straight from the hip." Having no silver left in his pocket, he passed a dollar bill to the Pullman porter, and shook his hand. "We appreciate your service, William."

"Sir, thank you. Pleased to be of service. Thank you, sir, thank you."

Without asking when, how often or how much, Leopold felt comfortable tipping the porter a dollar a day. Earlier in the afternoon, the valet returned his brushed, sponged suit, Phryné's laundered dress, and the rest of their clean, folded, personal items back to the compartment. He was a young

Oriental man dressed in a double-breasted white denim jacket and oversized pants secured with black ties rather than buttons. He gestured with a small, quick bow at the waist that bounced the small, tight ponytail on the back of his collar. He handed Leopold an itemized bill for sixty-five cents inside a small envelope. Phryné gave the young man two of her badly wrinkled dresses, her scuffed, black T-strap pumps and two of Leopold's suits. One dollar at a time, the cost of the trip was adding up.

Command Performance

Tuesday, August 30, Aboard The California Limited

Rolling across the Kansas prairies, the view from the windows was an ongoing theatrical performance in its natural setting. For the entire afternoon and hundreds of miles, the scene and the actors did not change. From daylight into darkness, The California Limited crossed the American breadbasket.

The cast took to the stage, found their mark and played their roles. Field after field of golden grain entered from stage left, without a costume change, or any other marked difference in color, texture, or appearance. The music resounding from the orchestra pit was the same monotonous, familiar, unchanged, mechanical drone. The symphony was hypnotic. The seasoned rhythm section played the repetitious clickity-click of American steel on steel. It was a perpetual encore.

The leading man wore a coat of black cast iron. He asserted his power, pushed the pistons and exuded passionate emotion with a flash of his chrome-plated throttle. With a signature hiss of steam, the conductor waved his signal lantern, his baton, to and fro. The chorus sang a mesmerizing *a cappella* medley: a sleepy song of wind that whooshed past a cocoon of man-made glass, steel, wood, and fabric.

From the balcony, the bawdy section of the urbanized crowd released steamy whistles and hand signals to the female performers. The audience was rocking, rolling and reeling with appreciation. One curtain call led to another and the wayward crowd either went wild or fell sound asleep.

Inside the all-weather cab, the engineer kept a firm hand on the controls. His elbow was casually resting outside the window when he tipped his denim cap to the flagman backstage. His keen eyes watched the drivers of the Baldwin locomotive roll across the rails. The brakeman stood in the wings and signaled for more fuel on the fire. Alongside the seasoned engineer, the faithful fireman labored diligently, anonymously, throughout the performance, hoping his labor would not go unnoticed, and was not in vain.

Of course, there was a curtain call. The engineer waved and gave the crowd an appreciative nod, and a smile of satisfaction. Everything was right with the world: *All The Way With Santa Fe.*

A Moving Meal

Leopold washed and shaved at the little white porcelain washbasin after Phryné had finished her morning ritual. He toweled off the rest of the shaving cream and checked his shave in the small round mirror. As he placed the razor back in its case, he paused and recalled something his father had said, *"Living without love is like shaving without hot water ... it stings."* He and Phryné were basking in love, and unlike his apartment back in Buffalo, there was no shortage of hot water on the Lake Union. The spring loaded nickel faucets shut off automatically, preventing waste. Their love, however, was overflowing.

Earlier, William asked what time they desired for seating in the Dining Car, and they selected the latest available; quarter to eight. Leopold and Phryné dressed in their best clothes for dinner; the newly cleaned outfits they wore when they were married in Chicago.

It was 7:30 PM and they were still traveling westward through Kansas, about 800 miles from Chicago. Together, they walked out their compartment door. After five steps down the hall, four past the ladies' salon, three through the connecting vestibules, they entered the Dining Car.

Another new experience awaited them eleven steps further down a narrow walkway, past the kitchen, and into the dining room. The Dining Car was about one third kitchen and two thirds seating area. Along the right side of the car were six tables for two. Each table was covered with snowy linen, gleaming silverware, and sparkling glass. Passengers were enjoying well-prepared meals served on pristine white bone china. Six tables for four were on the right side of the Dining Car, opposite the smaller tables. At first glance, every table seemed occupied. The steward was a tall, thin man with a milky complexion and pronounced freckles, dressed in a white dinner jacket and black slacks. He checked his watch, then Leopold's seating card. "Follow me … sir, ma'am." He carried his left arm outward, bent at the elbow, with a pure white towel folded over it.

He moved with poise down the center aisle, moving aside for one waiter, then another. He stopped at the fourth set of tables and motioned for them to be seated. Leopold took the window seat, and the Harvey steward helped Phryné with her chair. They were seated across from a portly man, likely in his late thirties or early forties, and an attractive young woman. They sat holding their menus, smiled across the table and gave a cordial greeting to Leopold and Phryné. There were three waiters in the car, all colored men, and like the steward, they were also dressed in white jackets. The menu was attractive, with a pencil-colorized photograph of the Grand Canyon on the cover.

"Irving Feinmann … call me Irv … this is Caroline Myles, a fresh little songbird from Chicago."

"Leopold and Phryné Throckmorton; we're from Buffalo, heading to Los Angeles on our honeymoon and seeking our righteous fame and overdue fortune. Well, maybe not fame … and just a modest fortune." He didn't know why he said that, or even offered that much information, correct or not.

Irv chuckled. "Pleased to meet you, Leo; Priny. I'm originally from the city myself, New York City. I spent a year in Buffalo one weekend last January on my latest visit to that great city. I was booked at some fleabag hotel room with no heat, right on the icy shore of Lake Erie, and that was long enough for me." He laughed at his own dry humor, his coarse laughter coming from deep inside his chest. His voice bounced hard and fast, like a Ty Cobb base hit to center field.

They checked the menu and its simple choices of two soup appetizers, three entrées, two desserts and several bottled water, juice or soda options. To encourage a rapid turnover of meal patrons, after-dinner coffee was served in the Parlor, or Lounge Car. As if on cue, a waiter magically appeared and stood at Phryné's elbow. He handed an order slip to each of them along with a small pencil. To avoid confusion or squabbles, verbal orders were not accepted. Harvey waiters let the customers make their choices, and read it back to them for verification. The waiter then submitted their cards back to the kitchen.

Irv ordered the roasted spring squab for himself and Caroline, Leopold the prime rib, and Phryné opted for the baked lake trout. Their dinners arrived immediately after their cream of celery soup. When Phryné noticed the roast squab sprawled across the white china plates, she kept her thoughts private. Crisply browned with shriveled little wings and skinny legs stuck between three tablespoons of applesauce, cranberry chutney and six asparagus spears, the main course looked helplessly cold and tiny on the white plate, like robins in an April snow.

Phryné was pleased with her menu choice, and enjoyed her fish, as Leopold did his beef. Irving and Caroline also seemed very happy with their fowl meals.

The conversation was interesting and lively, despite the efficient, hurried service. "Tell me, Irv. What brought you to visit Buffalo back in January? It sure wasn't the weather."

Irving's awkward attempt to lean back in his chair failed; a gentleman at the next table prevented that. The quarters were cramped, and just too close. He jumped at the opportunity to ramble. "I'm in the music business, scouting acts for sound recordings, night club talent, and occasionally I stumble across an actor. I travel regularly looking for new talent and sometimes I get lucky enough and sign one. That's why Caroline is here, I just snatched her up in Chicago. Back in January, I was checking on a dance band at Shea's, you must know it, that burlesque theatre on Main Street there in Buffalo, I'm sure you know where it is. Some band that was promoted and branded like Paul Whiteman. Of course, only Paul Whiteman is Paul Whiteman. Peppy Humes and His Novelty Band was good, but not what I was looking for. They were not Paul Whiteman. Their name said it all; something you can dance to, but forget as soon as the night is over."

Leopold recalled the name of the band. "We know that band from one of our nights out. They played the Hippodrome, remember Phryné?" His excited reaction to good memories quickly passed, and the qualm and trepidation from Saturday returned. His mood became somber, and he looked to Phryné. For the present, it was a feeling he needed to live with.

She shared his brief anxiety and fought through it. "Yes. I thought they were pretty good. At least when we were there. It must have been right around the same time, and we could have bumped into you, Irv. Maybe you remember seeing me … I was the flapper girl in the green dress dancing with that dapper* Leopold over there." She jerked her thumb toward her husband, and they chuckled.

162

Irving broke into a hearty belly-bouncing laugh. He gave them an affirmative nod. "See that? That was funny Priny … it's something how people can connect, isn't it? After we're done here, let's go back to the Lounge Car for coffee."

Leopold and Phryné found Irv and Caroline intriguing; Irving more so than Caroline, who was reserved, and did not have much to say over dinner. January's coincidence of proximity prompted her to join in the conversation. It was not long before she and Phryné were in each other's confidence about women's suffrage and fashion trends.

After their meal, the four of them made their way to the Lounge Car, the next car in the consist. It was further than Leopold or Phryné previously explored on the train, and like everything else about their trip, was uncharted territory for them.

The windows were wider than those in the Dining Car, and had drapes in a geometric Indian pattern of crisp sienna, turquoise and carmine. Irving casually pulled a hand-rolled Phillies Perfecto from his vest pocket, and made a half-hearted gesture offering it to Leopold, who declined. He carefully bit off the leaf end, methodically took it from his lips, and gently disposed of it into the stand ashtray. Next, he placed the cigar into a stubby, amber colored Bakelite cigar holder. It appeared to be a ritual with him: gently twisting the large cigar into the holder, then gripping it between his teeth, and wrapping his two red lips around it. He then ignited a wooden kitchen match with a flick of his thumbnail and forefinger, and placed it to the Phillies. He drew a long, deep breath into his round chest, holding and savoring it before he slowly exhaled. The smoke curled around his plump face and subtly wafted over his balding scalp. Standing, he appeared very round with legs too thin for his rotund shape. With his stiffly starched white shirt, pin stripe vest tugging at its buttons, and dark navy suit jacket, he had the pink face and physique of Humpty Dumpty. His voice was brusque and rough around the edges, but exceedingly high-pitched for his size. When he smiled, he exposed a set of very small, but gleaming white upper and lower teeth. Phryné tried to imagine exactly how this man could have such a comely young woman on his arm, and then scolded herself for imagining him naked and cavorting with Caroline.

Irv chose a central seating area on the side of the car almost at the far end. It had a chaise lounge love seat, two claw foot Queen Anne parlor chairs, and a round coffee table. The upholstery was a tucked and buttoned, dark Sherwood Forest green brocade. A gold-fringed Oriental patterned area rug rested on the floor. Half-round, frosted ceiling lamps glowed softly along the length of the car and smaller wall lamps glimmered between the windows. Leopold lit a Chesterfield, and Irv continued creating his personal smoke screen with the Perfecto.

Caroline had been the first to take a seat. She hesitated, and quickly looked around before she took her spot at the armless end of the settee. She was wearing a white polka dot, dark blue sheath dress with a beaded, low hanging belt. A brunette, with soft finger curls and carefully applied rouge and lipstick, Caroline's voice was as smooth as vanilla custard. When she spoke, her words mimicked the song of a nesting meadowlark in spring. Phryné admired Caroline's eyelashes, and was aware of the time and mascara that must have been spent perfecting them. Caroline sat with her hands on her lap, one holding her sequined pocketbook, and the other resting on top. She had gentle brown eyes, and a smile as smooth and soft as a spring breeze. She looked comfortable in her skin, but appeared a bit uneasy, as if she was expecting the teacher to summon her up to the blackboard. When Phryné took the seat next to her on the small sofa, her shoulders relaxed in relief. They exchanged smiles and Phryné offered her a Marlboro filter cigarette, which she accepted. Leopold took a chair, then Irving.

A Santa Fe steward took their drink orders: coffee, bottled mineral water, cream soda, ginger ale and a Bromo seltzer for

Irv. Phryné and Caroline ordered a plate of water biscuits, ripe olives and cucumber slices. The muffled din of subdued conversation throughout the car mixed with the dull mechanical drone of the train.

Irving Feinmann explained that he was a talent scout who worked on commission with travel expenses in advance. He recruited, auditioned and signed singers, bands and occasionally, actors to either studio or theatrical agent contracts. He also claimed to be connected to Famous Players movie studio. To Leopold and Phryné, it looked like he fit the job perfectly. He oozed braggadocio and self-confidence. No doubt, he was good at what he did, and he was dropping names like sand through an hourglass to prove it.

"Caroline here, she's got the moxie*, I got to tell you. You need to come down to our connected Drawing Room on *Lake Winnipeg* and listen to this girl sing. We can do that tomorrow, right Caroline? I'll put a record on the talking machine*, and you can warble your songs for … for … Leopold and his wife here." He awkwardly stumbled with Leopold's name and forgot Phryné's. Caroline held a little smile, and nodded in agreement. "And we can chat and nibble, have a little something or whatever to drink and listen to Caroline warble. It will be grand; I got to tell you. You need to hear this girl. She'll be bigger than Marion Harris. You can put money on that."

Caroline flushed with embarrassment, and gave a hand gesture for Irving to stop.

"Anyway, I got to tell you how I found this little gem. Last week Monday, my old pal Snooker Pearson called me on the blower from Chicago and says to me 'Hey Irv, you better come and listen to the pipes* on this little Polack. This dame sings her ass off. She's at Dreamland Gardens and opening for Essie.' He was talking about that Essie Waters. When he said that, it was all I needed to hear. If you are good enough to be the opening act for Essie Waters, you are damn good. So, I

165

packed a bag and me and Harry Mumford … he's my protégé … my assistant … he's a good egg … anyway … we were on the next train. You will meet Harry tomorrow. Right now, he's sleeping in the compartment with some stomach thing he caught back in Chicago. Anyway … well, I got to tell you, I went to South State Street and listened to this girl sing. She's got it. I met her mother on Tuesday, and we signed a contract on Thursday. And now I'm taking her to Hollywood, and on Friday, I am going to present her to Arne, who ran Nordskog Records. And maybe even Paramount on Saturday. I am taking her there myself. And I got to tell you, she is going to be big. She changed her name on Friday ... go ahead and tell them what your name used to be, Caroline, Sugar."

When Phryné heard *Hollywood*, she began to pay very close attention.

Caroline giggled softly, "Karolin Wawrzyniak. Nobody could pronounce it or spell it. It was a pile of letters all mixed up. W-A-W-R-Z-Y-N-I-A-K. See what I mean?"

Irving let out a guttural guffaw, tapped his Phillies and knocked off a long ash. "So now she is Caroline Myles, the Kankakee Songbird."

Phryné put an arm around Caroline and gave her a hug. "Congratulations! Good for you! That's nice. I cannot wait to hear you sing. Isn't this something, Leopold … to be right here and witness a star being born? This is so exciting! It is just like a story out of Motion Picture magazine!"

Leopold crushed out his cigarette. He raised his eyes and looked at the women over the crooked bridge of his nose. He nodded in agreement and exhaled the smoke from his lungs. "That is a heart-warming story, Caroline. I wish you the best. It seems that Irv is handling things perfectly for you. He sure seems good at his job."

Caroline's head was in the clouds listening to Irving's story and praise. She smiled, "Irv's a good man. He has proven himself to me and my mother. And let me tell you, my mother does not fall for any line of baloney. Irv knows this

166

business, and I am lucky to have an exclusive contract with him."

Caroline's 'road to stardom' story quietly ran out of steam. Irving Feinmann waved for the steward and ordered two more coffees, another Bromo for himself and two small cream sodas for the women.

From the front of the train, they heard a Baldwin five-chime steam whistle sound one lonesome blast followed a few seconds later by another. Out of curiosity, Leopold had been attempting to decipher steam whistle code. He supposed that a long burst indicated arrival at some point. He also tried to train his eyes to comprehend flashes of images, and to look quickly for clues as the train flew past countless fleeting little specks on the prairie. He thought he read 'Coleg' illuminated by the lights of the station. When the steward returned with the coffee he asked, "Still in Kansas, are we?"

Strange places all look the same in the dark.

The steward set the drinks on the table, stuck the metal tray under his armpit and glanced at his pocket watch. His movements were remarkably mechanical. "We should be in Colorado right now, sir. It's nine thirty and we just passed Coolidge, Kansas, sir. At approximately eleven o'clock a new power crew will come aboard, and the train will take on water and coal in La Junta, Colorado, sir." Leopold had no sooner thanked him, and he was gone.

Irving drank half of the small bottle of Bromo and asked a question he knew the answer to. "First time west, Leo?"

"Yes, it is. Other than Niagara Falls, Canada, this is the first time either Phryné or I have been beyond Erie County, and I've got a question for you, Irv. I am curious about something I know you can help me with. I wonder just how much I should be tipping the help. You know: the porter, waiter, valet and conductor."

Phryné wanted to hear more about Hollywood, not nickels, dimes and quarters.

"Well, you need to consider their wages. The colored Harvey waiters get their meals and about thirty dollars a month. The Chinese and white waiters make about five dollars more, but there ain't many of them. The porters, Pullman hires all Negroes you know, and they are all unionized now, and make just fewer than seventy dollars a month, but they buy their own meals and uniforms." Irving paused and took another drink of Bromo. "Everybody has their own idea about how much to tip, so I can only tell you what I leave, Leo. What you get is what you pay for. If the service is what you expect, a dollar a day should suffice for the porter. The waiter: I generally leave him a quarter, sometimes a half a buck, but you are in the dining car usually more than once a day. I have even seen some skinflints leave a nickel or dime." Irving paused for a puff from his cigar and continued, "The valet and barber: a quarter or fifty cents. If you get exceptional service, anything additional is up to your discretion. The conductor is a railroad employee, and I have never tipped a conductor. Some do, I don't. And think about it; nobody tips the engineer or fireman, and those are the two men who get you to where you are going." With that said, Irving finished his bottle of stomach relief and coughed with a throaty gurgle. "Now I got a question for your sweet wife. What kind of name is Priannee and how is it spelled?"

Phryné extinguished her cigarette. "I guess Caroline isn't the only one with a difficult name … mine is Greek. My grandmother, my mother's mother, was from Athens, and I am named after some lady in ancient Greece. It is: P-H-R-Y-N-E and it is pronounced *'fry-nee'*."

Irving drew another puff on his cigar, blew two perfect smoke rings, and exhaled sideways. "You know, Phryné, that's a charming story. Charming; you honestly look the part. You look like a Greek goddess. That's a perfect name. You are a lucky man, Leopold." He leaned back in his armchair, stretched his neck, wriggled his shoulders and set his cigar into the ash stand. "How about another round of drink? One more round before we say goodnight to Colorado. It goes on my expense account." He waved his pudgy arm in the air.

"So, what have you got lined up in Los Angeles, Leo?"

Leopold clenched his teeth, knowing that question was coming sooner or later. He wanted to avoid the uncomfortable and embarrassing honest answer. An overweight Los Angeles talent scout forced his hand.

"I don't have anything *lined up*. I'll find something when we get there. I can do anything from fixing a carburetor to driving the truck it goes in. And people say that I am a fast learner, so I don't think I should have a problem finding work. I am confident of that."

"Really? Sort of a jack-of-all-trades? How about your wife, Phryné? What about you, Sweetheart? Any special skills that you care to put on the market?" He rolled the cigar holder from one side of his mouth to the other. Stray ashes dropped off and onto his vest.

His question seemed innocent enough, but it caused the hair at the nape of her neck to prickle. She glanced quickly to Leopold and answered, "Nothing in particular. In Buffalo I worked at a beauty salon, cutting hair, doing nails and makeup."

The waiter returned with their order of two split Coca Colas and an Orange Dry. Irving handed the young fellow a dollar bill who then seemed to disappear into thin air. Irv reached inside his vest pocket and brought out a business card and handed it to Leopold. It was printed on silky, ivory-colored paper and embossed in black: *Irving A. Feinmann. ~ Theatrical Agent and Bookings. ~ Los Angeles, California. ~ 400 Figueroa Street. ~ Phone (Main) 4920.*

"Here's my card. We can talk about this tomorrow at length, but you young folks will find work as soon as your shoes hit the sidewalk in Los Angeles. That is not a dream. It's a promise, a fact. And I can get you in with *Famous Players Paramount Pictures*, the both of you, if you want.

169

Phryné can work makeup, and we'll talk about you tomorrow, Leo. How's that? It's booming in Hollywood, too, and not just L.A. There is so much work that the place is overflowing with wetbacks. You will be able to find work all right, but I can help you get better work, and better pay than the Mexicans."

Once again, Phryné picked up on Irving's mention of 'Hollywood'. The name sent a tingle down the length of her spine one more time. Names flew through her mind; names like John Barrymore, Vilma Bánky and Lillian Gish. The beauty parlor in Buffalo always had the latest movie magazines, and from the windows of Ritzy Rita's, she could see those names in lights on the marquee of Shea's Theatre. "How far is Hollywood from Los Angeles?"

It was a question Phryné had thought of, but never asked until now. Leopold looked interested also. Irving answered, "Some people say Hollywood is Los Angeles and vice versa. Let's just say that the two go hand-in-hand. I imagine that you could call them a two-headed cow with the temperament of a mule. To be totally accurate, Hollywood is up in the western hills, about eight miles from downtown L.A."

Seating in the Dining Car was generally on a first come-first served, basis to avoid waits or lines, but the foursome agreed to request seating together in the Dining Car tomorrow evening at seven o'clock. Afterwards, they planned to hear the voice that Irving bragged so much about.

For the first time in days, Leopold and Phryné were thinking about the future more than the past. They went to bed that night rocking with the rhythm of the rails and rolling with the thrill of the future.

Phryné was convinced that the train triggered her already zealous libido. Leopold was intrigued by her desire and captivated by her passion. She took possession of his mind and complete control of his body. Phryné timed her movements to the rhythm of the rails, rolled, writhed and teased him by skipping a beat at her whimsy. Secluded and secure in the compartment, she devoured him. He was consumed by her warmth. Their bodies united, writhed and wrapped in love until motionless. Never before were they so completely spent.

After The Limited stopped in La Junta, and switched out the power and crew, they fell asleep together, holding one another and their dreams.

Chapter Nine

Detroit City

Tuesday, August 30, Detroit, Michigan

It was ten minutes past six when Nicholas got off the Sandwich Street ferry from Canada and started along the bustling waterfront toward downtown Detroit. He had no particular reason to walk downtown; he was drawn to it by metropolitan magnetism. The buildings were twice as tall as anything he had seen in Buffalo, and ten times as numerous. The sky was aglow with the reflection of countless streetlights. The traffic was relentless, so much more than he ever witnessed. Pedestrians crowded the sidewalks just as streetcar and automobile traffic struggled for their rightful positions in the streets. A very few horse-drawn wagons dodged precarious interaction with anything mechanical. In every way imaginable, the population was much more diverse than he had ever seen back in Buffalo. Nicholas walked straight downtown, between the towering brownstones and stucco façades, through Campus Martius, past City Hall, the Opera House, and north on Woodward Avenue. Ladies in flowing dresses, men in suits, horse-drawn carriages, and automobiles of every type available to man surrounded him as if on display, seeking his approval, and asking if he would like to join the party.

He spent that first night in a flophouse* on Alfred Street, directly off Woodward Avenue, about a half mile from downtown. The shaded side street was a mishmash of homemade signs nailed to the porches or front doors: *Rooms, Beds,* or *Hot Meals.* Some were neatly hand lettered, perfectly painted, and some were written in an illegible scrawl. Some included the price range, a few were audacious, and others were outright discriminatory: *No Riff Raff; No Darkies; No Irish; No Women,* or simply, *No Harlots.* It was a city full of

172

migrants, fortune seekers, and immigrants with one thing in common: they were looking for work and needed someplace to sleep.

The entire block was made up of nondescript, run-down, nineteenth-century wood frame construction. His room was on the first floor of the two-story rooming house. A quarter bought a bed in a four-bed room for the night, and he decided to spend a nickel more for a bowl of watery oatmeal porridge and a cup of coffee. The cost of a private room was a dollar, something he could not afford that night. Along with the two-inch straw mattress, came a cold shower that bordered on Oriental water torture. Despite the inhumane discomfort, the shower was necessary. Nicholas washed his clothes as they hung on his body, rinsing the smoke, dust, sweat and tears of two days down the drain and into the Detroit River. The smell of the pea-green bar of Fels Naptha sent his memories back to his brother's apartment on Howlett Street, and the bathtub of lonesome clothes. He wondered if his brother was in a better situation tonight than he was. At the very least, Leopold had someone to keep him warm.

He dried himself with a worn, rough diaper-weave linen towel, walked to the back stoop in his Topkis athletic* union suit, and mercilessly wrung and shook the wrinkles out of his clothes. He hung them to dry over the foot of his bed, and planned to sleep with one eye open anyway. He still had a folded dollar bill and twelve cents in his wallet. He decided that tomorrow's worries could wait until morning. He fell into a deep sleep as soon as his head hit the pillow.

No, No, Nora

Wednesday, August 31

Sunlight struggled through the film of dirt on the rooming house windows. Nicholas did not get a comfortable night's sleep, but it was markedly better than curling up on a pile of burlap sacks in a tobacco shed. Much like the drunkard that passes out, he had caught some sleep, but he did not rest. At times during the night, it seemed the bedroom walls shook to their foundations with the sounds of snores, coughs and gags. The old house on Adams Street was busy, but it was a far cry from the turmoil in this fleabag. That morning, the room was a rancid potpourri of body odor, dirty clothing, stale smoke, feet and chlorine bleach. He looked around the room, and it appeared that he was the first soul to wake.

That day was the first time since he withstood the trauma of the fire that his state of mind was calm enough to take stock of his situation. His gaze went from the bulging, cracked plaster ceiling, to the naked windows and around to the dirty walls of the ten by ten foot room. The squalor around him was his motivation to get up, move out, and get a job. 'Hit the bricks and get a job' was his self-imposed command for the day. It had to be done that morning, no doubt. Ready to get dressed and go, he sat up, put his feet on the worn floorboards and discovered he had been robbed.

"Son of a bitch!" His complaint was loud enough to stir two occupants of the other three beds. He slept with his wallet under the pillow, his shoes under the blanket at his feet, his trousers and shirt hanging on the headboard, but somebody, somehow, managed to get away with his socks. He calmed quickly and didn't say another word. His brief outburst was enough to quell his riled emotions. Nicholas reasoned that there was something to be said about the sock thief: someone was apparently worse off than he was.

In the bathroom down the hall, he used the last four inches of toilet paper, washed his hands and brushed his teeth with a stiff forefinger and the gurgling, burbling rusty water from the tap. He had no idea what time of day it was, only that it was early, and it appeared that he was one of the first out of the house. He turned and looked back from the sidewalk, and decided that tonight, if at all possible, he would stay somewhere else. He also decided to spend thirty cents on a Gillette safety razor.

He retraced his steps of the evening before, and traveled downtown again on Woodward Avenue. The city was awakening, the citizenry was heading for places of employment, and machines and vehicles were beginning the grind of another day. By the time he reached Gratiot Avenue, the sun was just clearing the roofline of the Majestic Building, and washing downtown in the bright glare of late August. Cadillac Square was already a mass of pedestrian traffic. Perhaps it was the name of the street or the sun in his eyes that forced his feet toward the Northeast and up Gratiot. Storefronts had their awnings wide open, spread out across the sidewalks to offer welcoming shade to summer shoppers and passersby. The open canvas was a visual dance of color along the streets; a patchwork of faded greens, blues, and red. Streetcar bells clanged and resounded between the towering walls of buildings. Trolleys snapped and popped sparks from the overhead power lines, and their wheels click-clacked along the tracks. It seemed so much like Buffalo, but so much more. It seemed the city was feeding upon itself, and hungry for more human activity, and more bodies to push through its throbbing veins of commerce.

Newsboys shouted their headlines from opposite corners, daring the common citizenry to read the whole story. The Detroit News brandished the headline 'Purple Gang Strikes Again'; suspected of yet another murder the day before. Across the street, a young newsy with a much stronger voice hawked the Detroit Free Press' edition about the half dozen 'Bootleg Arrests' linked to the Chicago mob when the Prohibition Police raided a speed boat slip on Belle Isle. Street sweepers were ending their night's work and pushing along full carts of litter and horse manure. Shopkeepers, butchers, grocers, and haberdashers were unlocking their front doors. In an alley off Mechanic Street, a lost soul oblivious to the world was peeing in the gutter, steadying himself against the brick wall with an open palm.

When Nicholas crossed Saint Antoine Street, his thoughts drifted, and a speeding closed-body Buick, nearly ran him down. The loud horn and near miss jolted his senses back into reality. At the corner of Gratiot and Catherine Street, half a block from Saint Mary's Hospital, a small sign read *'Man Needed'* in the window of Garwood Detroit Machine Works. Nicholas' heart jumped and he felt his pulse at his temples. An alley ran alongside the shop, ending at a tall, weathered, wooden fence with a man-door. Next door was a bakery and pastry shop. His empty belly ached, and the smell was deliciously tempting, but the need for regular employment was the hunger that required his immediate attention.

He tried the door, and it was unyielding, locked. Frustrated, he wondered what time it was. Across the street was a long brick wall with only a few windows. The words 'Anderson Carriage Works' and 'Custom Vehicle Frames' were painted on the building, and ran for fifty feet down the side. On the sidewalk, a woman inside a colorfully decorated lunch cart was folding open its counter walls, and propping up the awnings with wooden poles. Nicholas crossed the street to ask the time. The woman in her early to mid-thirties lit the kerosene stove with a sudden, hollow whoosh. A girl in her teens was unwrapping bread rolls, and stacking them on narrow shelves. A younger girl was sorting paper plates and napkins. Three pair of eyes studied Nicholas.

"Good morning, Ladies. Do you know the time?"

From inside the wagon, he heard: "Getting close to eight o'clock. I'll have coffee in about five minutes and hot hash and eggs in ten." The voice spoke in a Slavic accent he did not recognize. The wagon was bright red, with black trim and yellow lettering. Along the side was *'Gabi's Goulash Cannon'* and *'Always Hot: Soup, Hash, Hungarian Goulash'*. His question about the ethnic accent was answered but still his curiosity was piqued. He wondered what sort of cannon could cause goulash to fly and several fleeting images crossed his mind. He fought the foolish diversion and allowed his eyes and mind to focus on the teenager with the raven hair. Her perfectly pert nose, deep cocoa eyes, and full lips had his attention.

"Do you know anything about that machine shop across the street, Miss?"

She had a demure manner. He noticed her bright white teeth, endearing smile and clear skin. She was wearing a dress of pressed cotton twill, white with tiny blue pin stripes, a large, buttoned, bib apron that ended just beneath her breasts, and clean, brushed brown boots. "They're busy, I can tell you that, sir. People and trucks and cars stop out front and in the alley all day long. There should be someone there by now." As she finished her words, a shining, dark green Peerless four-door sedan pulled to the curb across the street. The driver was not dressed like the typical Peerless owner, but rather wore a light brown pair of coveralls, a straw boater, and a white shirt with a red bowtie. He unlocked the front door of the shop and entered. Another car pulled into the alley and two men in dungaree work clothes exited and walked around to the front entrance.

Nicholas thanked the women for their help. "If I land me a job over there, I'll be back and get breakfast. My name is Nicholas ... Nicholas Throckmorton." He nodded and stepped off the curb, his heart in his throat. All three at the lunch cart watched with curiosity as he crossed the street.

He was hired on the spot that morning. It was his fresh face, determination and attitude that convinced Garfield Wood to hire the young man from Buffalo, New York, and inform him, "You may start tomorrow morning."

Nicholas replied, "I am ready now, sir, but I would like to get something for breakfast across the street if it's possible." His new boss studied him again, nodded and agreed. His employment with Garwood Machine began immediately after

177

his breakfast of hash and hard-boiled eggs. He began by sweeping sawdust, greasing gearboxes, and anything else that needed done under the roof of 139 Gratiot Avenue. By the time five o'clock came around, he had a five-dollar advance of his twenty-dollar salary in his pocket. In ten hours, he impressed a half dozen men with his attitude and willingness to learn. He got advice about where to find a respectable room and board, as well as where he might purchase another pair of socks and a change of clothes.

That afternoon, he had a big lunch at the Goulash Cannon. It was then he formally met Dominik and Gabi Sterescu, and their daughters Nora and Marie. At lunchtime, he sat on a small three-legged stool, had a hearty bowl of the Hungarian specialty, and a short but very cordial conversation with sixteen-year-old Nora, albeit under the scrutiny of her mother and father.

A hole needed to be filled. He was alone for the first time in his life, yet unaware of the emotional emptiness in his heart. His soul yearned for companionship. Up until two days ago, he had four women in his life: his mother and three younger sisters. He was accustomed to being around people: particularly around women.

The front door to the rest of his life opened just a crack that morning. Young, innocent Nora asked him, "Why did you leave Buffalo and come to Detroit?"

For a split second, a fleeting glimpse of his destiny passed in front of him. His answer was short and puzzling for the youthful, blooming Nora. "I had a bridge to cross, that's all."

That was the first of many enigmas that Nicholas Throckmorton would present to Nora.

After work, he bought a pair of socks and a Gillette safety razor at Waterman's Mercantile. A bit farther down Gratiot Avenue and two blocks away from the machine shop, he found room and board off Rivard Street for two dollars a day. The home was in a respectable working class neighborhood, and on the main trolley line. He was able to take a hot shower, shave and finally wash the stink of burnt timber completely off his body. Before he fell asleep, he thought briefly about Leopold, and realized that he would probably never see him again. His thoughts drifted to a girl named Nora.

Nick had no way of knowing that his brother Leopold and his gal Phryné were two thousand miles of railroad track away in Albuquerque, New Mexico.

Altitude In Climax Canyon

Aboard The California Limited, Trinidad, Colorado

Phryné awoke feeling Leopold's passion pressing against her loins. Last night's ardent desire returned. Feigning sleepy movement, she raised her leg ever so slightly and welcomed him between her thighs and against her warmth. A tender purr signaled her arousal to her waiting husband. She rolled herself on top of him, holding him selfishly between her legs. Flashes of sunlight streamed through the small, swaying drapes and danced across her breasts. She straddled him with zeal and devotion, timing her movements with the sounds of steam. Phryné again moved with rhythm and privilege, compulsion and ecstasy. Leopold managed to control his empyreal eruption until Phryné signaled her impending climax. He waited until he heard her soft fluttering whimpers, and felt her repeated contractions around him. Their sexual liaisons were normally intense as well as lengthy, but this morning's seemed unusually tiring and arduous, leaving them short of breath and lightheaded. Consumed with emotion and spent by passion, blanketed in their musk, they fell back to sleep. They would remember this morning for years to come, and it was to become a topic of private conversation. Phryné associated their physical exhaustion with the intense lovemaking of the night before, and their prolonged mutual climax this morning. Leopold attributed it to the novelty of marriage combined with their euphoric love for one another. It was the only reasonable explanation; never before were they so drained as they were that past night and again that morning.

They awoke when a Baldwin helper locomotive gave the Limited's consist a gentle but forceful nudge and bump in Trinidad, Colorado. The train required help for the climb up the steep grades through the Sangre de Cristo Mountains to Raton pass and around Climax Canyon. There were two Berkshire locomotives, each with a set of eight powerful drivers pulling The Limited along the tough uphill grades, cutbacks and long curves. Quite different from the Kansas prairie, the terrain restricted the train's speed, despite the power. An experienced engineer and his fireman were an invaluable asset through the mountains. Like so many other professions, if everything was working well, their expertise went unnoticed.

Once beyond Raton Pass, the Santa Fe rolled through the Canadian River Valley to Springer, New Mexico and across the high mountain plains south to Albuquerque. They noticed a marked difference in the air during a three-minute water stop, prompting Leopold to turn on the baseboard steam heat. The louvered vents clicked and snapped as the radiators warmed. He moved the drapes apart just enough to peek outside. Next to the water tank sat a small, nondescript station with the usual small white sign nailed above the door.

"Phryné, take a look where we are." She held the blanket across her bare chest, leaned over Leopold and looked out at the little building. The sign read *Dillon.*

"Well … if they only knew …"

"It's an appropriate name, Phryné. A jerkwater* town with the name of a real jerk."

Two long steam whistles, and the consist started rolling south through New Mexico again. The baseboard radiators continued to ding and pop, and it was not long before the compartment quickly warmed to a comfortable temperature. They performed their morning routines, washed and dressed in the fresh clothing delivered yesterday by the valet. It was mid-morning, and many of the Pullman sections still had the curtains pulled tight as they walked through the car. The passengers within were either still asleep or hiding from the light of day.

Once they were in the Dining Car walkway, the smell of hotcakes, butter, coffee and bacon drifted through the doors. Inside, the tinkle of china and glass and the ding of silverware blended with the hum of conversation. They were seated at a small table that morning, on the right hand side of the rail car. Outside, the high mountains were covered in a blanket of brown, green and grey. Early snows could arrive at any time now and instantly paint the mountains white. The air was so clear and dry, the view extended beyond eyesight.

After breakfast, they returned to their compartment, and of course, everything had been refreshed. William brought them copies of the Kansas City Star and McCall's. He asked cordially, "Did you folks sleep well last night?"

Phryné answered, "Yes we did, but it seemed we were still dog-tired this morning." His question and her polite response started a small back-and-forth. William explained the thin mountain air was probably the culprit. They were over a mile above sea level in Colorado and, at times, more than a mile and a half. William continued with an interesting anecdote about something that occurred on a train just over a year ago. He denied any first-hand knowledge of the event, and he would not confirm that it happened on a Santa Fe train, but he vowed it was a true story. He began by saying the world heavyweight boxing champion, Jack Dempsey, was traveling to Hollywood with his movie star wife, Estelle Taylor. They were to begin filming *Manhattan Madness*, in which Dempsey, the 'Manassas Mauler', had a small part. Dempsey and his wife had a custom private car for themselves, along with her ladies' maid, his manager and trainer. Somewhere in the mountains of Colorado, the champ collapsed in a heap after a vigorous workout with a top and bottom, double-hung, punching bag.

William explained, "You see folks, even the world champion can get worn out in the mountain air." After listening to William's tale, they understood that it was nothing more than altitude and thin air that caused the exhaustion they experienced after their back-to-back romps between the sheets. It was a relief, especially to Phryné, that neither of them had actually lost any of their stamina or zeal.

They were looking forward to the half hour stop in Albuquerque, and the opportunity to walk on terra firma for a few minutes and stretch their travel-weary limbs. William told them it would be the last power and crew change for The California Limited, and there would be scores of Indian and Southwest souvenir vendors and a very impressive Harvey House restaurant in the terminal. They were scheduled to arrive in Los Angeles the next afternoon at quarter past two, and so far, the train had been right on time.

The showpiece of the Albuquerque Terminal was the Alvarado Hotel, another Fred Harvey enterprise. It was a massive complex, unlike anything ever seen by Leopold and Phryné. Gigantic, shaded entry portals into the station, restaurant and hotel were along the length of the quarter-mile long building. Bell towers, huge fountains, granite floors and stucco walls, all in a Pueblo, southwestern style, made it appear as a fantasy paradise. Indian and Mexican artifacts, crafts and souvenir shops were in large separate halls. Craftsmen were making their wares on-site, creating a living museum atmosphere for traveler and tourist alike. Artisans were weaving rugs and styling silver jewelry. Newsstands, coffee shops, food vendors, barbershops, shoeshine benches and curiosity shops packed the halls.

The stop was only a half hour, and they could not spend the time that they would have liked. As soon as they arrived in the station, an Indian silversmith captured Phryné's attention and had no trouble holding on to it. Four Indian silversmiths were working around a small open-hearth furnace creating silver and turquoise jewelry. Smoke from the little foundry fire drifted up and out of the arched portico. Tiny red sparks appeared and disappeared magically into the glowing embers. Small hammers, long bladed knives and needle nose pliers tap-tapped, shaped, shaved and smoothed the silver into time-treasured keepsakes and personal ornaments.

They spent most of their half hour in Albuquerque ardently discussing whether Leopold could, or should, spend thirty dollars on a silver ring with a turquoise stone. Phryné based her argument on practicality. She promised that she would love him just the same if he waited to purchase her wedding ring until they were settled and held steady employment in Los Angeles. They had no way of knowing when that would be.

That's Entertainment

Wednesday evening, August 31

The couple was looking forward to that evening's dinner and show. The next day they would arrive at their destination, so they eagerly anticipated their last Harvey meal and service in the Dining Car. The highlight of the evening would be listening to Caroline Myles sing in Irving Feinmann's combination Drawing Room three cars down; something Phryné was especially looking forward to.

"You know, Leopold, I am really excited about tonight." Phryné limited her words, and did not mention she sincerely hoped that Irving could help them get started and get on their feet in California, be it either Hollywood or Los Angeles.

"I feel excited too, Sweetheart … and confident. I really am confident about Irv's help. But there is an underlying fear I cannot explain. It's not about Irving, it's just that Dillon had us both bamboozled so bad and he got away with it … right up until the time when he decided to run the border, and we were getting shot at. He led you, me and Ellie on, all right. And he kept pulling the rope. I am not going to let that happen again. Ever."

She thought about it. Leopold was right. They needed to be careful.

Phryné worked on her coiffure that afternoon, putting waves into her bob, and she took time with her makeup, carefully forming her crimson lipstick, applying the right amount of mascara, and deep purple eye shadow. The final touches were dabs of HoRoCo Heliotrope perfume behind her ears, and lacquering her nails with the Cutex** she purchased at Ritzy Rita's. She had one good pair of lace patterned, thigh high, smoke grey stockings she could wear to enhance the short knee duster* hemline of her peach chiffon dress. It had a slim waistline with tucks and pleats, and six-inch slits down the front and back. Her beige hook and eye boots would have to suffice. Phryné decided not to wear that restrictive camisole, and she would let her form show. She had nothing to be ashamed of, not in the least.

Leopold wore his three-piece sand-colored Sacque suit, a red silk tie, and a very seldom-used pale green shirt. He had asked the valet to polish his black and white patent leather wing tips. Together, dressed to the nines, Phryné and Leopold did not look at all like the truck driver and his beautician wife from Buffalo.

The foursome was seated together for dinner, something that could not be guaranteed given the rapid turnover necessary in the Dining Car. Just as their meals arrived, the Steward announced that the train had just crossed the border into Arizona. A few of the tables let out a cheer of approval, especially those passengers who were taking the Grand Canyon excursion. They would overnight in Williams, Arizona, and take the sightseeing train the next day. The Santa Fe railroad took tourists directly to the South Rim of the canyon and of course, to a Harvey House restaurant and hotel for those who desired a longer stay.

After dinner, they made their way through the cars to the Lake Winnipeg and Irving's drawing room and compartment. The rooms were adjoined, sharing one wall and connected by a door. The drawing room was a bit larger than the compartment, with a sofa along the hallway wall and a private bathroom. Caroline took a seat on the sofa. Phryné and Leopold sat on the fold-down bed window seats.

Irving stepped to the armoire and brought out a wicker basket with split bottles of ginger ale and a fifth of Canadian Club, neatly snuggled with white linen napkins. He set the basket of libation on the little table next to Caroline and brought out four glasses from the small wall cupboard. With a bottle opener in one hand, he began talking as he opened and poured the soft drinks with the other.

"I thought we could wet our whistles first, and then I can show you the little surprise I arranged for us all. I had the Conductor reserve us four a spot in the Parlor Car for half past eight. And then I had Harry set up the Blue Bird Talking Machine for us. There's a lot more elbow room in the Lounge, and I figure Caroline's voice will sound better outside of this cramped space, won't it, sweetie?" He did not wait for an answer; the words kept coming. "I got this bottle back in Chicago, imported from Canada by way of Detroit." He chuckled, "Who knows? Maybe it was one of Capone's boys that sold me this. Anyway, you cannot leave Chicago and not bring a jug or two of Canadian booze back to California. I got three more stowed away. We can get hooch in L.A., but Mexican tequila just isn't whiskey." He chuckled again, took the time to hold the bottle up for approval, and continued immediately with his speech. "You will join us in a drink, won't you?" He poured an ounce or more into each glass before he took a seat next to Caroline on the sofa. "We can have a quick one before the show. This is what they call a 'Horse's Neck'; ginger ale and rye." Irving raised his glass, "Here's to the future ... to Caroline, the songbird ... and Leo and his wife ... Phryné." He worked to get her name right, and managed. He was pleased. "Here, here! Glass clinks, then whiskey drinks!"

As soon as they entered Irving's drawing room, the mood had heightened. The big man's voice bounced off the walls of the rail car with the cadence of a carnival vendor. He brought out, and poured the whiskey with ceremony. He created a party atmosphere in a few short minutes. Caroline sat on the sofa, her hands folded on her lap, smiling like a kid in a candy store.

Irving reached into his vest pocket and handed Leopold an envelope. "Take a look at that, and let me know what you think, Leo." Phryné moved close to him, her hip against his and her eyes on the paper that her husband was unfolding. It was a typewritten letter of introduction to Abner Mandelbaum, personal assistant to Bernard Balaban, Famous Players Studios, Gower Street, Hollywood, California. The letter was concise, on point, and requested that 'all possible consideration be given for suitable and sustainable employment to Mister and Missus Throckmorton; Leopold and Phryné'.

Phryné's eyes were as big as half dollars. Leopold folded the letter, placed it back into the envelope, and said, "I am speechless, Irving. Thank you."

Phryné added, "Thank you so much. That is so nice of you to help us like this." Leopold stood, then Irving, followed by the women. Handshakes and hugs made the little room look like a scene from a family reunion.

Irving explained that his assistant Harry Mumford typed it up for him and he was able to get Leopold's last name from the Conductor. "You two seem like good folks. I could tell the night we met. That letter will get your foot into the door, anyhow. And Phryné, you be careful, and don't fall for anybody trying to sell you an acting deal. I mean it, there are some real villains roaming them Hollywood Hills, and I don't mean the kind that ties you to a railroad track. So, you keep your eye on her, too, Leo; you got a jewel there. And if things work out, maybe we will run into each other on the Players Paramount lots someday, and you can buy me a drink when

186

they get rid of this senseless Prohibition. Now, drink up, and we can get this party started. We can come back for a nightcap later, right?"

An answer to his question was neither required nor expected.

They sat in the same area of the Lounge Car as they were yesterday. The Blue Bird Talking Machine was near the right side of the car, and four or five Victor sound recordings sat on a hassock alongside it. Caroline was ready to go, standing next to the record player, her hands in front of her. The big man wasted no time, walked to the machine and lifted the lid. Curious eyes from the other passengers seated throughout the car watched closely with keen anticipation. Irving carefully slid a recording out of its paper sleeve and set it onto the turntable. He switched the record player on, lowered the arm, propped the lid, and sat down. Paul Whiteman's band started playing *California Here I Come*. Fifteen seconds later, the second chorus began, and the sweet, vanilla custard voice of Caroline Myles filled the Parlor Car. Heads nodded, smiles appeared, whispers passed from lips to ears and most noticeably, Phryné became so elated, her eyes misted. The song, and what the song brought to her heart, overwhelmed her. She had hold of Leopold's hand, and was not about to let go. Her happiness found its way to her husband and filled his heart with her essence. In a little over three minutes, the rail car filled with a hearty applause that clearly moved Caroline, pleased Phryné, and excited Irving Feinmann.

He took a moment before he changed the record, and stood in the center of the car like a circus ringmaster. He raised both arms, and in his peculiar high-pitched voice, presented Caroline Myles to the dozen or more other passengers in the car. He invited them to keep their eyes and ears open for future appearances and Victor sound recordings of the Kankakee Songbird.

For the next three quarters of an hour, Caroline sang to the big band accompaniment of Paul Whiteman's Orchestra on Victor Talking Machine Recordings. Irving had three double-sided heavy shellac records of *My Blue Heaven, Do It Again, Somebody Loves Me* and two others. As Caroline continued to sing, the crowd grew. Word quickly spread up the consist, and by the time the show was over, it was standing room only in the Parlor Car. Caroline Myles' debut railroad performance was a hit. She sang *California Here I Come* three times, and was asked for autographs. When Caroline sang, she lived the song, felt the words in her heart, and sang them from her soul. The audience, most of all Phryné, noticed. The performance was well received and appreciated.

Back in Irving's Drawing Room on the Lake Winnipeg, engaging conversation, shared laughter, and a few drinks rounded off Leopold and Phryné's night of entertainment. The most significant circumstance of the evening was the revelation of Irving's letter to Paramount. Leopold and Phryné were euphoric. Irving seemed genuinely gratified by their response, and after her evening performance, Caroline felt her dreams were coming true. A good time was had by all.

Phryné and Leopold returned to their compartment as the train was making a fifteen-minute stop in Williams, Arizona to pick up and drop off passengers for tomorrow's railway tour of the Grand Canyon. At eleven o'clock, The California Limited began its slow, tedious, winding trek across the mountains to Ash Fork. A mere twenty-one miles, the serpentine section from Williams consumed an hour.

They fell asleep knowing that the next day was California.

See Level

Aboard The California Limited, Thursday, September 1

Without festival or fanfare, rolling across the harsh, arid Mojave Desert mountain plateau, The California Limited crossed the Colorado River at Topock, Arizona, into California.

Both windows were slid halfway down, open to their maximum. Curiously, the drapes wafted only gently in the wind. Two six-inch electric fans whirred without noticeable effect. Phryné and Leopold were lying propped up in bed, watching the scrub grass, scattered tumbleweeds, sand, rock and distant mountains pass by. They could smell the heat rising from the tortured, parched earth. The desert deviously stole moisture from their nostrils and throat with every breath.

Leopold thought about the men tending the black beast powering the train: the engineer holding the throttle and the fireman stoking the flames of Hades itself.

It was just past seven in the morning, and already the blazing sun was baking the landscape. There were no secrets lurking in any shadows; there were none, excepting those of the skinny telegraph poles.

The newlyweds washed and dressed once again in the best clothing they could without repeating the previous day's outfits. They ordered their breakfast in the Dining Car to be as refreshing as possible: half honeydew melon, sparkling water, sliced apples and pears, toast and a minty orange chutney.

As the morning progressed, the sky blackened, and opened wide with a spontaneous, torrential, early autumn thunderstorm. Raindrops the size of quarters pelted the roof of the rail car, creating a crashing chorus of dinging metal. Puffs of dust rose from the desert and disappeared immediately into a haze of evaporating rain. It was a storm on an unimaginable scale for Leopold and Phryné. Torrents of rainwater formed instant miniature rivers, pushing sand and mud further into the desert. Bolts of lightning struck the earth without mercy, crashing violently with an endless rumbling roar, trapped within the heat. They sat astounded, watching the storm from their window. They acknowledged that this trip was an education, a learning experience and they discovered more about their country than they ever imagined.

Mile after mile, approaching Barstow, the desert gradually faded, distant mountains became a little greener, and the grass a bit thicker. Low desert shrubs such as creosote bush, fan palms and Aleppo pine appeared. The temperature was still hot, but bearable, and not nearly as oppressive. The train was speeding toward the Pacific. Just past noon, they arrived in Azusa, California, a water stop for the locomotive, and where they had their last meal aboard The California Limited. Anxious and curious, their eyes constantly drifted to the windows, looking for a glimpse of the Promised Land. They descended to the Los Angeles basin down the San Gabriel Mountains, and closer to their final stop. The waiters, porters, everyone seemed familiar and commonplace by now. The immaculate table linen, spotless glassware, silver coffee pots and glistening china: everything had lost its luster over the past three days.

Phryné mentioned that they had not seen Irving or Caroline since the previous night, and hoped they could at least catch them at the terminal in Los Angeles to say goodbye. Leopold noted that they never did meet Irving's assistant, Harry Mumford. They could only imagine the reason why.

After lunch, they packed their suitcase, Phryné's shoulder bag, and Leopold's duffle sack. All their possessions were in better condition now than when they left Buffalo. Their shoes were cleaned, brushed and appropriately polished; their jackets, slacks, shirts and dresses pressed, cleaned or laundered; ties and hats brushed, and everything else washed. Leopold checked his wallet and Phryné passed her cash to him. After everything was totaled, including the change in his pocket, they had $242.72 between them. They agreed that the next day, Friday at the very latest, they would find Gower Street in Hollywood, and knock on the door, humble, hopeful and smiling, looking for work.

The train was slowing; the tracks moaned and squealed with the strain. The rhythm diminished and the sway calmed. They sat holding hands, looking out the window. William knocked on their door and stuck his head inside. "We are approaching Pasadena, about ten miles from Los Angeles, folks."

Leopold stood, as did Phryné. He reached into his pocket, handed his last silver dollar to the porter and took his hand. "Thank you for your help, William. We have had a fine trip."

Phryné was standing beside Leopold, holding onto his arm. She smiled and nodded. "Thank you, William."

"And thank you, folks. I hope you find Los Angeles to your liking, and I especially want to thank you for using my name." He gave a brief gesture of a bow, and was out the door. Neither Phryné nor Leopold knew what he meant with the reference to his name. They could only assume that some passengers may not have been as polite as they were.

One long whistle blast and Leopold knew. "We're here, Phryné." She moved as close as she could to him, and peered out the window like a kid looking under the tree on Christmas morning. Another long blast, a pause, and another. They watched as La Grande Station appeared. A large gold colored dome was atop the roof of the red stone and brick station. The parapets and archways, cedars and palms painted a canvas of old Spain.

Their pulses quickened. A short burst, then another, and the sound of air brakes, the moan of steel, and the hiss of steam all mixed into a bubbling stew of sound under the roof over the platform. Feathers fluttered inside their chests, electricity tickled through their veins, and their skin danced with goose bumps. They had arrived.

When the train came to a complete stop, they looked out the window to the seemingly endless expanse of the terminal. The rush of bodies created a coordinated confusion and a bulging tide of humanity within the station. Leopold grabbed their bundled blankets, duffel bag, and suitcase. Phryné picked up her crescent shoulder bag, handbag, and the wrapped comforter. Passengers from the forward sections of the car were still exiting through the hall outside their door. They waited patiently, smiled at one another and looked around the room that had been their home for the previous sixty-six hours. A moment of silence and a break in the foot traffic outside their door signaled it was their turn to exit the Lake Union and put their footprints on California.

On the platform, a warm brisk breeze brushed at Phryné's curls, and ruffled her dress. "I think I smell the ocean, Leopold. I really do."

The Limited's passengers blended with the cross section of humanity inside La Grande. Different people with different destinations and their life stories packed in sacks, suitcases or blankets. Indians, farmhands, Mexicans, and even a cowboy or two were immersed with the businessmen, professionals, and society's finery. The varied headgear told the rest of the story: fedoras, bowlers, sombreros, bonnets, boaters, feathered cloches, ten gallon, scarves, and beanies. Los Angeles held a population of one million souls in its unique, booming melting pot.

Leopold and Phryné walked slowly into the passenger hall, and continued to look for Irving and Caroline, who evidently had been swallowed by the crowd, and apparently had vanished into obscurity. To become friends, be so close, so quickly, sharing life experiences, and then to part ways without ceremony, perhaps never to be seen again, leaves a feeling difficult to ignore and a nagging curiosity.

They stopped at a bench and set their baggage down. It was a bench like so many other benches they had seen at train stations in Buffalo, Chicago, Albuquerque, and now Los Angeles.

"Now what, Leopold?"

He did not speak. He opened his arms; she filled them. They held one another for several minutes. They felt closer than ever before.

Optimistic Realism

Leopold left Phryné watching their belongings on the bench and walked toward the booth. "Travelers' Aide" was neatly lettered in black, on all four sides of the red pyramid roof. It was a small, ten foot square, isolated kiosk standing in the center of the station like a piece on a game board, alone and unassuming, a lonely haven of help in the middle of ordered chaos, surrounded by travelers moving in an inconsistent direction.

"Can I help you?" An eager, ginger-haired young man with plentiful freckles stood behind the counter.

"Well, I have one simple question. If you only had a sawbuck in your pocket, and you were two hundred miles from home, alone and hungry in Los Angeles, where would you spend the night?"

The young fellow looked surprised, and had to think about his answer. Trained not to show favoritism or selectivity, and to provide only advice and options as unsolicited suggestions, he seemed a bit befuddled.

Leopold encouraged an honest answer. "Come on, buddy: you are alone and only have ten bucks, and you are not sure how long you will be stuck here. Where would you go?"

The young fellow looked around, as if looking to see if anyone was watching, and answered. "Well, sir, right across the street is the Hotel Wheeler, and behind it, on Carey Street, sits the Hotel Abbott. I think the Wheeler charges four or five dollars, but the Abbott is just as good, and they charge three; probably because they are farther away and not visible from the station."

Leopold slid a quarter across the counter. "See that, kid? It was simple. Thanks a lot."

They chose to stay at the Abbott, in a double room on the second floor. The linens were not crisp and fresh like the ones on The Limited, but they were clean. After a shower and change of clothes, they had dinner at the train station, at the

Harvey House. One discovery they made on their trip west was that the Harvey people knew food and the price was right. That evening Leopold also learned first-hand, that if you were not wearing a jacket, they would provide one for you.

Because the hotel was only a block and a half from the busy train station, the singular drawback was the noise. That aside, it was a perfect Southern California night, a gentle west wind wafting off the Pacific, clear starlit skies, and a wisp of crescent moon. They sat in the hotel courtyard at an umbrella table with two bottles of Coca Cola, talking about their completed cross-country caravan and immediate future. Mexican whippoorwills darted in and out of the beam of the yard lights, catching insects on the fly, and chattering their lonesome song. And not to be forgotten, an occasional steam whistle from La Grande Station sliced through the night air.

There were times when Leopold and Phryné experienced reoccurring motion, the sensation of movement and feeling the world continually fly by. The click-click of the rails hung stubbornly on, like a hangover.

They took stock of their situation, knowing fully well that they had a mere two hundred and forty dollars between them. Like Woodrow Wilson, the liberal optimist would argue that at $3.25 a day for a hotel room and $4.75 for meals, they could sustain themselves very well for twenty-five days. Phryné and Leopold agreed it had been wise not to squander thirty dollars on that turquoise ring back in Albuquerque.

A conservative realist such as Calvin Coolidge would ascertain that in case of a trip, stumble or fall, their modest bankroll was somewhat of a cushion, but by no means was it a feather bed. Leopold pointed out that nothing breaks a fall like a big bag of balled up bills.

"Tomorrow, Phryné, I get a job. That's first and foremost. I'm going over the top and getting it done."

All That Glitters

Friday, September 2, Los Angeles, California

The couple's adventure had spoiled Phryné. A shower was no longer a concept, something that she never before experienced, or a fixture that some people had and she did not. She informed Leopold that eventually, wherever they finally found a nail to hang their hats on, there had to be a shower.

When they arrived in Los Angeles the previous afternoon, they'd had no concept of the thriving metropolis surrounding them. There were pedestrians, trolleys, and vehicles everywhere they turned. They were in the middle of one of the largest commerce centers in the world. The three block area on the west side of the Santa Fe rail station was wall-to-wall wholesale grocery distributors, meat processors and packers, printers, produce distributors, lithographers, vendors of paper and products, lumberyards, and anything else that could be shipped anywhere, anytime on the railroad. Every other business they walked past either had a sign that read 'Help Wanted' or simply 'Inquire Within' on the door.

They had breakfast at a little diner called Louigi's Kitchen on Second Street, around the block from their hotel. Not to be out-done by the big boys, the little diner had a sign at the back of the counter *Waitress Needed*. Leopold had beef for the first time in months, at a price he could not believe. He enjoyed a Delmonico steak, two eggs, a two-inch-thick piece of toast and a strong cup of coffee for a dollar and ten cents. Phryné's morning meal was identical, without the steak, at a mere forty cents. She teased him about it, prompting him to promise that his breakfast would last until dinner.

They began their trip to the studio on Gower Street at the information booth inside the train terminal. Pacific Electric, the largest system in the country, operated the trolley cars in Los Angeles. Their excited anticipation peaked as they boarded the Hollywood - Melrose car and paid the ten-cent fare. The trolley was painted in a red and orange color scheme. Fifty feet in length, the cars were twice as large as those in Buffalo. The trolleys brandished 'Pacific Electric' in gold letters along the side.

A motorman and conductor greeted passengers at opposite ends of the car, and when compared to a steam locomotive, the trolley was virtually silent. Hum, whirr, snap, and click were the sounds of power. The car itself, wood and steel, creaked and squeaked with strain. The rails and wheels emitted the groan of steel on steel. Warm September air drifted throughout the car for the duration of the twenty minute, six-mile trip to the corner of Melrose and Gower. In bold white letters, an imposing sign stood on the hillside, framed by the San Gabriel mountain range, boasting its unique location to the entire world: HOLLYWOODLAND**. The conductor's voice reverberated throughout the car, "Gower Street ... exit right hand side of car".

Leopold stepped off the trolley and offered his hand for Phryné. They stood and watched No. 37 click away. They were standing in the shade, under the wide roof of the trolley stop shelter.

In every direction, the buildings were wood frame structures with clapboard or cedar shingle siding. Some appeared as if they were either erected overnight, on a whim without any forward planning. The few buildings with brick and stucco construction seemed to proclaim their solidarity in permanence. Alders, myrtles, oaks, and laurels were scattered among the buildings, not by design or transplant, but merely spared by the clearing saws. The yards were beaten, packed earth, or newly planted grass. In the hills to the northwest, development was occurring as they watched. Earthmovers on every scale from pick and shovel to bulldozers labored in the soil. It was construction at a dizzying pace.

Leopold took Irving's letter of introduction from his vest pocket. Phryné took a seat on the bench, crossed her legs and reached into her pocketbook.

"Cigarette, Leopold?"

He sat next to her and glanced at his pocket watch. He announced the time, "quarter to twelve" for no apparent reason, and held onto the envelope.

Phryné repeated herself, "Would you like me to cig you?"

"Sure." She took a Chesterfield from the pack, lit it, passed it to him and lit a Marlboro for herself. Automobile traffic spun little puffs and tiny whirlwinds of dust into the wind as it passed. Trolley No. 26 appeared from the opposite direction, displaying 'Santa Monica' and 'Beverly Hills' on the front marquee. A dozen or more passengers got off, and walked up Gower Street or one block down to Vine. It was a strange hodgepodge of citizenry; either gaudy, plain or overdressed. They all appeared to be in costume either by design, error or exaggeration.

Phryné and Leopold sat and watched the people parade disappear down and up the street. She moved close and pressed beside her husband. With her leg crossed, she gently rocked her foot and wriggled her ankle. She looked into his eyes. Phryné reached inside for the impetus to speak. Her words struggled to form on her lips and tongue.

"I do not think we belong here, Leopold. I have been keeping some thoughts to myself since yesterday, and I am sorry I have not said anything earlier, but we do not have to do this. I do not think we would be happy doing this. This Hollywood, movie star life, I mean." She set her pocketbook on her lap and put her hand on his thigh.

Leopold knew her courage. Sometimes she kept her thoughts locked up for days, until either the problem solved itself or she could no longer justify her silence. Phryné had her limits. Bold as she was, she had the fault of occasionally second-guessing or even intimidating herself to keep quiet.

He'd had the same thoughts while he showered that morning. "Well, it's not like we cannot do anything else. We really do not need help to find a job in this town, it seems. I think Los Angeles is like a beehive in the middle of a herd of

197

dairy cows. Like they say: *the land of milk and honey*. But, the guy who milks the cow has to be damn careful he doesn't get stung. And to tell you the absolute truth, Phryné, I remember something Irving said back on the train about this town being full of bastards looking for the chance to take you to the cleaners." She nodded. He inhaled and released the smoke between pursed lips. "Tell you what … to hell with this movie studio business. We are normal people, Phryné. I love you as you are. Let's stay normal." She leaned into her husband, kissed him on the lips and held him around the shoulders.

"You are an honest man, Leopold."

They walked down Gower Street and caught a glimpse of the business of movie creation on both sides of the street, inside what looked like large livestock barns, sheds, backyards, and even garages. An archway across a wide driveway off Lexington was perhaps the most glamorous, postcard view of the area. A curved placard read 'Famous Players Paramount Studios' supported by wrought iron and brick pillars. It was accented by climbing red roses, but Mary Pickford or Ronald Colman were nowhere to be seen among all the spectacular nothingness. The scope of Leopold and Phryné's vision was only the tip of the ever widening, spreading iceberg. It went on and on for blocks, around corners and downhill to Santa Monica toward the Pacific. Hollywood proved to be a bustling metropolis of nondescript, repetitive mediocrity. The glitter did not fall from the beauty queen's tiara, but the sulphuric truth tarnished it.

A Touch Of Home

They got off the trolley at Echo Park and spent an hour walking the paths, and feeding bits of crackers to the geese. Their decision to forego the presentation of Irving's letter was by no means binding, but they mutually agreed to try another path to the future other than Famous Players. Leopold commented, "I do not think we would be comfortable being players in this land of make-believe, Phryné. Maybe I am wrong, but for now, it does not seem like that shoe would fit. Think about it: everything is phony. It is the nature of the beast."

Perhaps he made that remark to convince even himself of the validity of their decision. Regardless, his wife agreed.

He got a pocketful of nickels from the conductor of the Virgil Avenue trolley, and they played hopscotch with the Pacific Electric interurban system for the better part of the afternoon. They explored a great deal of Los Angeles from trolley car windows by catching rides blindly, slap-dash up and down the city's streets. The trolley system allowed them to traverse the city as an erratic pin-the-tail-on-the-donkey game, one nickel at a time.

The Fourth Street trolley came to a dead stop at the corner of Main, and they exited the car along with several other impatient riders. A team of six mules pulling a petroleum wagon apparently had a mix-up with a bicycle and a Chevrolet coupe in the middle of the intersection. Two policemen and scores of interested citizens were milling about and trying to find a resolution to the problem. The oil wagon was a massive round tank, twenty feet long and six feet in diameter, with six-foot wooden spoke wheels on ten-inch axles. The driver remained in his seat on top of, and on the front of the tank, holding the reins of the team and trying to talk to the police over the noise of the crowd. The side of the tank read *Garrison Oil Company: Our Mule Brings Your Fuel.*

There were impressive buildings on each corner. The Westminster Hotel, with its parapets and main tower piercing the sky, stretched nearly half a block each way down both Fourth and Main Streets. On the opposite side, stood the Van Nuys Hotel with towering bay windows, and kitty-corner was the nine-story San Fernando Building, and Merchants' Bank next door. Everything looked like it was brand new and fresh out-of-the-box. Twenty feet overhead, like everywhere else in the city, was an ominous maze of power lines for the Pacific Electric trolleys. It appeared as a thick, black spider's web, dangerously close, ready to drop, capture and devour its prey.

The city was twice as large in population as Buffalo, and twenty times as busy. Eventually, they found their way back to the familiar vicinity of La Grande Station, just as dusk began covering Los Angeles in its blanket of grey. They were not overly hungry and settled for a hot dog, mashed potatoes and ginger ale at the Harvey lunch counter. They had kept well under their six-dollar-a-day meal budget. On the way out of the terminal, they stopped at the Santa Fe News stand, purchased a pack of cigarettes apiece, two picture postcards, a copy of the *Los Angeles Times*, a packet of Wrigley's Doublemint gum, and for no particular reason, a two-day old copy of the *Buffalo Evening News*. Of all the papers from all the cities, the *News* caught Phryné's eye. The clerk wrapped everything in a sheath of brown paper and tied it with a string.

Back at the Abbott, in room 214, they kicked off their shoes, collapsed on the settee and stretched out their legs. They caught their breath, and let the events of the day settle into their memory like so much dust on a grand piano. Leopold snapped the string off their little packet of purchases, glanced at the *Times* and told Phryné that tomorrow he would devote the day to finding a job. He would make it his mission.

The headline "Three Companies Fight Flames" on the masthead of the Buffalo paper did not warrant Phryné's attention back at the newsstand or Leopold's there in the room, but the lead story itself did. One sentence into the story, Leopold held the paper in clenched fists. Phryné watched her husband's eyes move across the page with dizzying speed. His expression was frozen. Her quick glance at the secondary headline revealed the reason for his torment.

SEVEN SOULS LOST IN BROADWAY BLAZE

Buffalo, NY. 29 Aug 1927. A great conflagration set skies ablaze during the early morning hours this Monday. It is the most devastating fire for this decade. The dwelling and boarding house that stood at number 31 Adams Street was burned to the ground, and neighboring structures at 29 and 27 severely damaged by fire and smoke, plus severe damage caused by an explosion of natural gas. The homes are considered uninhabitable pending further city inspection.

At approximately 2:30 AM next door neighbor Mrs. Mildred Hutchinson noticed flames at the front stoop of number 31 and sprang to the Broadway alarm box to summon the fire brigade. At 2:40 Station No. 3 of the Buffalo Fire Department responded but could not immediately sustain sufficient water pressure to effectively battle the flames. It has been reported the building was fully ablaze at that time. A tenant from the building, Mr. W. McTell who leapt from a second story window to ground below is now in hospital suffering a broken limb and burns about the body. When the pumping truck of the brigade arrived at 2:45 gas supply lines inside the structure apparently burst to create an explosive fireball that alit the skies orange and blue in color. Alas, total ruination ensued and the building is not to be salvaged. Two adjacent structures withstood severe fire and smoke and water damage plus debris spoilage. Broken window glass was reported on homes cross street. Three fire houses battled the flames, Stations No. 3, 7, and 1. The blaze was under full control at 6:45 am. The remains of seven were discovered in the abolition, four females believed to be homeowner Wilhelmina Throckmorton, her three daughters Johanna, Ottilie and Hilde. An elder son, Leopold, was not located, nor believed to reside in the home. Younger son, Nicholas, was reported to be at his work at Russell Miller Inc. However, his whereabouts at this writing remain unknown. According to city records at time of press, three male boarders are believed deceased: Mr. Richard Arbuckle of no known address, Mr. Archibald Phillips of Schenectady, and Mr. G. Lopenzky of Rochester.

Recently, as reported by this paper, Mayor F. Schwaub has been active with Fire Department officers concerning apparent equipment failure and shortfalls, which could prove to be an official concern in this latest fatal blaze. The city Commissioner's office has renewed his call to legislate the removal or permanent service disconnect of gas light systems in all private dwellings with electric service by year end and co-ordinate this with Ward Presidents. The investigation into the cause of the fire is ongoing. Contact: Brig. Comm. Abenstern BFC, Capt. D. Patterson II, BPD

Leopold sat with his jaw set and teeth clenched. His eyes moved to another smaller article in the left-hand column.

SUSPICIOUS DEATH INVESTIGATED

Buffalo, NY. 29 Aug 1927. At 4:30 am. Monday a badly beaten body was discovered under the Michigan Street bridge at the river ship canal. It is suspected the death occurred sometime this past week-end. Identification was tentative made of the remains as those of Mr. Dillon I. Cafferty aged abt. 25 of Buffalo who is known to the Pct. No. 2 police as a possible assoc. conspirator with the Black Hand mafia of the Canal District and New York City. Footprints of three men discovered on the soft riverbank are being examined. The Black Hand has been in the past implicated with prostitution rings in New York as well as Rochester and bootleg liquor smuggling from Lockport to Erie, Penna. No arrests have been made. The incident is under scrutiny by BPD Precinct No. 2. Contact: Lt. G. F. Krungel, BPD

Phryné sat looking over his shoulder, reading bits and pieces without disturbing him. He was not moving a muscle. Under a photograph of the new Peace Bridge, the center three columns covered the secondary story.

PEACE BRIDGE VIOLENCE LEAVES REVENUE OFFICER DEAD

Buffalo, NY, 29 Aug 1927, Shortly after 1 AM August 28, Sunday morning, an incident without precedent at the newly opened Peace Bridge resulted in the death by automobile collision of Customs and Revenue Officer Lionel P. Wiggins of Eggertsville, Erie County, NY

It has been revealed that the violent confrontation occurred Saturday night into Sunday early morning hours. Not all details have been released to this newspaper but what is known is that a newer model, black or maroon, four door sedan, possibly a Cadillac model, was involved. In addition to the hit-and-run driver, the total number of passengers or armed suspects inside the automobile is not known or released by the Immigration Dept. The public is informed the sedan will have impact damage to the front as well as gun-fire damage. It was reported shots came from within the automobile, and officers then returned fire after shots were reported coming from the passenger side. The total number of shots fired is uncertain. Pending further investigation, Border police and customs officials will not reveal if Thompson type automatic machine-rifles were used.

At press time it is also not clear what provocation led to the violence. It is reported that the suspect automobile was to be inspected by the Customs and Revenue Secondary Inspection Unit when it violently drove past the barricades and struck and killed Officer Wiggins. The automobile subsequently exited the confines of the Customs Inspection Compound driving at high speed and escaped the pursuit of two squad automobiles of Revenue and Prohibition Police, in addition to Customs

Officers. The suspect automobile was last seen erratically driving south on Niagara Street, Buffalo. It is therefore suspected that the driver of the automobile suffered one or more gunshot wounds. The incident is under joint investigation by the Buffalo office of the United States Bureau of Investigation, Customs and Revenue Dept., Ontario Provincial Police, Canada Excise and Tax Dept., and Buffalo Police Dept. Law enforcement officials welcome information from the public. Contact: US Dept Customs and Revenue; Canada: Ontario Provincial Police.; Cmdr. James P. Hines, Precinct 4, Buffalo Police Dept.

Leopold released his grip on the newspaper and passed it slowly to Phryné. He turned his head and looked into her eyes. He struggled, "The shit hit the fan, didn't it? We were, sure as hell, right about that, sure as hell."

His voice did not sound right. It was different; it did not sound like the Leopold she knew. He walked to the end table and picked up his pack of Chesterfield. Phryné was glancing over the articles, picking out bits that she missed. Leopold sat back down, lit a cigarette, filled his lungs then exhaled slowly, pushing the smoke through his nostrils. Inside his skull, the roar of a thousand cannon sounded with every beat of his heart. His ears stung with the clamor of a million church bells. His eyes burned with the image of his mother's blazing home.

Phryné picked up the cigarette that fell from his fingers. She watched as her husband began to weep.

Abruptly, his chest heaved, and his breath choked as he gulped for air. He struggled to exhale. Just as suddenly, he seemed to expel his complete essence with the air from his lungs. What began as a convulsion, ended as heartbroken sobs. She had seen men cry tears, but never endure this level of grief. Phryné put an arm over his shoulder, held his head with the touch of a mother, whispered and rocked him like an infant.

Chapter Ten

The Morning After

Saturday, September 3, 1927, Los Angeles, California

After Leopold read and re-read the news about the death of his mother and sisters, and the question regarding the whereabouts and safety of his brother Nicholas, he remained sequestered in room 214 of the Abbott Hotel for two and a half days.

At wit's end and without her husband's knowledge, Phryné took a bold initiative. On the morning after the bad news, she told Leopold she was going downstairs to the restaurant for a bit of breakfast. She offered to bring him back something, but he refused and remained in bed just as she had feared he would.

It was nine o'clock on Saturday morning; noon in Buffalo. From the manager's desk of the Hotel Abbott, she placed a trans-continental telephone call to her parent's home. After yesterday's shocking revelations, it was a necessary course of action. Phryné had realized that there was a barrelful of things that needed to be cleared up.

During the conversation, she managed somehow to control her emotions and remained calm. Her father spoke quickly and directly. First and foremost, he asked if they were all right and if they had heard about the fire. Phryné did a lot of listening. Her father informed her that on Friday, they'd attended the funeral for the Throckmorton family at Reformation Lutheran. Her friend Eloisa and her family were also in attendance along with a handful of family and a large number of the curious public. Eloisa had expressed her condolences and was eager for more news than what was written on the postcards Phryné had sent from Chicago. Phryné tried to fight it, but she started to tear. "How is Ellie doing, Papa?"

Her father continued, "Eloisa explained that Dillon had started a fight that Saturday night in Canada, and that she was injured by a broken chair someone had thrown in the ballroom fracas … and that you and Leopold decided to elope after you were back in Buffalo. Is that correct? Then on Sunday … there was the fire … and Dillon turns up dead, beaten and broken. You and Leopold are married now … I understand … like you wrote on the postcard we got in yesterday's afternoon mail? Is this true?"

"Yes, it is. And yes, we are married. We bought Pullman tickets to California, and we got married in Chicago. Last night we read about everything in the Buffalo paper, and I had to call you. Leopold and I were shocked, shaken and very distraught over the news of the fire, Papa. And we were very sorry to hear about Dillon, but it seems that trouble followed that man wherever he went. But I am very happy to hear that Ellie is all right."

There was just a few seconds of silence before her father continued. She was surprised and relieved to learn that her father met Fire Commander Wilbur Abenstern at the funeral and that he was Leopold's uncle, his mother's brother. It was Abenstern who had arranged the funeral, and had spoken with Nicholas on that horrific Monday morning, at the scene of the fatal fire. While no one knew what became of Nicholas, it was comforting to know he was alive. The official cause of the fire had not been determined due to the devastation caused by the gas explosion, but Commander Abenstern had considered the careless use of tobacco products by one of the upstairs boarders.

Phryné promised her father a long letter, and assured him everything was all right. The call ended after brief well wishes between Phryné, her mother and brother. After she placed the earpiece on the receiver, Phryné sat motionless in the chair next to the little telephone table for minutes, collecting her thoughts and emotions. She and the hotel manager waited for the American Telephone & Telegraph operator to call back with the charges. There was genuine relief and peace of mind after that telephone call. Phryné felt comfortable paying $22.20 to

206

the hotel manager for the four-minute, thirty-second conversation with her father. The time was rounded-up to five minutes.

Phryné told the desk clerk her husband was ill, and got around room service by bringing a pot of coffee and some toast up to their room.

When she told Leopold that she spent twenty-two dollars and placed a telephone call to her father, it seemed to lift his spirits, at least temporarily. The story that Eloisa made up about her injury made sense, and thus avoided any mention of the incident at the Peace Bridge. When Phryné recounted her father's conversation with his uncle Wilbur, Leopold said that he had not noticed his name at the bottom of the article, and probably would not have realized their relationship, explaining that he had not seen Abenstern in years. Like Phryné, he too, was relieved that his brother Nicholas did not perish in the fire. But the troubling questions about the cause of the fire and his brother's whereabouts were not answered.

Epilogue

Leopold & Phryné

With Phryné's patient persistence, Leopold came out of his depressive state on Sunday, the afternoon of the second day. Tuesday morning, Leopold swallowed his pride and went to Famous Players Studios, hat-in-hand, and presented Irving's letter to Abner Mandelbaum. He was hired as a driver and laborer for set creation and maintenance. Leopold and Phryné immediately rented a partially furnished, two-room, one-bath apartment off Figueroa Street for twenty-five dollars a month. To Phryné's delight, it had a shower.

Time rolled along and the money was good. In early October, Phryné began working at an up-scale beauty salon and spa on Alvarado Street.

In February 1928, a new family moved into a new two-bedroom bungalow home south of Laurel Canyon. In May, Phryné gave birth to a daughter: Millicent Mae. Eloisa arrived in Los Angeles in early April for an extended visit.

The dark times and long soup lines of the Great Depression did not dampen the film industry's clamor, nor did it dim Hollywood's glittering lights.

Nicholas & Nora

Three days after his eighteenth birthday, on October 15, 1927, Nicholas Throckmorton married Nora Sterescu in the rectory of Detroit's Saint Hyacinth Roman Catholic Church.

They were blessed with a son, Alexander, on May 14, 1928. The family relocated to Port Huron, Michigan, in the autumn of that year following Nicholas' employment with an Ann Arbor fertilizer and crop dusting firm. He eventually achieved his dream of becoming a pilot, and in 1938, left his young wife and son behind to join the US Army Air Corps.

(Phade to blaque)

THE STORY CONTINUES WITH:

Dollar To Doughnut

The Glossary: 1927 Slang

applesauce	flattery, nonsense, BS.
athletic union suit	men's one-piece buttoned underwear, short sleeve top, knee length underpants
baby vamp	an attractive female
bearcat	a sexually aggressive female
behind the eight ball	in a difficult position; in a tight spot
berries	perfect
big six	a new six cylinder engine
billboard	a flashy dresser
bimbo	tough guy
blind pig, blind tiger	a speakeasy; a bar or nightclub operating illegally during Prohibition
blue nose	prudish person
blower	telephone
Bog Irish	(derogatory) impoverished
bootleg liquor	term originated from the form-fitting flasks made to be stuck in boot tops for illegal liquor
bull	policeman, federal agent
breezer	automobile without a top (or windows)

camiknickers	half-slip and panty combination
"cig me"	cigarette, please
chin wag	conversation
chump	gullible person
clam	a dollar
classy chassis	a fine figure
consist	cars of a train, either passenger or freight
copacetic	popular term among flappers; wonderful
cuddler	a promiscuous woman
Cupid's Bow	to apply lipstick to outline and emphasize the upper lip in the shape of an inverted bow
dapper	lively, flashy, well-dressed man
dimbox	taxi
dressed to the nines	dressed up
drugstore cowboy	a man that hangs around sidewalks trying to pick up women
egg	a person living the high life
gams	legs

get a wiggle on	hurry up
glad rags	fancy clothes; Sunday dress
guappo	(mafia) thug, bully, braggart (derogatory)
flapper	stylish, brash young woman in short skirt
flimflam	swindle, truck, ruse
flophouse	cheap rooming house with many beds per room
greaseball	(derogatory) Italian
hack	taxi
Harp	(derogatory) Irish
hard-boiled	tough guy
ish kabibble	a retort: "it figures" or "baloney"
jerkwater (town)	a small stop for locomotives to refill water tenders. The chain would be pulled, or jerked, to open the spigot on the water tanks.
knee duster	short dress or skirt; hemline at the knees
know your onions	knowledgeable
middle aisle	getting married

stroll	
moxie	vigor, pep (after the soft drink *Moxie*)
noodle juice	weak, bad-tasting tea
over the top	(out of the trench), into the battle (WWI); excessive
palooka	an inexperienced, clumsy oaf
pipes	singing voice
rake	scoundrel, immoral individual
rattler	train
Ritz	high class, fancy (after the NYC hotel)
rube	(derogatory) an ignorant, rural person
sawbuck	ten-dollar bill
Sheba	woman with sex appeal (movie *Queen of Sheba*)
Sheik	man with sex appeal (Rudolph Valentino movie *The Shiek*)
snake charmer	an accomplice used to distract attention from the police
spifflicated	drunk
spiffy	elegant, fancy
talking machine	record player

tomato	a woman
windsucker	braggart
Wop	(derogatory) Italian; immigrant (WithOutPapers)
zotzed	killed, murdered, dead

The End Notes

Chapter 1:

Phryné was named after a feisty Ancient Greek champion of women's rights born about 370 BC; actually, a *hetaira,* an educated, beautiful and worldly courtesan. Phryné (Ancient Greek = Φρύνη) lived during the age of Alexander The Great and the wars between the city-states of Thespiae and Thebes. Because of her perfect form, it is said that Phryné was the model for several statues depicting love goddesses such as Philotes and Aphrodite.

Peerless, Packard, and Pierce Arrow were known as "the three Ps" of the automobile world: the ultimate in affordable luxury transportation. Peerless (the car nobody heard of) was made in Cleveland; the Packard was manufactured in Detroit; the Pierce Arrow was produced on Elmwood Avenue in Buffalo, New York. All were assembled by hand.

The name *Throckmorton* was bastardized at Ellis Island, New York by an immigration clerk in 1894. The "Durchmorgen" family were Prussian immigrants aboard the *SS Spree* from Bremen, Germany.

Rag-and-bone men collected unwanted household items and sold them to merchants. Traditionally, this was a task performed on foot, with the scavenged materials (which included rags, bones and various metals) kept in a small bag slung over the shoulder. Some wealthier rag-and-bone men used a cart, sometimes pulled by horse or pony.

Dark Red was the only color of lipstick. It contained lead.

Fergie's Foam, the 4.4% beer legal in Ontario, was stronger than the 3.2% "light beer" of today.

"Always bring American cigarettes if you go to Canada." Phryné created this axiom from a remark that Leopold made on one of their first trips to Niagara Falls: "Since the War of 1812, Canada has had a secure border. The cigarettes that the Canadians make from Burley tobacco have kept Americans from invading and occupying their country."

A thimble was the common betrothal gift for the bride-to-be in the late 19th Century and early 20th. Engagement rings with diamonds did not become popular until after the 1930's, when DeBeers Diamonds began a fervent advertising campaign.

In the early 1900s, car dealers created publicity for their automobiles by hosting car races. In 1922, a championship race was held in Pikes Peak, Colorado. Noel Bullock entered his Model T, named 'Old Liz.' The car was unpainted and lacked a hood. Spectators compared the car to a tin can. By the start of the race, the car had the new nickname of 'Tin Lizzie'. She won the race.

Chapter 2:

Grape farmers enjoyed a booming business during prohibition. 'Wine blocks' or 'bricks' of grape concentrate were sold with the following warning: "*After mixing with one gallon of water, DO NOT place in a cupboard or basement for 20 days or product will ferment and turn into wine.*"

'Lucky Lindy', the 'Lone Eagle'; American aviator Charles Lindbergh made the first solo trans-Atlantic flight, May 20, 1927.

Chapter 6:

Mercurochrome (merbromin) was a popular topical antiseptic for cuts and abrasions from the 1920's to 1998 when its use was discontinued for fear of mercury poisoning. When dry on the skin or dressings, it was bright orange in color.

Chapter 7:

Marlboro cigarettes were introduced by Philip Morris in 1924, and marketed them to women: "mild as May" with red tips on the filters to hide lipstick marks.

Chapter 8:

Harvey advertised for and hired "white, young women, 18 to 30 years of age, of good character, attractive and intelligent".

The girls were paid $17.50 a month to start, plus room, board, and tips. Makeup was absolutely prohibited. They were required to sign a one-year employment contract, and forfeited half their base pay should they fail to complete the term of service. Marriage was the most common reason for a girl to terminate her employment; half of them married customers. Before *Harvey House* opened the restaurants along the Santa Fe railroad, it was said *"There are no ladies west of Kansas City, and no women west of Albuquerque"*.

2,231 miles in *66* hours: Ironically, world famous *US Route 66* (established 1926) runs parallel to the tracks used by The California Limited (inaugural run 1896) much of the way from Chicago to Los Angeles.

Chapter 9:

Cutex was introduced 1917 as the only paintable nail polish. Nail polish remover was first introduced in 1928.

Hiram Walker, an American citizen, owned a distillery in Walkerville, Ontario that produced *Canadian Club* rye whiskey. Boot-legging during Prohibition made him a millionaire.

Pullman rail car company was founded by George Mortimer Pullman, born in Brocton, New York. Many sleeper cars were manufactured at the company's 38-acre Buffalo, NY factory.

Pullman porters were often called *"George"*: a derogatory reference to hired help.

HOLLYWOODLAND - the famous sign was erected in 1923 for a Los Angeles housing development. In 1949 the word "LAND" was removed.

Art by Amy.©

"Go pack your bags, sailor."
~ Phryné Truffaut, August 28, 1927

Kilroy was here

As a self-published author, my readers are my best advocates.
Please consider a simple rating or brief review
on Amazon or Goodreads.

It is appreciated.

Some More Odd Stuff

Some prohibition-era mixed drinks:
Fog Horn: 1 part gin + 2 parts ginger ale; add ice
Gin & Sin: Equal parts: gin, lemonade, and orange juice
Horse's Neck: 1 part rye whiskey + 4 parts ginger ale
Horse's Ass: 1 part soda water + 1 part ginger ale (This drink was
a reference to the Prohibitionists who would actually drink it.)
(you decide how big the "part" is.)

*"The introduction of so powerful an agent as steam to a
carriage on wheels will make a great change in the situation of
man."*
~Thomas Jefferson … 1802~

It is written in stone.

Carved at : Sandman's Workshop, Pigeon Forge, Tennessee

Music To Consider

Tea For Two	Marion Harris
Sweet Georgia Brown	Ben Bernie & Orchestra
California Here I Come	Paul Whiteman & Orchestra
Am I Blue	Ben Selvin & Orchestra
Oh! Katharina	Ted Lewis Band
Six Or Seven Times	Blue Roseland Orchestra
My Blue Heaven	Gene Austin
Who's Boogie'n My Woogie	Oscar's Chicago Swingers
Stardust	Hoagie Carmichael
At The Jazz Band Ball	Bix Biederbecke
No, No, Nora	Eddie Cantor
Charleston	Lanin's Roseland Orchestra
Pussy Cat Blues	Big Bill Broonzy
Positively Absolutely	Piccadilly Hotel Band
Sleepy Time Gal	Art Landry & Orchestra
A Precious Little Thing Called Love	George Olson And His Music Makers
Waiting For A Train	Jimmie Rogers
Lookin Over Four Leaf Clover	Gene Goldkettle & Orchestra
Tonight You Belong To Me	Gene Austin
Blue Skies	The Knickerbockers
It Had To Be You	Isham Jones & Orchestra
Heebie Jeebies	Boswell Sisters
The Varsity Drag	Frank Black & Orchestra
Rainbow Round My Shoulder	McKinney's Cotton Pickers
Baby Face	Jan Garber & Orchestra
Snowin' On Raton	Townes Van Zandt

Post Script.

THE TITLE SPRING:

(From Chapter Nine, "No, No, Nora") For a split second, a fleeting glimpse of his destiny passed in front of him. His answer was short and puzzling for the youthful, blooming Nora. "I had *a bridge to cross*, that's all."

"This novel contains 100% recycled and rearranged
alphabetic symbols, words and post-consumer thought."

"All that jazz ..."
~ Leopold Throckmorton

"Thank you!"
~ Edward R Hackemer

f5abcedc-4812-4145-a324-837fd477c16cR01